Where t

1

Where the Silence Fell

Luke Osborne

UK | USA | Canada | Ireland | Australia
India | New Zealand | South Africa

Publication U.K.,
Worthing

First Edition Published in the U.K. 2025

The moral right of the author has been asserted.

Set in 11.5pt / 14.75pt Baskerville

ISBN: 9781036934101

For Florence and Arthur.

The earth drinks blood, the sky bleeds fire,
Men vanish into mud and wire.
Shells scream truths no mouth can voice,
Death marches where we had no choice.

Hands tremble over ghosts unseen,
Eyes wide, staring at what has been.
Names carved in smoke, in ash, in rain,
Nothing returns, yet all remains.

Silence grows in the hollows of the mind,
A witness to horrors we cannot unwind.
We walk among ruins, hollowed and worn,
Bearing the loss the world has torn.

One

Mediterranean Sea – March 1941

The Mediterranean was too peaceful.

Fred Bennett stood at the starboard rail of HMS Warspite, his fingers white against the steel. The water stretched out in a perfect sheet of pewter-grey, as though the sea itself was holding its breath. A thin veil of smoke drifted along the horizon, the only sign of the Italian fleet that lurked somewhere beyond.

Fred had seen the sea in every mood, restless, playful, violent, but it was the quiet that unsettled him most. It was the silence before the guns spoke, before men screamed and steel was torn apart. A silence that made the heart drum too loud in its cage.

Behind him, sailors went about their work with brittle chatter, adjusting ropes, checking weapon sights, tightening helmets already damp with sweat. One lad, Evans, barely old enough to shave, was rubbing a rosary bead so fiercely it looked like he might wear it smooth before the night was done.

Fred forced himself to breathe slow, deep. His chest was tight, that familiar coil of tension, the waiting game that always came before battle. Once the first shot was fired, he knew the fear would steady into something manageable. But for now, it gnawed at him, cold teeth on the edge of his mind.

"Lieutenant," a voice called. Petty Officer Thomas, broad-shouldered and soot-smudged, came striding across the deck. "Captain wants you sharp. Italians are closing."

Fred gave a short nod. He pushed away from the railing and made for the gunnery station, his boots clanging against the deck plates. All along the battleship, the crew was braced, the Warspite alive with the tension of men who had done this before but never found it easier.

The first enemy flare bloomed in the distance, casting the sea in ghostly white. An Italian cruiser loomed into view, guns already lighting like lightning across a storm cloud. Shells screamed overhead, crashing into the water with geysers that drenched the deck in icy spray.

"Enemy cruiser at two o'clock!" someone shouted.

Fred raised his binoculars. The Zara. Sleek, lethal, her decks ablaze with fire as she opened up. The sight should have inspired terror, but Fred felt something else, a grim clarity. This was what they had trained for. This was why they were here.

"Prepare to return fire!" he barked.

The Warspite's gunners moved like a single organism, shells manhandled into place, breeches slammed, sights adjusted. The captain gave the signal, and the great guns roared. The whole ship shuddered, Fred's bones rattling with the recoil.

Through his lenses, he saw the first salvo fall short, the sea exploding in white plumes. The second struck true. Flames leapt across the Zara's hull, black smoke rising like a funeral pyre.

"Direct hit!"

A ragged cheer went up, but Fred silenced it with a sharp gesture. "Keep steady. Again!"

The Warspite's secondaries thundered. The night became a strobe of fire and smoke, the air thick with cordite and burning oil.

Then came the counterblow. A shell slammed into the deck just aft, showering Fred with splinters. The world went white with heat and dust. When his vision cleared, he saw one of the gun crews sprawled across the deck, one lad clutching a mangled leg. Blood seeped fast between his fingers.

Fred dropped to his side. "Medic!" He tore a strip from his own sleeve, binding the wound as tight as he dared. "Stay with me. You'll be alright."

The sailor's grip clamped like iron around his wrist, eyes wide and terrified. Fred squeezed back once before Petty Officer Thomas knelt beside them, his face set. "Bridge wants you, sir."

Fred hesitated. He hated leaving a man like this. But orders were orders. He gave the wounded lad's shoulder a last squeeze and forced himself to his feet.

The bridge was a storm of voices. Captain Cunningham leaned over the chart table, his jaw set like stone. "They're moving to encircle. We break their line here. Bennett, take charge of the starboard batteries."

Fred saluted, heart pounding, and returned to the guns. The Pola was sliding into view now, her silhouette sharp against the burning horizon.

"Gunners, ready!" Fred's voice cut through the chaos. "On my mark, fire!"

The first salvo went wide, crashing into the sea. He swore, adjusted, and ordered again. The second ripped into the Pola's decks, silencing one of her forward turrets in a burst of flame.

"Good! Again!"

But before they could fire, the deck convulsed beneath him. An explosion ripped through the hull, throwing Fred into the air. He hit the sea hard, the cold shock smashing the air from his lungs. For a moment, he was just another body tumbling in the dark water.

He kicked, hard, breaking the surface just in time to hear the thunder of guns overhead. Beside him, a scream cut through the chaos. Petty Officer Dawson flailed, one arm useless, a jagged shard of metal buried deep in his shoulder.

"Hold on!" Fred struck out towards him, the salt burning his throat with every gasp. He caught Dawson under the arm and hauled, stroke by desperate stroke, until a rope splashed between them.

He shoved it into Dawson's good hand, bracing them both as the deck crew hauled with brutal strength.

They collapsed onto the planks in a spray of blood and seawater. Medics swarmed Dawson at once, plunging morphine into his arm and carrying him below. Fred lay heaving, coughing up seawater, watching the dark trail Dawson's blood left behind. He didn't need to be told, the man wouldn't last the hour.

Fred forced himself back to his post. A medic intercepted him, hand already reaching for his shoulder. "Sit down, sir, you've swallowed half the sea. You need to be checked over."

Fred shook him off, wiping brine and blood from his face. "I'm fine."

"You're not. Look at you…"

"I said I'm fine." His voice came sharp, steel over fatigue. "There are men out there who need you more than me."

The medic hesitated, eyes narrowing. "At least let me…"

"Back to your wounded, lad." Fred fixed him with a glare that brooked no argument. "That's an order."

The medic swallowed, gave a reluctant nod, and vanished back into the chaos.

Fred straightened, chest still burning, and turned to the men who waited, wide-eyed, for direction. He gave it, though every breath felt like broken glass.

"Fire at will!"

The Warspite roared. Salvo after salvo hammered into the enemy line. One by one, the Italian ships faltered, burning, retreating into the smoke. At last, the Zara sank, her stern rising like a final salute before vanishing beneath the waves. The others fled.

The cheer that followed was ragged, broken with exhaustion, but it rippled along the deck. Fred lowered his binoculars, scanning the wreckage-strewn water. Bodies and burning oil, it was all part of the sea now. Somewhere down there, Dawson's blood was gone, absorbed by the depths.

Captain Cunningham appeared at his side. His face was lined with fatigue but lit by weary pride.

"We heard you went over," the captain said. "For a moment, I thought we'd lost you."

Fred swallowed, the salt still burning his throat. "Would've, if not for that rope. I owe whoever threw it more than I can say."

Cunningham gave a tired nod, eyes softening. "Good work, Lieutenant. You kept your head."

"Thank you, sir," Fred managed.

As the Warspite turned for port, the guns cooling, Fred leaned into the wind. The sun was rising, painting the horizon in strokes of gold, but his chest felt heavier, not lighter. The history books would mark this as a triumph.

But Fred knew better. Victory always came with ghosts.

Two

Worthing, England - 1939
Two years earlier

The small seaside town of Worthing lay tranquil under the late summer sun, its streets lined with neatly arranged houses and gardens in bloom. The sea glittered with a calm, deceptive beauty, and the sounds of seagulls calling overhead blended with the gentle lapping of waves against the shore. For Lieutenant Bennett, this was home, a place of quiet comfort before the storm of war changed everything.

It was early September 1939, and Fred, then a fresh-faced twenty-one-year-old, strolled through the familiar streets of Worthing. He was carrying a crisp new uniform from the local tailor, his mind a whirlwind of excitement and uncertainty. The shadow of war loomed over Europe, and Fred had made a decision that would alter the course of his life.

In Worthing, Fred's world was small and tightly woven. Aside from his parents, who had always been his pillars of guidance and warmth, there was only Rose. She had been a part of his life since they were children, the girl who grew up just a few streets over, always with a quick laugh and a reliable friend whenever he needed one. Rose had a way of grounding him, balancing his restless energy with her quiet strength. Their friendship had deepened over the years, and as time passed, he had come to feel something more for her, an affection that words never quite captured. She was the one person who could steady his nerves about leaving, even though he knew it worried her deeply.

Rose's presence was as much a part of Worthing to Fred as the familiar shoreline or the narrow streets of their quiet town. She was woven into his memories and dreams, and though he hadn't yet spoken of the future with her, part of him couldn't imagine one without her in it.

As Fred approached the Navy recruitment office, his heart began to quicken. The office was a modest building, its windows displaying posters urging young men to join the Royal Navy.

"Oh, I see! Volunteering without me, then, Fred?" Tommy had appeared from nowhere, landing a slap on the back.

"Tommy! What are you doing here?" Fred gazed at the office entrance and then back at Tommy. "I thought you weren't going to volunteer yet?"

"Ah, yes, I wasn't going to old friend. Not properly. Not like you are! I've been assigned a desk job, Fred. I know what you're thinking. That I've joined the army to push papers somewhere warm and safe while other men are freezing. And maybe part of me thought that too, when the assignment came through. I won't lie, I felt a bit sick reading it. But I did volunteer. I didn't have to; they would've let me stay at the Ministry, tucked behind a desk, same as before. But it didn't sit right. All this talk about doing your bit, and there I was, about to start shuffling requisition forms while lads like you were going to get shot at. So I requested a change this morning, hoping they'd send me where I could make a difference. It turns out that the difference they wanted me to make is... well, more forms. Just in uniform for now. Royal Army Ordnance Corps. Not exactly a glamour post, is it? But apparently, they think I'm more use keeping supply lines running than charging over some blasted hill."

Fred smiled. Tommy only ever knew how to speak at the fastest rate possible. Fred went to start talking, but Tommy wasn't finished yet, "I don't know. Maybe they're right. Perhaps it's cowardice, disguised as logistics. But I promise you this, Fred, just because I'm not carrying a rifle doesn't mean I'm not part of this fight. I'm still in it. Just... in a different way."

"Cowardice?" Fred scoffed, shaking his head.

"Don't be daft, Tom. If everyone were out waving rifles about, who'd keep the lot of us fed, clothed, and firing in the right direction? You lot behind the lines, you're the reason we don't all end up fighting each other over a tin of corned beef. And anyway, the way I see it, you've done your bit twice over. Once in civvies, and now in khaki, alright, with a fountain pen instead of a bayonet, but still. I'd trust you over half the red-tabbed buffoons running things. As for me, well, I've always fancied the sea. Fewer forms, more fresh air. Figured I'd rather take my chances with a destroyer than sit waiting for Jerry to drop one on my roof. Navy'll keep me busy, and at least if I get blown to bits, I'll be clean when I go. Besides, someone's got to keep the Empire afloat, eh? Might as well be me. Don't worry, I'll be swanning about in a greatcoat on some windswept deck while you're drowning in carbon paper and tea rations. We'll both suffer in our way."

Fred clapped Tommy on the shoulder, "You did the right thing, mate. You're where you're meant to be. Just promise me you won't get so buried in filing cabinets you forget how to write to your oldest friend, alright?"

The two stood in silence for a moment, the consequence of unspoken things hanging in the space between them. Then Tommy offered his hand, firm and steady, the trace of a smile tugging at his lips. Fred took it, gripping hard, not out of bravado but because there was nothing else to say that hadn't already been said.

"Look after yourself," Tommy murmured.

Fred nodded once, eyes bright. "You too."

Tommy hesitated, then added, "And if you ever get in over your head, don't be too proud to ask for help. Even from an old pen-pusher like me."

Fred smirked. "If it comes to it, I'll send for you, and a crate of carbon paper to build a barricade."

Tommy rolled his eyes, but his grin lingered as Fred turned on his heel, shoulders squared, and walked up the first steps of the stairs leading to the naval recruiting office, and whatever came next.

Fred paused for a moment on the second step, taking a deep breath before venturing further. The room was sparsely furnished with wooden chairs and a desk where a stern-looking officer sat, pen in hand.

"Good morning," Fred said, steady but tinged with nerves.

The officer looked up, his eyes sharp behind round spectacles. "Morning, lad. Here to enlist, are you?"

Fred nodded, his resolve firm. "Yes, sir. I want to join the Navy."

The officer regarded him for a moment, then nodded and began to fill out the necessary forms. "You're aware of the risks?"

"Yes, sir," Fred replied, unwavering. "I'm ready."

The enlistment process was straightforward, but Fred could feel the importance of the decision settling on his shoulders. He had always felt a sense of duty, a desire to contribute to something greater than himself. With Europe on the brink of war, it was a call he could not ignore.

He had arranged to meet Rose by the river following his enlistment. He hadn't even told her what he was doing that morning, and he worried about how she would take the news.

Fred and Rose sat together on the bench by the river, the late afternoon sun casting a warm glow over the water. Rose traced patterns in the dirt with her foot, her brow furrowed in thought. "Fred," she began, barely above a whisper, "why the Navy? Why now?"

Fred looked at her, searching for the right words. "I can't sit here while everything's happening out there," he said, his tone a mix of conviction and unease. "This isn't just some adventure, Rose. It's about doing something that matters… something bigger than me."

Rose met his gaze, her expression torn between admiration and worry. "But I worry it'll change you," she murmured, her hand reaching for his. "You're already enough, Fred. For me, you're enough."

He squeezed her hand gently, his thumb tracing circles over her knuckles. "I know," he replied softly, "but this is something I need to do." The words hung between them, filled with promises and uncertainty, as they both tried to hold onto the moment for as long as they could.

Back at home, Fred's parents were a mixture of pride and concern. The small semi-detached house in Worthing, with its creaky floorboards and sun-bleached curtains, suddenly felt both comforting and suffocating. It was strange to think how quickly the ordinary could begin to feel like something he was already leaving behind.

His mother, a kind woman with gentle eyes and a soft touch, had been apprehensive from the moment she had seen the papers. Yet, true to her nature, she didn't let fear overtake her support. She fussed over Fred with quiet urgency, moving about his room like a woman trying to hold back time by folding it into neat piles. His shirts were ironed with extra care, his socks counted and paired with military precision.

"I just don't want you to get hurt, Fred," she said, trembling slightly as she folded a navy jumper and placed it gently into his suitcase. "This is such a dangerous period. It's not just drills and training anymore; boys go off to these things and come back different. If they come back at all."

Fred took her hand in his, squeezing it reassuringly. Her fingers were cold, as if the worry had seeped into her bones. "I'll be fine, Mum. I need to do this. I need to do my bit."

She gave him a watery smile, brushing her thumb across his knuckles like she used to when he was small and sick in bed. "I know you do. You've always had that in you. Just promise me you'll write. As often as you can."

His father, a stoic man with a weathered face and broad, work-roughened hands, stood in the doorway, arms folded, watching the scene with quiet intensity. He hadn't said much since Fred announced he'd be leaving. Now, he stepped forward, his boots sounding heavy on the old floorboards.

He extended a firm, unwavering hand, and Fred took it. His father's grip was firm, the kind of strength that carried more than just muscle. It was pride, fear, and a lifetime of quiet example wrapped into one gesture.

"Make sure you stay safe out there," he said, his voice gravelly. "Do us proud."

Fred nodded. "I will, Dad."

They stood like that for a moment. Father and son. Man and Boy. On the verge of becoming something more, before the silence softened into a mutual understanding.

In just four days, Fred would board a relatively short train journey bound for Portsmouth, where the next chapter of his life would begin. The thought filled him with a nervous energy he couldn't quite shake. He could already imagine the whistle of the train, the smell of smoke in the air, and the gentle jolt as it pulled away from the platform. Portsmouth wasn't far in miles, but it felt like another world altogether.

The Royal Navy training depot awaited him, its strict routines, its cold dormitories, the barked orders of instructors determined to strip him down and rebuild him in the image of a fighting man. It would be the end of comfort, of lie-ins and home-cooked meals. The end of peaceful Sunday mornings with the paper crackling in his father's hands and the smell of bacon drifting from the kitchen.

Leaving Worthing meant leaving behind more than just a town. It meant stepping away from the safe, known world and placing his trust in something larger than himself. He didn't yet know the shape of what was coming, but he could feel the scale of it settling on his shoulders, both a burden and a calling.

He glanced once more around his room. Everything was still there, but already it felt like it belonged to someone else.

Four days. Then everything would change.

Three

Leaving Worthing - 1939

The morning of Fred's departure arrived with a grey sky that hung low over Worthing, heavy with the promise of rain. A brisk wind tugged at the edges of coats and skirts, and the sea, barely visible beyond the rooftops, was a sheet of dull steel. Even the gulls seemed subdued, their cries distant and mournful.

The streets were quiet as Fred walked the short distance to the station, his suitcase clutched in one hand, his cap tucked under his arm. He wore his civilian coat buttoned to the throat, collar upturned against the chill, though it did little to stop the wind from finding the cracks in his resolve. The world around him felt muffled, like he was moving through something thick and invisible, each step harder than the last.

At the platform, a low whistle sounded as the train idled, steam curling up around its great iron frame. Soldiers in long coats and woollen scarves stood in clusters, some smoking, some laughing too loudly, all of them pretending not to notice the anxious faces of those they were leaving behind.

Fred's parents were there, standing a little apart. His mother dabbed her eyes with a handkerchief, trying to smile, while his father gave him another one of those firm, silent nods. Words had already been said at breakfast, over lukewarm tea and barely-touched toast, but they didn't need repeating.

And then there was Rose.

She stood just a few feet from the edge of the platform, her hands buried deep in her coat pockets, curls whipped about by the wind. Her eyes found his and held them, steady and unblinking, as though she could will the clock hands to slow with the force of her gaze alone.

Rose reached up and adjusted the collar of his coat, her fingers brushing lightly against his neck. "Don't do anything stupid, all right?"

"I'll try not to." He gave her a crooked smile, though it didn't quite reach his eyes.

She looked like she wanted to say more, but the words caught in her throat. Instead, she leaned in and pressed a kiss to his cheek, quick, warm, and trembling at the edges.

The guard's whistle blew once. Fred turned, lifting his suitcase, and stepped toward the carriage. He paused at the doorway, looking back one last time.

Rose raised a hand. She didn't smile. She didn't need to.

The engine gave a sharp hiss, a shuddering breath of steam and heat. Fred climbed aboard.

As Fred settled into his seat, his gaze drifted back to the platform, searching through the thinning steam until he spotted her, Rose. Her face was a mix of emotions, her bright eyes filled with warmth and a hint of worry. She raised a final hand in a hesitant wave, her lips pressing together as if to hold back words that would only make his departure harder.

Fred leaned out the window, cupping his hands to project his voice over the din. "I'll be back before you know it, Rose. I promise."

She smiled, a little tremulous, and called back, "You'd better, Fred. I'll be waiting right here for you." Then, as if gathering her courage, she added, "And don't forget to write."

He nodded, smiling, trying to imprint every detail of her face in his mind, the curve of her cheek, the determined set of her chin, and the softness in her eyes. "Every chance I get," he said, grinning. "Just you wait."

The train jolted, and with a final, lingering look, Fred watched as Rose lifted her hand a final time, her petite figure gradually fading into the haze of steam and distance.

Worthing began to blur behind him.

Outside, the familiar landscape of Sussex rolled by, green fields, scattered cottages, and the distant outline of the South Downs.

The train was filled with young men like himself, all wearing the same expression of anticipation and determination. Some sat in silence, lost in their thoughts, while others chatted animatedly about the adventures they imagined lay ahead. Fred joined a conversation with a lad named James, a wiry fellow with bright eyes and a quick smile.

"First time leaving home?" James asked, glancing at Fred's crisp new uniform.

Fred nodded. "Yeah. Just signed up. Figured it's time to do my bit."

James grinned, nudging him with an elbow. "Same here. My old man was in the Navy, so I guess it runs in the family. What about you?"

"Just felt like the right thing to do," Fred replied, looking out the window as the train sped towards Portsmouth. "Guess we'll all be in it together now."

As the train drew closer to the naval base, Fred's excitement was tempered by a sense of trepidation. The sprawling complex of buildings and ships came into view, a hive of activity with sailors and officers moving with purpose. The train finally came to a halt, and Fred stepped onto the platform, the sea breeze ruffling his hair.

A sergeant barked orders, herding the recruits into formation. Fred stood tall, taking in his surroundings. The base was larger than he had imagined, with rows of barracks, training grounds, and the constant hum of activity. He was assigned to a group and led to a long, low building that would be his home for the next few months.

Inside, the barracks were plain but functional, lined with metal bunks and wooden lockers. Fred found his assigned bunk, neatly made with pristine sheets and a woollen blanket. He set his kit bag down, the reality of his new life settling in. This was it, the beginning of his journey. The room buzzed with the nervous energy of young men, all eager to prove themselves.

An older sailor, a grizzled petty officer with a weathered face, entered the room. His voice boomed over the chatter, commanding attention. "Alright, listen up! I'm Petty Officer Jenkins, and for the next few months, you will follow my orders. Training starts at 0600 sharp. You're here to become sailors, so you'd best be ready to work. Dismissed!"

Fred exchanged glances with Tom, who was assigned to the bunk above him. "Looks like we've got our work cut out for us," Tom muttered, a hint of a grin on his face.

Fred smiled, feeling the effect of his decision but also a growing sense of camaraderie. "Yeah," he agreed, glancing around at the other recruits. "But I reckon we can handle it."

As he lay on his bunk that night, the sounds of the base outside lulling him into a restless sleep, Fred thought of Worthing, of his parents, and of the uncertain future that lay ahead. He was far from home, but for the first time, he felt a part of something bigger, a part of history in the making.

And despite the uncertainty, he knew he was exactly where he was meant to be.

Four

Portsmouth - February 1940

The transition to Navy life had been stark. Training had begun at the naval base, and it was a world away from the serene landscape of Worthing. Fred's days were filled with rigorous drills, physical training, and maritime instruction.

The discipline was demanding, and Fred struggled at first to adjust. The early mornings and late nights left him exhausted, and the constant drill of routines was a far cry from the leisurely pace of his life back home. Yet, amidst the sweat and exhaustion, Fred found a sense of purpose. The growing camaraderie with his fellow recruits made the gruelling training bearable.

The training was not just physical; it was also mental. Fred learned about navigation, seamanship, and the intricacies of naval warfare. He found solace in the structured routine, in the clear goals and objectives that replaced the ambiguity of civilian life.

Fred found himself alone on his bunk most evenings, usually wondering where his first posting would take him. But it had dawned on him that he hadn't received any letters from Rose recently, or his mother for that matter. He missed home, he missed that distinct smell of seaweed in Worthing and the warmth of the summer grass on the Downs.

Although there was the familiar sound of seagulls every morning, it wasn't the same as home.

He didn't allow himself to give it too much thought; his focus needed to be on being the best he could be.

Fred found a thrill in the discipline of long-range shooting. The stillness it demanded, the precision it rewarded. He approached every shot like a calculation, accounting for wind drift, distance, and breath control. It wasn't just about pulling the trigger; it was about mastering the moment before it. Over the weeks, the rifle became second nature to him, as if it responded to thought more than movement. His focus turned surgical, his patience unshakable.

That same control bled into every weapon he trained with. The Webley revolver, never meant for accuracy at a distance, became another challenge to overcome. He worked it harder than most would bother, pushing past its limitations.

During a session on the range, after landing three shots clean at over seventy-five metres, one of the instructors barked out, "That's not shooting, that's witchcraft." Lowering his binoculars, he added, "I've trained commandos, snipers, you name it, but I've never seen someone ring steel with a bloody Webley from that far." Fred only gave a faint shrug, reloading without a word, the corners of his mouth betraying the hint of a smile.

Fred nodded, eyes still on the target. "It's all the same, really," he said. "Just slower breathing, steadier hands... and a lot of hours."

What he learned with the rifle, he carried into his use of the Webley revolver. He practised relentlessly, adjusting for wind, distance, and drop, pushing the limits of what the stubby service pistol was designed to do.

With each session, Fred's respect for the skill deepened, and he realised that, just like every other part of his training, this too was an art, one that demanded discipline, patience, and trust in his abilities.

As the months passed, Fred's initial apprehension transformed into confidence. The Navy had a way of moulding its recruits, shaping them into disciplined and skilled sailors. Fred excelled in his training, driven by a sense of duty and the desire to prove himself. He made friends and formed bonds that would later be tested in the crucible of battle.

Thinking of how he was back in Worthing, Fred realised how much he had changed. The carefree days of his youth, games by the green, the distant clanging of St Andrew's bells, Rose's laughter echoing through the alleyways, now felt like dreams he wasn't entirely sure he'd lived, and those days had been replaced by the rigid structure of naval life and the grim weight of war. Yet, even amidst the cold regimentation, he carried with him the warmth of his upbringing, the values of duty, honour, and quiet resilience passed down like heirlooms from his father, his mother, and the coastal town that shaped him.

He returned to his room late that afternoon, salt still clinging to his coat from the harbour air. On the corner of his bed lay a small envelope. Cream paper, slightly smudged. The moment he saw the handwriting, his heart dipped.

It was his mother's.

They had exchanged letters steadily since his training days, news from home, careful questions, Sunday weather, a recipe now and then. But this envelope looked rushed. The loops in her writing were less measured, the ink darker in places where the pen had lingered too long. Fred sat on the edge of the bunk and slowly opened it.

Dear Fred,

I hope this finds you safe and warm. I have tried to write this letter more times than I care to admit, and still, I don't know if these words will be correct. I've always believed in speaking plainly, but I'm not sure how to tell you this without hurting you.

There was a raid last week, not one of the big ones, not one anyone thought would matter. A lone bomber, cut off from its group, perhaps. He dropped his load over Broadwater. One of the bombs landed near Leigh Road. Rose was there.

She had gone to collect her rations. I suppose she didn't hear the siren in time. They told us it was quick. That it was over before she even turned her head. I don't think she would have felt it. That might not comfort you. It doesn't comfort me.

The house feels impossibly quiet without you, and more so without her visits. I still catch myself looking out the window for her walking by. Your father has said little, but he walks the prom each morning before the town wakes up, as if he's looking for something he's lost in the sea air.

I didn't want to write this. I didn't want you to carry this weight into whatever you're facing. But you deserve to know. And you would have seen it in my words eventually anyway, I cannot hide the crack in them.

She loved you, Fred. She always thought you were made for something bigger than this town. She was right. Write when you can. I'll still be lighting the candle in the window.

With all my love, Mum

Fred let the letter fall to his lap.

The breath caught in his throat wasn't a sob, not quite. But something trembled inside him like a bridge about to give. He stared straight ahead at the bare wall, unblinking.

He couldn't take it in. He wouldn't. Not now. Not when there was so much still to endure.

A shadow passed across the foot of his bunk. "You alright, Bennett?"

It was Davies, red-haired, the lad from Cardiff who snored like an artillery barrage. Fred had barely spoken more than a dozen words to him in the past month.

"Yeah," Fred said quickly, sliding the letter back into its envelope. "Just tired."

Davies nodded, yawning. "Aren't we all. Food in ten." He moved off, boots clumping on the floorboards.

Fred lingered a moment, the aroma of his mum's lavender mixed with hearth smoke still in his nose. Home, he thought.

Then he lay down on the bunk, folded the letter under his pillow, and told himself she was fine, that she'd write again soon. That she was still laughing, somewhere just beyond memory.

Fred looked deep into a mirror, "Dad always said, 'Keep your boots dry and back straight, lad.'"

And that's what he would do.

Tomorrow, he would be walking onto his first assignment, HMS Warspite.

He needed to be ready.

Five

Portsmouth - September 1940

Fred's heart beat heavy in his chest as he stood on the crowded dock at Portsmouth, the pre-dawn air thick with smoke, salt, and the clang of chains. Around him, sailors, marines, and army lads jostled with kit bags and shouted last-minute farewells. Above them, gulls circled in the grey sky, calling out like old ghosts.

A transport ship loomed at the quay, its hull streaked with rust, its deck lined with lifeboats and canvas-covered crates. It wasn't glamorous, not a sleek warship, not the famous Warspite, but it would carry him to her.

"Hurry it up, lads! Get aboard!" barked a petty officer from the ramp. "Convoy leaves with or without you!"

Fred clutched the strap of his bag and took a final glance behind. Portsmouth, the narrow streets, the familiar pub near the base, the cool sea breeze, was already beginning to feel like a memory. Somewhere out there, in a hotter sea and under a different sun, HMS Warspite was waiting.

"Bennett?" came a voice from his left.

He turned to see Petty Officer Jenkins, clipboard in hand, eyes scanning the boarding list.

"Sir."

"You're assigned to Warspite, correct?"

"Yes, Petty Officer."

Jenkins nodded, ticking his name off. "You'll meet her in Alexandria. It could be a month before you're aboard, depending on how the Med behaves. You'll join a draft en route and transfer from Port Said. Understood?"

Fred nodded. "Yes, sir."

"Then get on with it. The bloody enemy isn't waiting for us."

A grin formed at the edge of Fred's mouth. He slung his kit bag higher on his shoulder and joined the stream of men boarding the transport. The gangway creaked beneath his boots as he stepped aboard, swallowed into the belly of the vessel.

Below deck, the air was already thick with sweat and diesel. Hammocks were strung tight in rows, sailors slinging gear into corners, joking, smoking, writing hurried letters. Fred found an empty spot, tied off his gear, and took a moment to steady himself. This was it. No turning back.

Above, the ship's horn blared. Dockworkers cast off ropes. Slowly, almost imperceptibly at first, the transport began to move. Fred climbed the narrow stairs to the deck and watched as England slipped away, the spires of Portsmouth blurring into haze, then swallowed by the open sea.

The wind caught his hair, sharp and salty. The engines groaned into rhythm, steady and purposeful. They were heading south, toward Gibraltar, perhaps, or around Africa, he didn't know for sure. But the destination was clear: Warspite. And war.

As the coastline vanished behind him, Fred felt a strange mix of grief and anticipation. He was leaving everything behind, family, certainty, home, to join a ship he had only read about in dispatches. A ship that had shelled Narvik, traded blows with Italian battleships, and would soon take him into the very heart of the war.

A voice beside him murmured, "Feels strange, doesn't it?"

Fred turned to see another young sailor, pale, wide-eyed, maybe eighteen.

"Like standing on the edge of the world," Fred said softly.

The days at sea blurred together in a steady, endless rhythm. Fred settled into the crowded transport ship's routine: early reveille calls, hastily eaten meals in the mess, hours spent leaning against the rail watching the horizon. The sea was a vast, restless expanse, grey under stormy skies, sparkling beneath rare shafts of sun.

He learned to read the ship's motions, how to steady himself when the waves rolled harder, how to keep his balance as the vessel pitched and yawed. Around him, men shared stories and fears, playing cards or singing old sea shanties. The air was thick with diesel and the faint, ever-present tension of war.

At night, Fred lay in his hammock, rocked by the ship's gentle sway. He thought of Worthing, the quiet streets and his parents' faces. Then, of the battleship waiting for him so far away in Alexandria.

"We're approaching Gibraltar," the captain announced one afternoon over the ship's loudspeaker. Fred felt a thrill run through the crowded deck as the fortress cliffs came into view, towering over the narrow straits where the Atlantic met the Mediterranean.

From Gibraltar, the convoy turned east, threading through the Mediterranean's blue corridors, ever watchful for Axis submarines lurking below. The ship's crew practised blackout drills, scanning the dark waters for any sign of danger.

One evening, as the sun dipped low, Fred stood on deck beside an older sailor who pointed toward a faint glow on the horizon.

"Port Said," the man said quietly. "The gateway to Egypt."

The ship anchored briefly in the busy harbour, the bustling port a jarring contrast to the quiet sea. Supplies were loaded and new orders relayed. Fred's heart pounded with anticipation; the moment to meet Warspite was near.

From Port Said, Fred and a small draft of sailors were transferred to a naval launch, a swift, chugging boat cutting through the calm Mediterranean waters. The sun beat down, and the salty spray chilled his face.

"Alexandria's just ahead," the launch's coxswain called out.

Fred's gaze fixed on the skyline as Warspite's unmistakable silhouette emerged through the haze. The massive guns and towering superstructure dominated the harbour, proud and unyielding against the backdrop of the city.

The launch drew alongside Warspite's port side, rocking gently. Fred climbed the ladder, each step bringing him closer to the reality he had dreamed of and feared. The deck was alive with sailors moving purposefully, carrying orders and laughter alike.

A tall, broad-shouldered man approached, his face weathered but kind.

"You must be Bennett," he said, extending a hand. "Chief Petty Officer Andrews. Welcome aboard, Warspite. You've got some training, I hear?"

"Yes, Chief," Fred replied, gripping the hand firmly. "At Portsmouth."

"Good," Andrews nodded. "You'll need it out here; the Mediterranean's no place for the fainthearted. The fascists are watching, and it won't be long before we're tested again. Ready?"

Fred swallowed and nodded, feeling the weight of the ship beneath his feet and the weight of the war pressing around him.

"Come on then. Let me show you where you'll be working."

As Fred followed the chief toward the main battery, the sun cast long shadows across the deck. The smell of oil and metal filled the air. This was no longer a dream; this was war. And Fred was finally part of it.

Andrews looked out at sea, "We won't be the same when we come back."

Fred looked out at the water, endless and grey. "No," he said. "I can't imagine we will."

Six

Alexandria, Egypt - March 1941
6 months later

The docks of Alexandria steamed under a high afternoon sun. Crates clattered, orders rang out in Greek, Arabic, and English, and the salt wind carried the scent of heat and the faint sour tang of diesel. HMS Warspite loomed in the distance, newly docked after the chaos of Cape Matapan, a victory, yes, but one that left Fred hollowed out inside.

Too many dead. Too much sea.

He should've gone back to quarters, maybe written the damn letter to his mother he had been putting off. Instead, he turned down a side street, pulled his collar loose, and let the noise of the port fade behind him. He didn't want to think. He didn't want to feel. He just wanted a drink.

The flavours of grilled lamb from the market fires clung to Fred's uniform as he ducked down an alley towards some lights. The bar he found was little more than a shack with chairs. Sailors, locals, and soldiers packed the narrow space, the ceiling low and thick with cigarette smoke. A fan turned lazily overhead, doing nothing.

Fred made it to the counter and ordered a beer in fractured Arabic. The bartender didn't care about his accent; he just shoved a warm bottle across and held out a hand for payment.

Fred turned to lean against the bar, just in time to see a glass fly past his head and shatter against the wall behind him with a sharp crack. Shards skittered across the tiled floor, and a hush fell over the room, brief, taut, the way the air hangs right before a storm.

The source of the disturbance stood near the centre of the bar: a broad-shouldered Australian soldier with sun-bleached fatigues hanging loose off his frame, buttons open to the navel, revealing a hairy chest slick with sweat. His face was red with fury, and he smelled faintly of dried blood and too much ouzo. Across from him, a cocky Irishman grinned with the crooked confidence of someone who'd seen one too many bar fights and always come out laughing. He held a shot glass like a weapon, set slightly back in his hand, the knuckles white where he gripped it.

"You've got the brain of a busted mule and the manners of a pig on fire," the Irishman said with a snort, his accent thick as a Donegal winter.

The Australian let out a roar and lunged forward.

Fred moved before the impulse could register.

He stepped away from the bar, boots skidding slightly on the sticky floor, and grabbed the Aussie's shoulder with both hands. The man was solid, a walking slab of outback muscle, but Fred used his momentum against him, yanking sideways and back, shifting his centre of gravity. The soldier staggered, arms pinwheeling.

Fred twisted, stepped in, and slammed his fist into the man's chin.

The movement was clean. The effect wasn't.

The Aussie toppled backwards into a cluster of chairs that buckled beneath him like matchsticks. A woman screamed. Bottles clinked violently behind the bar. The tension snapped, and chaos erupted.

The Irishman leapt in with the gleeful shout of a boy back on the schoolyard. A punch came flying from the side; Fred ducked under it, feeling the breeze on his ear, and countered with a left jab to the ribs of a second soldier joining the fray. The man folded with a grunt, but another came right behind him, swinging wildly. Fred took a glancing blow to the jaw, a flash of white light in his skull, then retaliated with a low sweep that knocked the man's legs out from under him.

The bar exploded into a full-blown melee. Chairs were hurled, fists flew, and boots pounded the wooden floor. Someone smashed a bottle. Someone else was shouting in Greek, fast, furious curses cutting through the clamour. Fred caught a glimpse of a sailor trying to climb over the bar for cover before a stool flew past and knocked him down.

The room stank of sweat, ouzo and cheap rum, stale smoke soaked into the old beams above, and something metallic and sour that Fred couldn't place. Beneath it all was the Mediterranean heat, thick as syrup, clinging to the skin.

He fought like he'd trained: sharp elbows, economical movement, using the chaos around him as a weapon. The Irishman stuck close by his side, weaving in and out of the brawl with uncanny grace, laughing like it was all a grand joke. At one point, he shouted, "Christ, I like you already!" as he head butted a man and sent him sprawling.

Fred had no time to reply. A bottle exploded near his feet. Glass cut across his calf. He barely noticed. Another soldier grabbed his arm from behind. Fred twisted, elbowed him in the gut, and drove a knee up into the man's chin.

Then, suddenly, a crack rang out above the noise.

The bartender had climbed onto the bar, a pistol in one hand, waving it overhead like a conductor's baton. He screamed something guttural in Greek, twice, then three times, and the room fell still.

Everyone paused, panting. Blood trickled from noses and busted lips. Chairs lay splintered.

One man moaned softly in the corner, curled around his stomach.

The bartender fired again into the ceiling. Plaster dust rained down.

That did it.

The crowd scattered like cats in a thunderstorm. Boots scrambled. Curses echoed. Fred caught his breath as the Irishman clapped him on the shoulder.

"Not bad, lad," the Irishman said, wiping blood from his split lip. "You've got a gift."

Fred grinned despite himself, jaw already aching. "You started it."

"Damn right I did. And you finished it."

They both laughed, still breathing hard, as the bartender muttered darkly and waved the pistol in their general direction. Outside, bruised and laughing, Fred leaned against a sun-warmed wall and rubbed his jaw.

"You've got a decent right hook for an Englishman," the Irishman said, still catching his breath.

Fred grinned despite himself. "You're welcome."

"Name's O'Malley," the man said, offering a hand. "Sergeant Colin O'Malley. Royal Marines. You?"

"Fred Bennett. Royal Navy. Lieutenant." He said it flatly; he hadn't quite gotten used to the title yet.

"Well, Lieutenant," O'Malley said, brushing dust off his shirt, "that was an excellent waste of an afternoon. And now that I owe you one, let me buy you something better than that camel piss you were drinking. Have you ever been to La Sirène Rouge?"

Fred raised an eyebrow.

"It's a cabaret club," O'Malley said. "Decent music. Dangerous girls. The kind of place the brass pretends doesn't exist."

Fred hesitated, then nodded. "Lead the way."

The club was tucked away behind a crumbling cinema, all red velvet and cigarette smoke. A pianist played sultry jazz in the corner while a woman in green satin sang into a silver microphone, her French drifting over the room like perfume. It was accompanied by a saxophone, which dripped slow, bluesy notes that cut through the heat like a knife through butter.

Fred nursed a bourbon. O'Malley had already disappeared to chat with the maître d', flashing that mischievous grin that made people either love him or hit him. Fred was surprised by O'Malley's warmth, considering his hardened look.

Then he reappeared, with two women in tow.

"Fred, meet Aya and Thalia," O'Malley announced. "Sisters, dancers, heartbreakers, and fluent in bad English."

Aya, the elder, was dark-haired, poised, with a faint scar above one eyebrow that only made her more arresting. Thalia was younger, louder, with golden curls bouncing as she laughed at something O'Malley whispered.

Fred offered his hand. Aya took it lightly, her fingers warm.

"You look tired," she said in a Greek accent softened by French.

"I am," he replied. "But not too tired for company."

They shared a bottle of wine, then another. There was dancing, close, slow dancing, and Fred let himself be pulled into the rhythm. Aya smelled of orange blossom and cigarettes. Her voice was low, her laughter rare but authentic.

"You're not like the others," she said softly, later, when they sat in a booth lit only by the flickering candle.

"No?"

"You watch everything. Like you're already somewhere else."

Fred didn't answer. Instead, he reached for her hand.

They ended up at a modest flat above a bookshop: wrought iron balcony, creaky steps, perfume in the air.

They stumbled in, laughter and kisses, shoes kicked aside. Thalia pulled O'Malley into the second bedroom with an excited squeal and the slam of a door.

Fred and Aya lingered in the hallway, her arms around his neck, their breaths slow and heavy. The kiss was deeper now, less playful. More urgent.

"I should go," Fred said quietly, even as his hands found her waist.

"You won't," she murmured, and kissed him again.

In the bedroom, she lit a single oil lamp. Fred sat on the edge of the bed, watching her as she slowly unpinned her hair.

"This is your world, isn't it?" he said.

Aya raised an eyebrow. "What do you mean?"

"Smoke, song, men like me. In and out with the tide."

Her smile was small. "Yes. But sometimes the tide brings something good."

She stepped forward, pulling him into a kiss that left no more room for doubt. Her lips pressed urgently against his, the taste of wine still lingering there, sweet and sharp. His thumbs brushed the line of her cheekbones before his hands slid to the nape

48

of her neck, then lower, tracing the curve of her back through the thin silk of her robe.

She leaned into him, her palms resting against his chest, fingers splayed as though to anchor herself to the solidness of him. Their bodies pressed closer, the warmth of her against the starch of his uniform, until the cloth between them felt unbearable. He kissed along her jawline, the angle of her throat, pausing at the hollow just above her collarbone where her breath caught sharply.

Her hands moved with equal curiosity, sliding over his shoulders, down the strong lines of his arms, before slipping below his waistline. Laughter, breathless and nervous, broke between kisses as buttons yielded and fabric fell away. Skin met skin at last, his palms finding the curve of her waist, then higher, tracing the shape of her ribs before resting against the rhythm of her heartbeat.

Her legs shifted beneath his, curling around him, drawing him closer still. Every touch carried them forward, his hands sweeping from her waist to her ribs, her fingers sliding across his back, tracing muscle and bone beneath skin.

The movements grew slower, deeper, each shift of their bodies an answer to the other, every kiss a wordless promise. For a moment, for one night, they weren't soldier and singer, survivor and shadow: they were simply two souls finding shape in each other's warmth in a world grown cold.

Fred woke with the light. The shutters let in slits of golden sun, warm across his bare shoulders. From the kitchen came the soft sound of humming, a delicate tune, old and unfamiliar. Aya was already up, wrapped in her robe, barefoot, moving through the morning like it belonged to her. The aroma of strong, bitter coffee curled through the air, dark and comforting.

Moments later, Thalia and O'Malley emerged from the other room, looking like a pair of devils who'd danced with angels. Tousled, grinning, slightly dazed by life or love or whatever the night had left behind.

O'Malley raised a hand in a lazy salute. "Morning, sailor."

Fred didn't speak. He just smirked and reached for the chipped mug Aya placed beside him, its contents hot and fragrant. Their fingers brushed briefly, unintentionally. Neither of them acknowledged it.

For a little while, the four of them sat together in the hush of the morning, a silence not awkward, but earned. The kind that followed noise and sweat and secrets. Four strangers, tethered for a night by a war too big to name and a city too old to care. In the eye of the storm, they'd found something, not peace, maybe, but a kind of stillness.

The clock hadn't stopped ticking. The world beyond the apartment was still burning, and he had to return.

Fred dressed in silence, pulling his uniform back on piece by piece, the fabric stiffer than he remembered. He adjusted his collar, ran a hand through his hair, and slung his kit bag over his shoulder.

On the street below, Alexandria had already come alive, market stalls opening, vendors shouting, smoke curling from rooftop chimneys. Somewhere, far out in the bay, Warspite waited.

Fred paused at the edge of the street and looked back.

Aya stood on the balcony, arms crossed, robe fluttering around her legs in the early breeze. She didn't wave.

But she didn't look away, either.

Fred held her gaze for a long, quiet moment, something unsaid stretching between them. Not regret. Not promise. Just recognition. A single night of closeness in a world that offered no guarantees.

He thought about saying something, anything, to make her remember him when the tide carried them apart. But words felt heavy, clumsy. Better to leave the silence unbroken.

Behind him, O'Malley's voice carried from the table inside. "You coming, sailor, or are you planning on marrying her?"

Fred gave the faintest smile, shook his head once, and turned away. The sea was to his left, the heat rising off the stones beneath his boots. He walked on.

Seven

Heading back to the barracks, Alexandria buzzed with activity. Ships were anchored in neat rows, their crews working to repair battle damage or restock supplies. HMS Warspite, Fred's ship, was among them, showing scars from the fierce Battle of Cape Matapan. The old battleship had proven her worth once again, but she was in dire need of repairs. Fred watched from the deck as cranes lifted crates of ammunition and supplies, sailors and dockworkers moving with a sense of urgency.

Despite the victory, Fred's thoughts were heavy. The war was far from over, and he knew this respite was temporary. He would soon be back in the thick of things. As if on cue, a young ensign approached, a sealed envelope in his hand.

"Letter for you, Lieutenant,"

"Thanks," Fred said, taking the letter and holding it tight.

Fred found solace in the shade of a stone wall behind the naval barracks, the sound of gulls overhead and distant Arabic voices rising from the harbour. Alexandria was always loud, markets, sailors, carts on cobblestones, but here, tucked away between sandstone and shadow, the noise faded.

He held the letter in his hands. The envelope was worn from heat and travel, addressed in the careful, slanted handwriting of his mother. It had taken weeks to reach him. By the time it had caught up with him, he was already preparing for his next mission.

He unfolded the letter, his fingers tracing the familiar script.

My dearest Fred,

It's bitterly cold here in Worthing. Your father swears it's nothing compared to the winter of '29, but I think that's just an excuse not to insulate the loft.

The garden looks bare now, but the winter jasmine has bloomed all the same. It reminds me of when you were small and used to dig through the flowerbeds with your tin spade, looking for Roman coins. You always said you'd be an explorer.

I hear the war on the wireless, names I don't recognise, cities I've never seen. But I listen, hoping your voice might somehow carry through it.

I lit a candle for you last Sunday. The vicar said a quiet prayer. Miss Harrow still thinks you're stationed in Portsmouth. I let her believe it.

Your father walks the prom every morning. He says it's for the air, but I know he's looking out to sea, waiting for you to return.

We miss you, Fred. Please take care.
With all my love,

Mum x

He read it twice. Then once more.

The perfumes of home lingered faintly on the paper, lavender, maybe, or something older, like the dust of old books. He folded it carefully, tucking the creases along their worn lines, committing each word to memory.

Boot-steps approached over gravel. Fred looked up to see Lieutenant Commander Hargrove, already in uniform, a folder tucked under one arm.

"You're underway at nineteen hundred. Briefing in thirty," he said, then nodded toward the letter. "Yours?"

Fred nodded. "My mother."

"Hold onto the memory," Hargrove said, his tone softening. "But you'll need to leave the letter here. If they find it on you… it could compromise everything."

Fred hesitated, confused for a moment, then nodded. Slowly, he passed the folded letter across. Hargrove didn't rush him. He took it gently, as if handling something sacred.

"She'll be proud," he said.

Fred forced a smile. "She always was. Even when I didn't give her a reason."

Hargrove clapped a hand to his shoulder. "Naples is no place for ghosts, Bennett. Let it rest here. You'll see her again."

As the officer walked away, Fred remained still, hand hovering for a moment where the letter had been.

Then he stood, straightened his shirt, and turned toward the waiting Mediterranean.

"Lieutenant Bennett," another ensign approached, saluting. "Orders from Commander Hargrove."

Fred laughed, "Something tells me I am going to Naples."

He took the envelope. Orders meant change, and change in wartime was never simple. He thanked the ensign, tore open the envelope, and read the typed orders. His eyes widened slightly as he read the details: reassignment to a covert intelligence mission in Italy, unsurprisingly, Naples.

Fred took a deep breath, folding the letter carefully and slipping it into his jacket. Naples. The name conjured images of sun-drenched coastlines and vibrant streets, but under Axis control, it would be a different reality. He would be walking into enemy territory, tasked with gathering intelligence on Italian naval movements, all while trying to remain undetected.

That evening, Fred found himself in the officer's mess, a glass of whiskey in hand. The room was filled with the low murmur of conversation, the clinking of glasses. He sipped his drink, savouring the burn in his throat, trying to process the mission ahead. He knew the importance of intelligence work, how crucial it was for the Allied efforts. But going undercover in a city swarming with the enemy was a different kind of battle, one that required a different type of courage. He didn't feel ready.

Lieutenant Commander Gregson, one of the Warspite's senior officers, sat on the seat across from Fred. He was an experienced hand, with a scar running down the side of his face, a souvenir from a skirmish in the North Atlantic.

"Got your new orders?" Gregson asked, his voice gruff but not unkind.

Fred nodded, taking another sip of whiskey. "Naples. Intelligence work."

Gregson raised an eyebrow. "That's a dangerous place to be right now. A lot of fascists. You'll need to watch your back."

He took a slow sip of his drink, then added, "When I was your age, they sent me to Brest. Thought I was just there to keep an eye on ship movements. First week in, the man I was working with disappeared. Turned out he'd been talking in his sleep." Gregson's gaze met Fred's. "They don't forgive mistakes over there, Bennett. Not the small ones, and certainly not the big ones."

Fred nodded, feeling the importance of the words. "I know. It's where they need me, but am I the best man for the task?"

Gregson grunted, raising his glass. "Someone must think so! To new missions, then. And to keeping your head down."

Fred clinked his glass against Gregson's, the sound ringing hollow in his ears.

As the night wore on, Fred found himself staring into his empty glass, thoughts drifting to the mission. He wondered about the people he would meet, the challenges he would face. Could he blend in to gather the information needed without drawing attention?

Fred stepped outside into the amber dusk, the smell of sea brine sharp in his nostrils. Somewhere in the distance, a gull cried. Home, thought Fred, felt so close in that moment and yet couldn't be further away.

Early the next day, Fred boarded a small, camouflaged fishing boat that would take him partway to his destination. It was a quiet departure; only a handful of men were aware of his mission. The journey was long, the sea stretching out like an endless blue expanse. The boat's engine hummed softly, a constant reminder of the distance growing between him and the familiar world of the Warspite.

As the coast of North Africa faded into the distance, Fred found himself lost in thought. The war had changed him, had taken parts of him he would never get back. He thought of the men he had lost in battle, their faces haunting his memory. He thought of his family back in England, wondering if they were safe, if they were thinking of him.

Hours turned into days, and Fred's mind drifted to the civilians he might encounter in Naples. War was different for those who lived under occupation. They bore the burden of it in ways soldiers did not, their lives upended, their freedoms stripped away. He wondered how they survived, how they found the strength to carry on amidst the fear and uncertainty.

Eventually, the boat reached its rendezvous point, where Fred was transferred to a submarine waiting to take him the rest of the way to Naples. The transition was swift, the submarine's crew efficient and professional. Fred felt the tension in the air as they submerged, the vessel gliding silently beneath the waves.

As the hours passed, the confined space of the submarine forced Fred into a state of introspection. The Gestapo and Italian secret police were relentless. If he were caught, there would be no rescue, no escape. He would be on his own, facing the full force of the Axis powers.

But it was more than the physical risks that weighed on him. It was the moral ambiguity, the need to deceive, to lie. He would have to blend in, to pretend to be someone he wasn't, to betray trust for the sake of his mission. It was a necessary part of war, he knew that, but it didn't make it any easier to accept.

Fred closed his eyes, the hum of the submarine's engines a distant lullaby. He thought of the faces of the men he had fought with, the comrades he had lost. He thought of his duty, it was this sense of duty that drove him, that gave him the strength to face the unknown.

When the submarine surfaced off the coast of Italy, Fred felt a jolt of anticipation. The city of Naples lay ahead, a sprawling metropolis under the shadow of Vesuvius.

He stepped out onto the deck, the salt air filling his lungs. The coast of Italy loomed in the distance, a dark silhouette against the morning sky. Fred squared his shoulders, set in determination.

As the submarine prepared the dinghy that was to take him ashore, Fred felt a strange sense of calm. For the sake of his comrades, for the sake of his country, Fred Bennett would not fail.

Eight

Fred disembarked from the submarine under the cover of darkness, easing himself into a small canvas dinghy with only a paddle and a compass to guide him. The sea was calm but heavy with tension, each stroke quiet and deliberate as he made his way towards the Italian coast. As the black outline of the shore drew nearer, he slowed, letting the tide carry him the final stretch.

His boots sank slightly into the wet sand as he stepped out, dragging the dinghy higher up the beach before concealing it beneath a tangle of seaweed and driftwood. Then he moved swiftly, his dark clothing blending with the shadows, heading up the coast toward the rendezvous point. He had been briefed on the plan: a resistance member would meet him at a small fishing hut and lead him into Naples. There, he would begin gathering intelligence on enemy movements in the region.

The journey was short, the sounds of the waves fading behind him as Fred approached the hut. His senses were on high alert, every rustle of leaves and snap of twigs sending a jolt of adrenaline through his veins. As he reached the hut, a figure emerged from the shadows, a man of medium build with a cap pulled low over his face, about twenty-six by Fred's guess, and unmistakably Neapolitan in his clipped accent and sharp features.

"Luciano?" Fred whispered, using the code name he had been given in his briefing.

The man nodded, his eyes darting around before he spoke in a low voice. "*Sei Fred?*" Are you Fred?

Fred nodded, shaking his hand. His handshake was quick but firm, the skin rough with old rope burns. "We don't talk more than we have to," he said, scanning the beach behind Fred. "Not out here."

Without another word, the man turned and gestured for him to follow. They moved quickly, sticking to narrow, winding paths through the underbrush, avoiding any signs of civilisation. After nearly an hour of walking, the lights of Naples began to appear in the distance, a sprawling tapestry of flickering lamps and darkened buildings.

The lights of Naples shimmered like fallen stars scattered across the bay. For a moment, it could have been any city on any peaceful coast. Then a spotlight swept across the water from the harbour fort, and the spell broke, beauty framed in barbed wire.

Luciano led Fred through the outskirts of the city, taking a wide route to avoid patrols. As they ducked through a narrow archway, Luciano's hand brushed the wall, fingertips trailing over the cool stone as though touching an old friend. "These streets keep their secrets," he murmured, more to himself than to Fred. There was an earthy aroma to the city. Eventually, they reached a narrow street lined with small shops, their windows dark.

The air was still thick with roasted chestnuts and motor oil, and the stone beneath his boots radiated the day's heat like a slow fever.

As they skirted a shuttered café, Luciano nodded toward the door. "Used to be my uncle's place. Best espresso in Naples. Now the fascists drink there." His voice was flat and his body tense.

Luciano came to a sudden stop in front of a tailor shop, its sign swinging slightly in the breeze. He glanced around once more, then pushed open the door, the bell above it tinkling softly. Fred followed him inside, the scent of fabric and cedar filling his nostrils.

The shop was small, with bolts of cloth stacked neatly on shelves and a counter littered with sewing tools.

Behind the counter, propped against a stack of folded shirts, was a small black-and-white photograph in a chipped frame. Two children, grinning at the camera, their hair windblown, the sea bright behind them. One corner of the glass was cracked. Luciano's gaze flicked toward it once, almost involuntarily, before he turned back to Fred and nodded toward the stairs.

Luciano gestured towards it, his voice barely more than a whisper. "Your quarters are upstairs. Please wait for me there. I will come with food and more information very shortly." Luciano stepped back toward the door but paused. "Don't open to anyone but me. Even if they speak your language." His gaze lingered on Fred for a beat, as if weighing something, then he was gone.

Fred nodded and headed up the stairs, his footsteps silent on the worn wood. The room at the top was modest but clean. A single bed stood against one wall, a small table with a lamp beside it. A window overlooked the street below, the shutters half-closed. Fred set his bag down, moving to the window to peer out. The street was quiet, only the occasional stray cat or shadowy figure moving in the night.

He turned back to the room, taking in the simple surroundings. This would be his base for the foreseeable future, a place to rest, to plan, to lay low. Fred moved to the bed, sitting down on the edge, his mind already racing with thoughts of the mission ahead. The contact with the resistance had gone smoothly, but he knew that was only the beginning. There would be challenges, dangers, and he would need to be ready for them all.

A soft knock on the door interrupted his thoughts. Fred tensed, his hand moving to the knife at his belt. "*Chi è?*" Who is it?

"It's me," Luciano's voice came through the door, calm and steady. Fred relaxed, standing and opening the door. Luciano entered, carrying a basket of bread, cheese, and a flask of wine. He set it down on the table, turning to face Fred.

"Your accent…it's not bad. Too clean for a Neapolitan. But still. You learned in school?" Luciano placed the basket down. "This is for you."

"No, my grandmother was from Liguria. I grew up with the language, mostly food, arguments and lullabies!" Fred smiled.

"Well, keep practising. Eat something and sleep. You'll need your strength. Tomorrow, I will introduce you to the others. For now, rest."

Fred nodded, his eyes meeting Luciano's. "Thank you," he said. He knew how much risk these people were taking, how much danger they were in simply by helping him. Luciano nodded in return, a silent acknowledgement of the unspoken bond between them.

As Luciano left, Fred sat down at the table, taking a piece of bread. He chewed slowly, his mind focused. The resistance was strong in Naples, he had been told, but they needed guidance and coordination. That was his role. To gather intelligence and to aid the resistance in whatever way he could.

Fred glanced out the window, the lights of Naples twinkling in the distance. The city was under occupation, its people oppressed, but there was still hope. As long as there were those willing to fight, to resist, there was a chance.

He finished his meal, setting the basket aside. The bed creaked as he lay down, the events of the night catching up with him. As he closed his eyes, the sounds of the city below lulled him into a restless sleep.

Nine

Naples, Italy - April 1941

Before the city stirred, the bay lay like a glass mirror, reflecting the pink bruises of dawn. Fisherman's boats creaked as nets were hauled, and shuttered cafés began to open.

Fred was lying on top of his bed, his mind still racing following his meeting with Luciano, when the knock came at his door. It was light, almost hesitant, but distinct enough to draw Fred from the light sleep he had finally managed to fall into. He sat up, reaching for his knife. He was still getting used to this, trusting people he barely knew, putting his life in their hands.

"*Chi è?*" he called out, his voice sharp.

A pause, then a young man's voice answered, "Enzo. Luciano sent me."

Fred hesitated, knife in hand, then decided to trust the contact. He slid the knife into his belt and opened the door. A slender young man stood in the doorway, no more than twenty, with a nervous energy that immediately set Fred on edge. His dark hair was unruly, and his eyes darted around the room before settling on Fred. The young man's boots were dusty, one lace frayed almost through. He shifted his weight from foot to foot, glancing down the corridor before meeting Fred's eyes. "Luciano's occupied, but said you're a friend. I hope he's right." Enzo said, his Italian tinged with the local Neapolitan accent. "He asked me to come instead. I will be your contact moving forward."

Fred scrutinised him for a moment. There was something about Enzo's manner, earnest, eager, that put Fred at ease, though he couldn't afford to let his guard down completely. "Come in," he said, stepping aside.

Enzo entered, looking around the small room with a curious eye. "Luciano says you need a supply drop," he said, cutting straight to the point. "Food, weapons, radios?"

Fred nodded. "We'll need enough for at least a month. And I'll need a new transmitter. Mine's been acting up."

Enzo nodded, making a mental note. "We can arrange that," Enzo said, a quick smile flickering. "You'll be surprised how much we can move under their noses if you know the right streets. There's a drop point near the old lighthouse, about five kilometres south of here. Midnight tomorrow."

"Midnight," Fred repeated, committing the details to memory. He studied Enzo, still wary. "You're new to this," he said, making it a statement rather than a question.

Enzo smiled, a little nervously. "New to this part of the city, yes. But I've been with the resistance since Mussolini sided with the Axis. My father was a fisherman. He smuggled food to the partisans in the hills before they caught him 6 months ago."

Fred nodded, his suspicion easing a little. Enzo's voice was sincere, a passion that Fred recognised. "You're brave to continue," he said. "After what happened to your father."

Enzo's face hardened. "I do this for him. For all of us. We can't let the Nazis win. And besides…" he paused, a small smile playing on his lips, "I want to see England someday. Maybe after the war, when things are different."

Fred raised an eyebrow, curious. "England? Why England?"

Enzo's eyes lit up. "My mother had an English friend before the war. She would tell us stories about London, the countryside, and the rain." He laughed. "She made it sound like another world. A world where people were free, where you could say what you wanted, do what you wanted. I've always wanted to see it for myself."

Fred couldn't help but smile. It was rare to find someone so hopeful, so untouched by the cynicism that war brought. "England has its problems," he said, "but it's a good place. A place where people fight for what's right. You'd like it, I think."

Enzo's eyes gleamed. "Is it true what they say? About the pubs? That you can walk in and order a drink, and people talk to you, even if they don't know you?"

Fred laughed. "Yes, it's true. And the beer is warm, which is something you might have to get used to. But the people are friendly, especially in the small towns. They'll welcome you like you're family."

Enzo looked wistful. "It sounds…peaceful. Like a dream."

"It can be," Fred said softly, thinking of Worthing, of the quiet streets and the sound of the sea. "But it's fighting its own battles now. Everyone is, in one way or another."

They fell silent for a moment, the immensity of the war hanging between them. Finally, Enzo spoke, his voice steady. "We'll win this. The Germans, the Fascists, they can't hold on forever. People like you, like me, we won't let them."

Fred nodded, feeling a surge of determination. "We won't," he agreed. "Tomorrow night, at the lighthouse."

Enzo nodded, standing up. "Midnight." He moved to the door, then paused, turning back. "Thank you, Fred. For trusting me. And…for telling me about England."

Fred smiled. "Thank you, Enzo. For reminding me what we're fighting for."

At the door, he hesitated. "My father says the sea always brings back what it takes, eventually. I don't know if that's true, but… maybe it will be for Naples." Then he was gone, footsteps quick on the stairs.

Ten

The night air was filled with silence as Fred crept along the rocky shoreline, Enzo just ahead of him and Luciano bringing up the rear. The moon hung low behind a veil of cloud, casting silver slivers of light across the water, just enough to see but not enough to feel safe. The old lighthouse loomed in the distance, its skeletal frame a silent sentinel above the cliffs.

They followed the ragged path along the cliff, the sea restless below. Enzo kept glancing at the lighthouse ahead, the beam sweeping out into the night.

"My grandmother used to say a lighthouse beam was like the eye of God," he murmured, "always watching, even when you think you're alone."

Fred gave a faint smile. "And what does she say about fascist patrols?"

"That God doesn't walk their streets." Enzo's grin was quick, but it didn't reach his eyes.

"Not far now," Enzo whispered, crouching behind a cluster of rocks and motioning for the others to do the same. His hand rested lightly on the grip of his revolver. Fred scanned the terrain. There was no sign of movement, no sentries or patrols. But that didn't mean they were alone.

Fred leaned in. "We stick to the plan. In and out. No sound, no unnecessary fire."

Luciano gave a tight nod, the fingers of his gloved right hand flexing. His left hand carried a small black satchel for the transmitter and supplies. He'd insisted on coming despite Fred's objections.

They moved again, inching closer to the drop site. The lighthouse was surrounded by rubble and cracked paving stones. Years of disuse had turned it into a crumbling husk, perfect for a covert exchange.

Fred reached the edge of the lighthouse grounds and signalled for the others to hold position. He slid forward, eyes scanning for the drop. There, beneath a rusted iron grate, half-covered in sand and driftwood, a dark canvas bag had been stashed. He reached for it, checking its weight. Radios. Rations. Ammunition. It was all there.

With the supplies in hand, they quickly headed through the narrow backstreet, shadows pooling between the shuttered shops.

"Hold," Luciano said under his breath, one hand coming up. His head tilted, listening.

Fred strained to hear over the faint hum of the harbour, catching only the creak of wood somewhere up ahead.

"Could be nothing," Luciano murmured.

"Or someone," Fred said, stepping forward. That was when the soldier rounded the corner.

Fred froze.

A voice barked, Italian, guttural, alarmed. A flashlight beam swept across the lighthouse ruin.

"*Merda,*" Luciano hissed, ducking behind a chunk of collapsed masonry.

Two boots thudded down the path, then another two.

Enzo pulled his revolver but held fire, his body tense.

Fred motioned for him to hold. "Wait."

An Italian soldier appeared at the path's edge, rifle raised. He shouted again, demanding identification. Fred stepped back into the shadow. Another soldier appeared. This one moved quicker, descending toward the lighthouse.

They'd seen movement.

Fred knew they had only seconds.

When the second Italian came around the corner, rifle drawn, Fred lunged. He tackled the soldier into the wall, silencing him with a swift stab of his knife to the neck. The man gurgled, slumping forward. Blood spilt across Fred's sleeve.

The other soldier shouted, rushing forward.

A shot cracked through the air, too loud.

Luciano fired, dropping the second soldier with a hit to the chest. But the gunfire would bring more. Fred turned.

"Move!"

They grabbed the supply bag and ran, boots slamming against the uneven ground. Enzo led the way back toward the cliffs, where a narrow goat path cut down toward the shore.

Another shot rang out.

Fred glanced back in time to see Luciano stumble.

"Luciano!"

"I'm fine," he growled, clutching his left hand.

Fred yanked his arm over his shoulder. "You're hit."

"Only the hand," Luciano winced. "Keep moving!"

They plunged down the path. Wind ripped through their coats, the sea crashing below. By the time they reached the hidden cove where a dinghy was tethered beneath camouflage netting, the sound of distant shouting echoed behind them. Reinforcements. They had minutes.

Luciano glanced down at the blood seeping through his sleeve and gave a short laugh. "It's nothing. I've had worse cuts shaving."

Fred raised an eyebrow. "What were you shaving with, a bayonet?"

"Close enough." He winced, but his grin stayed.

Enzo jumped into the boat, untying it. Fred and Luciano followed, Fred keeping one eye on the cliff above.

"Push off!"

The dinghy glided out into open water, paddles slicing through the dark. Fred exhaled only once they were well beyond the rocks.

They rowed in silence, only the splash of oars and the occasional grunt of pain from Luciano breaking the calm.

Half an hour later, they beached at a hidden inlet and dragged the dinghy ashore. Fred finally turned to inspect Luciano's hand by the light of a covered torch. The bullet had passed cleanly through the fleshy part between thumb and forefinger.

"You're lucky," Fred muttered. "Another inch and you'd be waving with a stump."

Luciano smirked, though his jaw was tight. "Wouldn't be the first time I've been lucky."

Fred looked to Enzo, who was kneeling beside the bag, inspecting the contents. "You did well tonight," Fred said. "Quick thinking."

Enzo gave a slight, proud nod. "We got what we needed."

Fred nodded, but his gaze drifted to the lighthouse, still visible in the distance as a shadowed silhouette.

They had supplies now, and they had survived, but dawn was still a long way off. Luciano's blood seeped steadily through the makeshift bandage, dripping dark against the pale sand. He tried to laugh, to make light of it, but the sound faltered in his throat. Fred caught Enzo's eye in the half-light; no words were needed. They couldn't risk a hospital, couldn't risk questions. Someone would have to be trusted. As the first grey light touched the horizon, Enzo muttered a single name, and they carried Luciano into the waking city.

Eleven

Fred and Enzo laid low in a crumbling loft above a shuttered bakery. Outside, the city throbbed with the fallout: boots striking cobblestones, truck engines groaning through the narrow streets, the echo of shouted orders that carried farther than gunfire. Luciano had found a safe house to get his hand looked at.

Fred kept watch through a cracked shutter, heart thudding each time a patrol moved past. The air still reeked of smoke and burned oil from the docks, acrid even at this distance. Somewhere behind him, Enzo paced like a caged animal, his boots whispering over the dusty floorboards.

"They'll be looking for someone," Enzo muttered. His voice was quick, tense. "Workers from the shift… they'll drag them all in. Ask questions until someone breaks."

Fred didn't take his eyes from the street. "That's why we keep still. We don't give them anything."

Enzo's footsteps halted. "You think they won't find something anyway? A neighbour swears he saw us? A dockhand remembers a stranger's face? Naples is full of eyes."

Fred turned then, meeting his gaze. "And most of them are too afraid to open their mouths. Fear keeps people quiet."

Enzo snorted softly. "Fear also makes them talk." He dragged a hand through his hair and resumed pacing, his shadow twitching against the bare wall.

Fred sighed. "Sit down. You'll wear a hole in the floor."

Reluctantly, Enzo slumped onto a sack of flour, sending a puff of white dust into the stale air. He leaned forward, elbows on his knees, staring at the floorboards as if the Germans themselves might come marching through the cracks.

For a time, only the muffled sound of trucks rumbled from the streets. Then Enzo said, quieter: "Do you think it was worth it?"

Fred closed the shutter and leaned against the wall. "It was worth it because we needed these supplies. Tonight, we have what we needed to delay them. Time matters."

Enzo glanced up, his dark eyes flickering. "You really believe that?"

"I have to," Fred said simply.

Enzo reached into his satchel and pulled out a chunk of stale bread, breaking it in half. He held one piece out. "Eat. Thinking is easier when your stomach isn't empty."

Fred accepted it with a faint smile. "Sound advice from a philosopher in hiding."

Enzo shrugged, chewing his own share. "Hiding is what philosophers do best."

Despite himself, Fred chuckled. The sound felt strange in his throat after so much silence.

They ate in quiet for a while. Outside, a German voice barked orders, harsh and guttural, followed by the slam of truck doors. Both men froze until the noise passed.

"They'll make arrests," Enzo whispered, voice barely audible. "If anyone so much as whispered about me…"

Fred cut him off gently. "No one whispered. You were careful. That's why I trust you."

Enzo stared at him for a long moment, as if testing the words for truth. Then he looked away, "Trust is a dangerous thing, Inglese."

The silence that followed felt different, less brittle, more weighted with understanding.

Later, lying back on the rough boards, Fred tried to rest. He listened to the city instead: the uneven rhythm of patrols, the barking of a distant dog, the wail of a child cut short by a soldier's shout. Sleep hovered just beyond reach, but paranoia kept him awake.

As Fred and Enzo waited for dawn to come, Enzo kept his head low, voice pitched just for Fred.

"Tomorrow, we smile. We drink coffee. We pretend nothing happened."

Fred nodded, adjusting his cap. "And if someone looks too closely?"

Enzo's mouth twitched into a humourless smile. "I'm more concerned about the coffee."

Twelve

Luciano sat on a wobbly wooden chair, sweat dampening the collar of his shirt, blood soaking through the makeshift dressing on his hand. His teeth clenched hard enough to crack, his jaw locked against the hot, pulsing pain radiating from his left palm. The distinct smell of vinegar and boiled cloth turned his stomach.

"Keep still," said Fabia, her tone sharp but calm.

Luciano hadn't known where else to go. Enzo had hauled him, bleeding, through the back alleys until they reached the bakery on Via Sprezanzella. Behind it, through a crooked iron gate and up two flights of stairs, was Fabia's flat, a place Enzo had sworn was safe. He hadn't questioned it. Enzo knocked in a particular pattern, and when the door had opened, Luciano collapsed across her threshold. Enzo had then disappeared back into the night.

"I am still," he ground out.

"You're twitching like a fish on a hook." She dipped a strip of linen into a bowl of steaming water. "You want to pass out and crack your head open, too?"

He shut his eyes and tried to breathe. The fire in his hand had dulled to a heavy throb, but when she peeled back the blood-soaked bandage, the agony returned in a rush. He bit down on a rolled scrap of cloth she'd shoved between his teeth earlier.

Fabia worked with practised hands, swift, efficient and no-nonsense. Her dark hair was pinned back under a scarf, and she moved like someone used to cleaning wounds and lying about how bad they were.

She wasn't a nurse, not officially. But she'd treated her fair share of bruises, burns, and bullet holes since war arrived in Italy. Her flat, hidden behind a bakery in the Quartieri Spagnoli, had become a quiet refuge for those who couldn't afford questions.

Luciano winced as she poured the vinegar over the open wound.

"You're lucky it wasn't your head," she said. "Or your lungs."

"It was my writing hand!"

"You're lucky you're alive," she snapped.

He looked up at her through gritted teeth. "That wasn't luck. That was Enzo pulling me out."

Fabia said nothing. She just wrapped the fresh bandage tighter than necessary.

She brought him tea afterwards, weak, bitter stuff that tasted like boiled leaves and metal, but it was hot, and he was shivering, so he drank it anyway. The room was small: one cot, a chipped washbasin, and a battered wooden cabinet filled with cloth, iodine, and whatever morphine she could smuggle from a sympathetic pharmacist. A crucifix hung over the door. The window had been painted black.

Fabia sat opposite him, hands wrapped around her mug. For a while, neither spoke.

"How do you know Enzo?" Luciano asked.

She didn't answer right away. "He helps people. So do I." She took a sip of her tea. "Sometimes that's all the reason we need."

"You knew my brother," he said eventually.

She raised an eyebrow. "Which one?"

"Mario."

Her gaze softened. "Yes. I did."

"He said you were a nurse during the last war."

"I was a student nurse. Barely old enough to shave my legs, let alone patch up soldiers. But yes. I saw enough."

"Why'd you stop?"

"I didn't like seeing young men die in front of me." She gave him a long look. "Still don't."

Luciano looked away. His hand ached like it belonged to someone else, an enemy attached at the wrist. The bandage was clean now, but the damage was done. The bullet had gone through the edge of his palm, shattering bone and muscle. He wouldn't be writing leaflets or smuggling parts in false-bottom crates anytime soon.

"What good am I like this?" he muttered. "Can't shoot, can't write, can't blend in with a hand wrapped like that."

"You're alive," she said again. "That's what matters."

"No," he replied bitterly. "What matters is what we do while we're alive. Otherwise, what's the point?"

She got up, crossed the room, and opened a drawer. From it, she pulled out a pencil and placed it on the table in front of him.

"Use the other hand," she said.

He stared at it. Then at her.

"It's not the same."

"No. It won't be. But you're not dead. So pick up the pencil and start again."

Later, as dusk settled over the city and the distant rumble of troop trucks echoed off the alley walls, Luciano sat by the shuttered window, his tea gone cold beside him.

He held the pencil in his right hand, clumsy, unfamiliar, and scrawled a single line across a scrap of paper.

'We are not done yet.'

He paused. Stared at it.

Then he drew a shaky line underneath and wrote a second sentence.

'Pain is the tax we pay for defiance.'

He smiled faintly. Not because it didn't hurt, but because it did.

And he was still here to feel it.

Thirteen

Naples, Italy - May 1941

With the rising sun progressing across his bed, Fred opened his second-storey windows and looked out. The narrow streets of Naples were alive with the sounds and scents of a city under occupation. Market vendors called out in rapid Italian, offering fruits, vegetables, and bread to passersby. Children darted between the adults, their laughter a rare note of joy amidst the sombre faces of those enduring the war. Fred Bennett walked through the bustling marketplace, his senses overwhelmed by the vivid tapestry of life unfolding around him.

Dressed in civilian clothes, Fred did his best to blend in, to move through the streets like any other local. His mission required him to remain inconspicuous, to avoid drawing the attention of the German and Italian soldiers who patrolled the city with their ever-watchful eyes. He had been in Naples a week now, and his assignment already pressed heavily on his shoulders.

Fred paused in front of a small café, its awning faded and worn, the paint peeling from the shutters. It was a modest establishment, nestled between a bakery and a jewellery shop, but it exuded a quiet charm. The sign above the door read 'Café Rossi', and the aroma of freshly brewed coffee wafted out, mingling with the warm smells of baked bread.

Needing a moment of respite, Fred pushed open the door, a small bell tinkling as he entered. The café was cosy, with a handful of tables scattered about and a counter at the back where an espresso machine hissed and steamed. Fred made his way to a table by the window, the sunlight streaming in, casting a warm glow across the wooden floor.

"Mum! You have another customer!" A small boy called before dashing out of sight.

He sat down, glancing around the room. The patrons were a mix of locals, older men sipping coffee, women chatting softly, their eyes flicking nervously towards the door each time a soldier passed by outside. The atmosphere was tense, as if everyone was holding their breath, waiting for the next disruption, the next knock on the door.

"*Buongiorno,*" a voice said, breaking through Fred's thoughts. He looked up to see a woman standing by his table, a notepad in hand. She was in her early thirties, with dark hair pulled back into a loose bun and warm brown eyes that held a hint of weariness. Her face was kind but guarded, as if she had seen too much of the world's harshness.

"*Buongiorno,*" Fred replied, his Italian careful but fluent. "*Un caffè, per favore.*"

The woman nodded, jotting down his order. "Subito," she said, giving him a brief smile before turning to the counter. Fred watched her go, noticing the way she moved with a quiet grace, her hands quick and efficient as she prepared his coffee. There was a strength in her bearing, a resilience that intrigued him.

She returned a moment later with a small cup, setting it down in front of him. She set the cup down with a practised hand. "It's not as good as it used to be, chicory instead of beans today." A faint shrug. "But if you close your eyes, you can almost believe." She spoke softly but clearly.

"You're not from here," she said.

"Does it show?" Fred asked.

"Only in the way you watch people before you speak."

Fred hesitated, caught off guard by the question. He had hoped to avoid direct interactions, to remain just another face in the crowd. "No," he admitted, keeping his tone casual. "I'm from the north. Just passing through, I feel I need to always be on the watch, considering the world we live in."

The woman studied him for a moment, her eyes narrowing slightly. "Times are dangerous," she said quietly, glancing towards the door. "People from outside are not always welcome."

Fred nodded, understanding the unspoken warning. "I understand. I'm just looking for a quiet place to rest."

She seemed to relax a little at his response, nodding. "We all are," she said, softening. "I'm Isabella, by the way. Isabella Rossi. My family has owned this café for years."

"Luca Gallo," he replied, extending a hand. "It's a nice place you have here. Was that your son earlier? You and your husband must be very proud of a handsome boy like him."

Isabella shook his hand, her grip firm. "Thank you. My late husband and I are very proud of Marco. We used to run this place together. Now it's just me and my children."

Fred felt a pang of sympathy. The war had taken so much from so many. "I'm sorry," he said sincerely. "It must be hard, you have two children?"

Isabella's eyes flickered with a mixture of pain and determination. "It is. But we manage. Life goes on, even in times like these. And yes, I do. I have a daughter called Sofia." As she spoke, her gaze flicked to the door each time it opened, a reflex so smooth it might have gone unnoticed, if Fred hadn't been watching.

Fred nodded, feeling a connection with her words. He knew the resilience it took to carry on, to find small moments of normalcy amidst the chaos of war. As he sipped his chicory, he found himself watching Isabella as she moved about the café, serving customers, wiping down tables. There was a quiet strength about her, a warmth that seemed to radiate despite the hardships she faced.

The soft chime of the café bell sent a ripple through Fred's nerves. He straightened in his chair, eyes flicking to the entrance. It had been a week since the supply drop at the lighthouse, since they'd left two soldiers dead in the dirt. So far, there had been no sign of retaliation, no whispered warnings on the resistance channels. Still, Fred's instincts kept him taut as a drawn wire.

Luciano stepped through the doorway, the morning sunlight catching on the polished black leather of his gloves. Fred's gaze dropped instinctively to the Italian's right hand, the one bandaged beneath the glove. It had taken the bullet cleanly, grazing the flesh but missing bone. Lucky, all things considered. But luck rarely lasted long.

"Luciano," Fred said, rising with a smile and offering a firm handshake. "Good to see you, as always. How did you know I was here?"

"And you, my friend," Luciano replied, his voice smooth, his tone casually upbeat, a little too casual. "I figured you wouldn't be able to resist the nearest café to you, and I just wanted to come say hello."

The café was quieter now, just a few regulars hunched over their espressos and cigarettes. From

91

behind the counter, Isabella approached with practised ease, a steaming cup in hand.

"*Caffè, signore,*" she said with a small smile as she placed it in front of Luciano. Her eyes shifted to Fred, warm but curious.

Fred caught her glance and offered a polite nod. "Isabella, this is Luciano. An old friend of mine, from the north."

"*Piacere,*" she said, brightly.

Luciano returned her smile with a courteous nod. "The pleasure is mine."

She lingered only a second longer before drifting back to the counter, where she resumed cleaning a set of glasses with the diligence of someone who paid attention to more than just smudges.

Luciano waited until she was out of earshot, then leaned in, lowering his voice. "Be careful with trusting her, Fred."

Fred took a slow sip of his drink. "I trust that she makes good coffee," he said evenly. "Beyond that, I keep my eyes open."

Luciano's lips twitched in a faint smile, but his eyes were hard. "Good. The walls here are thin, and the wrong word travels quickly."

Fred nodded. "I haven't forgotten where we are."

The conversation turned to the incident. Luciano glanced briefly out the window before speaking again. "The bodies were found. The army is blaming looters. Desperate thieves trying to steal weapons. No mention of resistance. No patrols sent out. No names circulated."

"That's better than I expected," Fred said, though his voice lacked relief.

"They're under pressure," Luciano continued. "Between the shortages and the local unrest, they don't want to stir more trouble unless they're sure."

"Or maybe they've grown too used to thinking no one here's brave enough to push back," Fred murmured.

Luciano finished his drink with a final swig and stood, brushing a crease from his coat sleeve. "Enzo sends his regards," he said casually. "He's out of the city until tomorrow, laying low. Smart boy."

Fred stood as well, his eyes following a pair of German officers passing outside the window. He waited until they'd gone. "Tell him to keep his head down, at least til tomorrow night."

Luciano nodded, then leaned in once more. "Normality is a luxury, Fred. Don't forget that."

Fred met his gaze. "I won't. But even luxuries can be useful, in the right dose."

Luciano gave a slight tilt of his head, not quite agreement, but not opposition either. Then he turned and walked out, the bell above the door ringing softly behind him.

Fred remained standing for a moment, watching the street. The city moved on as if nothing had changed, but beneath the cobbles, the pressure was building. And somewhere out there, the next step in this silent war was already being planned.

As Luciano left, the café returned to its lull: spoons clinking, chairs scraping, a radio murmuring a Neapolitan waltz in the corner. Fred sat alone for a while, watching the swirl of sugar dissolve into his hot drink.

Outside, the street hummed with life, but beneath it, tension thrummed like a distant drumbeat.

He checked his watch. This time tomorrow, he and Enzo would be at the docks, crawling through shadows and praying no one sees them.

It wasn't espionage. Not exactly. But it was war. The kind fought in alleyways, with fuel valves and careful timing.   And tomorrow, it was his turn to light the match.

Fourteen

Fred crouched behind a stack of abandoned crates near the eastern pier. The sharp diesel bit at the back of his throat as he crouched beside the crate, fingers trembling against the cold steel casing.

Enzo glanced toward the water. "I used to fish off this pier with my brother when we were boys. We'd sell to the men who unload here. Now it's those damn fascists who take the catch, and pay nothing."

The night was warm, humid, and loud with the creaking of moored ships and the distant bark of a German officer's orders. A full moon hung low in the sky, its light diffused by a veil of coastal mist. Not ideal, Fred thought. Shadows were fewer. Risks were greater.

Tonight's mission was pure sabotage: anything to delay the war machine. Fred doubted himself; he wasn't a saboteur, not a trained one anyway.

Beside him, Enzo adjusted the strap of his satchel, its contents clinking faintly. "We've got ten minutes before the shift change," Enzo whispered, nodding toward the patrol route beyond the dock gate. "That's our window."

Enzo's confidence fed into Fred, who checked his watch, then his surroundings. A German fuel truck was parked twenty yards away, its metal tank glinting beneath a single overhead lamp. Soldiers were unloading crates from a nearby barge, distracted, their rifles slung lazily over their shoulders.

A boot scraped nearby. Fred froze, blood roaring in his ears. His shirt clung to his back with sweat, the damp cotton itching beneath his collar as he waited, unmoving, in the alley's shadow.

"This one's your idea, remember?" Fred muttered, glancing sidelong at Enzo. "So if we end up floating face-down in the harbour..."

"I'll buy the drinks in the afterlife," Enzo grinned, unbothered.

The plan was simple in theory: make the fuel tank rupture and ignite after the saboteurs had gone. It had to look accidental, or at least uncertain. No gunfire. No dead bodies. Fire and Chaos will be enough.

Fred moved first, darting low across the open stretch of dock. He crouched beside the truck's rear wheels and retrieved a small satchel from under his coat. Inside: a homemade timer rigged to a weak incendiary charge and a modified bottle of engine oil. Just enough to ignite the puddle of leaked fuel, they would fake with a loosened valve.

Enzo reached the other side, nodding. Fred gave a quick thumbs-up and slid under the truck.

Minutes ticked by. The scent of petrol increased as Fred carefully loosened the fuel outlet. A slow trickle began pooling on the concrete. He worked fast but precisely, securing the timer behind the rear axle where it would be hidden from casual inspection.

"Done," Fred whispered as he emerged, wiping his hands on a rag. Enzo passed him a small bottle of their faux oil spill mix, and they added it to the pool, extra smoke, extra panic.

Then came footsteps. Two soldiers, laughing, boots echoing on the metal ramp of the docked barge. The boots echoed somewhere beyond the cargo sheds. Fred paused for a moment. A chain clinked, swaying on a mooring post, and the noise seemed deafening in the quiet.

"Go," Fred hissed, and both men slipped into the shadows, ducking behind crates just as the soldiers strolled by. Fred held his breath. The timer was set for six minutes. If the Italian soldiers lingered near the truck, they'd have to intervene somehow.

One soldier paused, lighting a cigarette. The other kicked at a loose bolt on the ground. Fred's fingers itched to grab his pistol, but that wasn't the plan. They waited.

Then, mercifully, one of the dock workers called over in broken German, pointing toward the crates. The soldiers ambled away, drawn to the distraction.

Fred and Enzo slipped out, hugging the wall until they reached a side alley. They rounded the corner just as a dull whump shook the air behind them. A bloom of orange light lit the harbour, followed by shouted orders and the rush of boots.

The fuel truck was engulfed in flames.

Enzo grinned as the plume of smoke began to rise. "They'll call it bad luck. Maybe they're right."

Fred kept his eyes on the fire. "Or maybe someone will start asking questions."

"Then we'll give them the wrong answers," Enzo said, already turning away.

They didn't look back.

Ten minutes later, back on the quiet streets away from the waterfront, Fred lit a cigarette with trembling fingers. "Enzo, do you think they'll buy it?" he asked.

Enzo was beaming. "Of course. You saw the way it caught, looked like a bad valve and a careless spark."

Fred exhaled smoke slowly, calming his nerves. "You enjoy this too much."

"Just the part where we make a dent without firing a shot."

Fred couldn't help the smile tugging at the corners of his mouth. "Let's hope Command sees it the same way."

"They will," Enzo said. "You've got them listening now, Fred."

Fred didn't answer, but he nodded.

As he got back to his apartment, he wiped soot from his face with trembling hands. The taste of smoke clung to his teeth, and his ears still rang from the detonation. The bed beneath him was lumpy, but he sank into it like it was a king's cushion.

In the days that followed, German lorries moved more cautiously through Naples. Rumours spread of sabotage, but no arrests were made. It had worked. A whisper of resistance had echoed through the city.

And that whisper led Fred, a few days later, to the quiet warmth of 'Café Rossi'.

Fifteen

Over the next few weeks, Fred returned to 'Café Rossi' with increasing regularity, finding solace in its peaceful atmosphere amidst the turmoil of occupied Naples. The café had become a sanctuary for him, a place where his mission could momentarily lift from his shoulders. Each morning, Fred would take his seat at the same table by the window, his eyes scanning the bustling street outside, watching the ebb and flow of daily life. The vibrant activity of the city persisted, even under the watchful eyes of the Italian patrols that passed by, their presence a stark reminder of the ever-present danger.

The café's interior was warm and inviting, a contrast to the tense reality outside. The walls were adorned with faded photographs of the city in better times, and the air was filled with the rich aroma of freshly brewed coffee mingled with the faint odour of vanilla from the pastries. Fred found a strange comfort in these small details, reminders of normalcy in a world that had gone mad. He had been getting to know both Marco and Sofia, Isabella's children, but his eyes were always cast upon Isabella.

A pot simmered on the stove, and the smell of garlic and rosemary softened the tension in Fred's shoulders. It was reminiscent of Sunday roasts back home.

Isabella moved gracefully between the tables, her presence commanding yet gentle. Her dark hair was always neatly pinned back, and her movements were fluid, almost as if she were dancing. She would bring Fred his coffee, a steaming cup of rich, dark espresso, always prepared just the way he liked it. At first, their interactions were brief, a simple exchange of pleasantries, polite comments about the weather or the state of the city.

"*Buongiorno, Luca,*" Isabella would say, placing the cup in front of him. "How are you today?"

"As well as one can be," Fred would reply, offering a slight smile. "And you?"

"Busy, as always, the children and I are delighted you are here," she would respond with a light chuckle, her eyes sparkling with a warmth that made Fred's heart ache with a longing he couldn't quite place.

She set down the tray and leaned on the counter for a moment. "So, Signor Gallo… do you miss home?"

Fred kept his expression light. "Sometimes. But home's a dangerous habit in wartime; once you get used to it, you never want to leave."

"And what brings you to Naples, then? The weather?" she asked, one brow arched.

"Among other things," Fred said. "Though I've been warned about the locals."

"You should be. We talk too much."

"Not all of you," he said, and she smiled despite herself.

He knew he was a fraud for not revealing his real name, but he took comfort from the idea that he was protecting her by not revealing who he was.

Over time, the nature of their conversations had begun to shift. They spoke longer, their words drifting from the superficial to the personal. Isabella would linger a little longer at Fred's table, her fingers brushing against the back of a chair as she stood beside him, her eyes softening as she talked about her children.

"Marco is growing so fast," she said one afternoon, with both pride and worry. "He's ten now, and already he talks about wanting to be a soldier. I try to tell him that there are better things, safer things to aspire to, but he's so headstrong. Like his father."

Fred nodded, listening intently. He could see the strain in Isabella's eyes, the lines of fatigue that marred her otherwise flawless complexion. "He's lucky to have a mother like you," Fred said gently. "Someone who cares enough to guide him, to protect him."

Isabella smiled, though the sadness lingered. "I hope I can protect them," her voice barely above a whisper. "This war…it takes everything. I want them to have a future, something beyond all of this."

Fred reached out, his hand covering hers where it rested on the table. "They will," he said firmly. "This will end, and they'll have a chance to grow up in a better world. We're fighting for that future, Isabella. For all of us."

Isabella squeezed his hand briefly before pulling away, her eyes glistening with unshed tears. "Thank you, Luca," she said. "For saying that. It means more than you know."

Their conversations provided Fred with a sense of focus, a reprieve from the clandestine meetings and coded messages that filled his days. It was in these quiet exchanges that Fred found a kindred spirit in Isabella, someone who understood the toll the war had taken on him, even if she didn't know the full extent of his involvement.

One afternoon, Fred was sitting at his usual table when Enzo entered the café. The young resistance member's appearance was always slightly dishevelled, his dark hair falling into his eyes, but his demeanour was cheerful as he made his way over to Fred.

"*Ciao,*" Enzo greeted him with a wide grin, sliding into the seat opposite. "I knew you'd be here again!"

Fred raised an eyebrow, his lips twitching into a smile. "Do I detect a hint of jealousy, Enzo?" he teased. "Are you afraid I'm spending too much time enjoying my coffee?"

Enzo laughed, shaking his head. "Not at all. I'm just glad to see you relaxing for once. You look less like a man with the burden of the world on his shoulders when you're here."

Fred chuckled, acknowledging the truth in Enzo's words. He turned as Isabella approached their table, a tray balanced expertly in her hands.

"Enzo, this is Isabella, the proprietor of this fine establishment," Fred said, introducing the two. "Isabella, this is Enzo, a friend of mine."

Isabella smiled warmly, setting down two cups of coffee. "It's a pleasure to meet you, Enzo," she said. "Luca speaks highly of you."

"What about me, Luca?" a young voice called out from behind the counter as Marco appeared.

"Ah, yes, and the man of the house, Marco."

Enzo's cheeks flushed with a mixture of pride and embarrassment. "The pleasure is mine, signora, and also you, young sir," he said, his tone respectful. "Luca didn't tell me he had such good taste in coffee shops."

Isabella laughed, the sound light and musical. "He's a good customer," she said. "One of the few who appreciates a quiet corner and a good conversation."

Enzo nodded, glancing around the café. "It's a nice place," he said. "A bit of calm in the storm."

Isabella's smile faded slightly, a shadow passing over her features. "We do what we can to keep things normal," she said quietly. "But it's hard, with fascists everywhere, the constant fear…"

Enzo's expression grew serious. "You're doing more than most, signora. Your café gives people hope. A reminder of what life was like before the war."

Isabella looked at him, her eyes searching his. "Thank you, Enzo," she said softly. "That means a lot."

The three of them sat together, the conversation flowing easily despite the tension that simmered just beneath the surface. They spoke of many things, of Naples and its history, of the war and the hope for its end.

As the afternoon wore on, Fred felt a sense of camaraderie growing between them, a bond forged in the shared experience of war, of loss, of hope.

Isabella returned to her work, leaving Fred and Enzo to their conversation. The café bustled around them, the clatter of cups and the murmur of voices creating a comforting background noise. Fred watched Isabella move through the room, her smile never faltering despite the weight she carried.

As she collected his empty cup, their fingers brushed. She didn't look away this time, and neither did he; just a moment, long enough to be noticed, short enough to be denied.

"She's remarkable," Enzo said quietly, following Fred's gaze. "To keep this place going, to stay strong for her children...it's not easy. You know, there are some around here who still believe we can win this without becoming monsters. Meeting people like Isabella gives me a chance to believe that."

Fred nodded, his admiration for Isabella growing with each passing day. "No, it's not easy," he agreed. "But she does it. Every day. She's the kind of strength we need right now."

Enzo looked at him, a knowing smile tugging at his lips. "And you, Fred? What keeps you going?"

Fred met his gaze, a multitude of thoughts swirling in his mind. His mission, his duty, the faces of the men he had lost, the hope of a future without war. And now, Isabella. Her quiet courage and the small moments of peace he found in her presence.

"I suppose it's the same as everyone else," Fred said finally, his voice steady. "Hope. The belief that this will end, and we'll be able to build something better from the ashes."

Enzo nodded, his expression thoughtful. "Hope," he echoed. "It's a powerful thing, isn't it?"

Fred smiled, a hint of sadness in his eyes. "Yes," he said quietly. "It is."

As the sun dipped lower in the sky, pulling darkness across the streets of Naples, Fred felt a renewed sense of purpose. He knew he wasn't alone.

Sixteen

Naples, Italy - July 1941

Fred found himself alone once again in the café. The sun dipped low in the sky, casting long shadows across the cobblestones. The other patrons had gone, and the streets outside were quiet. Isabella was cleaning up, her movements slow and deliberate. Fred watched her, feeling a sudden urge to speak, to break the silence.

"You're a strong woman, Isabella," he said, his voice breaking the stillness. "To keep going, to keep this place running. It can't be easy."

Isabella paused, looking up at him, a tired smile tugging at her lips. "We do what we must," she said. "For our families, for ourselves. It's the only way to survive."

Fred nodded, understanding the truth of her words. "You remind me of someone I knew," he said quietly. "A friend. She had that same strength, that same determination."

Isabella's eyes softened, and she set down the rag she had been holding, moving to sit across from him. "What happened to her?" she asked gently.

Fred hesitated, the memories surfacing, sharp and painful. "She didn't make it," he said finally, his voice thick. "The war took her, like so many others."

"I'm sorry," Isabella said, reaching out to touch his hand. Her fingers were warm, a comfort against the chill of his thoughts. "Loss is never easy."

Fred looked at her, feeling the weight of his grief lift just a little. "No, it's not," he agreed. "But being here, talking to you, it helps. It reminds me that there's still good in the world, even now."

Isabella smiled, a genuine warmth in her eyes. "We have to hold on to that," she said. "To the small moments of kindness, of connection. It's what keeps us human. I am thankful for the neighbours, they have given me the evening off from the children today." She handed him a cup, her fingers brushing his once more. Neither moved away for a moment. Outside, a tram bell rang faintly in the distance, then the quiet closed in again.

Fred felt a flicker of something he hadn't felt in a long time. In Isabella's presence, he found a brief escape from the harsh realities of war, a moment of peace in a world turned upside down. As they sat together, the light fading outside, Fred realised that in this small café, amidst the turmoil, he had found a glimmer of solace, a reminder of what he was fighting for.

He was reminded of the humanity that still existed, even in the darkest of times.

As the soft lamplight cast a gentle glow over the café, Fred found himself lost in Isabella's eyes. The warmth in her gaze and the understanding in her words made him feel more alive than he had in months. They sat in silence, the unspoken words hanging in the air between them. Isabella's fingers still rested on his hand, a slight, comforting touch that sent warmth through his body.

"Luca," she whispered, barely audible over the quiet hum of the room. He looked up, meeting her eyes, and in that moment, the world outside seemed to fade away. There was only her, only this moment.

Before he could respond, Isabella leaned forward, her breath warm against his skin.

Fred felt his heart quicken as she drew closer, his senses heightening. Her lips brushed his, tentative and soft, a question more than an action. Fred's eyes closed, his hand moving to cup her cheek, his thumb brushing lightly against her skin. He kissed her back, feeling the gentleness of her lips, the soft sigh that escaped her as their kiss deepened.

When they finally pulled away, Fred's breath was shallow, his thoughts spinning.

"You're very sure of yourself," she said.

"Not always," Fred replied, almost before he could stop himself.

She tilted her head, studying him. "Then you hide it well."

Isabella's eyes were dark, her pupils wide with a mixture of emotions he couldn't quite decipher. She stood, her hand slipping from his, but only to extend it towards him, an invitation, a silent plea.

"Come upstairs with me," she said, her voice low, filled with a vulnerability that mirrored his own. "I don't want to be alone tonight."

Fred hesitated for a fraction of a second, the reality of war and its shadows lingering at the edges of his mind. But the pull was too strong, the need for connection too overwhelming to ignore. He took her hand, standing up and allowing her to lead him through the dimly lit café, up the narrow staircase to the small, private world above.

As the door clicked shut behind them, the outside world vanished entirely. Fred turned to Isabella, his hands finding her waist, pulling her close. Her hands threaded through his hair, and he kissed her again, with more urgency this time, a need to feel, to escape, to find solace in her touch.

Isabella responded in kind, her body pressing against his, her kisses fervent, searching.

They moved together, shedding the remnants of their day, the ache of exhaustion, the feeling of fear, until there was nothing left between them but bare skin and the quiet blaze of desire. Isabella's room was modest, the bed narrow and worn, but as they lay there tangled, their limbs a labyrinth of warmth and comfort, it felt like the safest place in the world. The faint scent of flowers from her pillow mixed with the lingering smell of woodsmoke from the fireplace, wrapping around them like a whispered promise.

Fred's lips traced slow, reverent paths along her neck, soft dips and gentle hollows, pausing to breathe in the delicate aroma of her skin, the faint saltiness of a day's sweat. His fingers followed, light as feathers, mapping the curve of her collarbone, the subtle rise and fall beneath her skin. Every brush, every sigh, was a wordless conversation, an exchange of trust in a world that had offered so little.

Isabella's hands wandered with purpose, tracing delicate, swirling patterns across Fred's back, each touch a quiet balm to the storm in his mind, grounding him, reminding him that here, here with her, he could be. The muscles beneath her fingertips twitched involuntarily, and he caught the flicker of surprise in her eyes as his hand moved slowly up the inside of her leg, before she smiled softly.

It was slow, savouring each second as though the moment might stretch forever. Every kiss was a promise whispered in silence; every caress a testament to the humanity that survived even amid the chaos and carnage of war. Time blurred, fingers tangled in hair, the warmth of breath mingling, hearts beating in a steady duet.

Fred paused to study her face, eyes closed, cheeks flushed, lips parted slightly as she breathed his name in a soft murmur. Her skin was flushed and glowing, radiant in the dim candlelight that flickered against peeling wallpaper. He traced the line of her jaw, memorising the curve of her cheek, the delicate flutter of her lashes.

Isabella's fingers lay across his chest, fingertips warm against his skin, memorising the scar on his ribs, the way his breath hitched at her touch. Their bodies moved in a slow, sacred rhythm, never rushed, never careless, each motion carrying the impact of longing and tenderness.

When at last they reached a climax, not a roar but a quiet surrender, an intimate sharing that left them trembling and breathless. They collapsed into one another, limbs entwined like roots beneath the earth, hearts beating loud in the small room.

Silence settled around them, thick and complete save for the soft, shared sounds of their breathing. Fred held Isabella close, his hand resting lightly on the curve of her waist, feeling the steady rise and fall of her chest beneath his palm. The rhythm of her heartbeat echoed against his own, a fragile but unbreakable tether in a world gone mad.

He felt at peace, as if the storm inside him had quieted, even if just for a moment. As sleep began to claim him, Fred pressed a soft kiss to her hair, whispering her name, a silent vow to remember this moment.

Seventeen

Fred stirred beneath the thin cotton sheet, blinking against the warmth that filtered through the room. The golden light of morning spilt softly through the shutters, illuminating the worn floorboards and dust motes that danced in the air. For a moment, he didn't move. The air was still. The usual weight in his chest, the pressure of danger, duty, and disguise, felt curiously absent.

He turned his head. Isabella was lying beside him, one arm tucked under her cheek, her breathing slow and even. A loose curl had fallen across her face. Fred reached out, brushing it gently aside. She stirred but didn't wake, her lips parting slightly in her sleep.

For a while, he just watched her. It was the first time in months, perhaps longer, that he felt anchored to something real. Not the mission. Not the lies. Just a moment. A person.

He slipped out of bed quietly, moving toward the narrow window. Naples lay beyond, already warming under the Mediterranean sun. From this high up, the street noises below were muffled. He could smell bread baking, salt on the breeze, and faintly, engine oil from the port.

A creak behind him.

"You're thinking too loudly," Isabella murmured.

Fred turned, a smile playing on his lips. "Old habit."

She sat up slowly, holding the sheet to her chest, hair tousled, eyes sleepy but sharp. "You don't have to apologise for waking before me," she said, reading his guilt as easily as if it were scrawled across his chest.

"I wasn't sure how this would feel in daylight," he admitted, walking back to the edge of the bed.

"And?" she asked, tilting her head.

Fred sat beside her. "It feels like something I shouldn't want... but do."

Isabella studied him for a moment, then reached for his hand. Her fingers laced with his, warm and certain. "We don't get many chances at something real. Not anymore."

They sat like that for a while, tangled fingers, bare knees touching. Fred leaned in, brushing his lips against her temple.

Eventually, Isabella rose, wrapping a thin robe around her body. "Coffee?" she offered, padding barefoot toward the tiny kitchen in the corner.

Fred chuckled. "If you have it."

"I always have a way. We live on the edge of a knife; there's no surviving that without coffee. You just have to know who to ask to get hold of it."

She poured two small cups from a dented moka pot, handing him one. The coffee was thin and bitter, but the heat in the cup warmed his palms, and for half a breath, he could almost be back in Worthing. Isabella's fingers brushed a folded ration card on the table, and, without looking up, she smoothed it flat as if ironing out an old worry. "What will you do when you leave?" she asked quietly.

Fred swallowed, the answer a taste he kept to himself. "The same as always," he said, and the word hung frail between them.

They sat at the tiny kitchen table, chairs too close, knees knocking gently with every movement.

"I dreamt of home last night," Fred said, surprising even himself. "Not the war. Just… home. My mother's garden. The smell of the sea."

Isabella's smile softened. "You miss it."

"I miss who I was there," he replied. "Before I became someone else for this bloody war." Fred asserted himself, realising he was slipping from his purpose.

She reached over, pressing her palm to his cheek. "You're still in there. Even if the world tries to take pieces of you."

Fred closed his eyes at her touch, leaning into it.

"I'm glad I found this place," he said after a beat. "Found you."

Isabella looked away, the tenderness in her gaze briefly clouded by worry. "You're not the only one with secrets, Luca," she said quietly. "But if I'm honest... I don't want to be alone in this world anymore."

Fred's brow furrowed. "Then we won't be. Not while I can help it."

A knock downstairs shattered the moment. It was light, tentative, but sharp enough to remind them both of where they were, and what waited outside.

Isabella stood, her back straightening as she pulled the robe tighter. "Customers," she said, tone shifting automatically. "I am the only café not serving roasted barley instead of real coffee in Naples at the moment, not sure how long that will be though."

Fred moved to dress, slipping on his shirt, tucking in the revolver he still carried. He caught her glance as he did.

"You'll be careful?" she asked.

"Always," he said, though they both knew it wasn't true.

She pressed a kiss to his cheek, brief but sincere, then turned toward the stairs.

As Fred followed, adjusting his collar, he felt the strain of the world settle back over his shoulders. But something had shifted inside him. He wasn't just fighting for orders or duty. Now, he was fighting for something that felt like home.

Eighteen

The following days passed like a dream wrapped in gauze, light, warm and surreal in their stillness. The tension that had gripped Fred since the moment he arrived in Naples had eased, if only slightly. The city, though still draped in the grey shawl of occupation, felt quieter. Rumours filtered in, enemy patrols reduced, the commandant replaced, or ill. Some whispered of internal disputes, of breakdowns in discipline. But no one trusted calm during a war. Least of all, Fred.

He had stayed the night at Isabella's, and again the next. They didn't speak much of what it meant. They didn't need to. Mornings were slow and quiet; coffee, silence, the brush of fingers over a collarbone. Fred had not known softness in a long time, and now that it had found him, he was unsure how to carry it without breaking it.

On the third afternoon, Fred slipped away. Not because he wanted to, but because he had to. There were codes to collect, papers to destroy, and contact points to refresh. He left Isabella sleeping in the café's attic flat, sunlight spilling across the curve of her bare back.

He walked the longer route through the back alleys, the smell of stale wine and rotting citrus hanging thick in the air. Naples pulsed beneath his feet. He cut behind the old marina wall, past a shuttered fish market, until he found the place. It was an old shipping yard, long abandoned, its concrete cracked with weeds.

Luciano was already there, leaning against a rust-streaked bollard, a small satchel at his feet.

"You're late," he said with a smirk.

Fred didn't rise to it. "You're early."

Luciano pushed off the bollard. He studied Fred for a beat, then narrowed his eyes, curious. "You've changed your coat."

Fred glanced down at the brown jacket, fresh, stiff. "Mine got soaked in the storm last week."

Luciano tilted his head. "Storm, eh?" He crossed his arms. "Alright. Want to tell me what's going on?"

Fred frowned. "What do you mean?"

"You've got that look," Luciano said, eyes gleaming. "Same one I saw on Tomaso after he met the midwife from Palermo. The same look Enzo gets when he writes letters he never sends."

Fred snorted. "What look?"

Luciano stepped closer. "The look of a man whose heart has been ambushed."

Fred looked away, nervously. "It's nothing."

"Fred." Luciano's voice dropped. "She's not nothing. I've seen the way your shoulders sit now. You're breathing again. Properly."

Fred exhaled sharply, then sat on the edge of a broken crate. "It's Isabella."

Luciano crouched beside him, his voice softer now. "How long?"

Fred shrugged. "A few days. Maybe longer, if I'm honest with myself."

Luciano nodded slowly. "The one who runs the café?"

Fred blinked and nodded.

"Come on," Luciano grinned. "I've been watching your patterns since March. You were always in and out. The last three days, you barely left. I had to make sure you weren't in trouble."

Fred gave a wry smile. "Not trouble. Not the kind you think, anyway."

Luciano grew serious again. "You know what I'm going to say."

Fred nodded. "Don't let it cloud my judgement. Don't get attached. War doesn't pause for love."

"But," Luciano added, "don't ignore it either. This isn't the kind of thing you throw away like an old mission briefing. It keeps you tethered. Reminds you what we're fighting for."

Fred met his eyes. "You think that's worth it? Risking that kind of grief?"

Luciano didn't answer immediately. He stood, walked a few paces, then turned back. "We're ghosts in the making, Fred. All of us. If something, or someone, makes you feel human again? Take it. Even if only for a while."

The silence that followed was heavy but not uncomfortable.

Luciano lifted the satchel. "Here. Codes and a new list of safe houses. Enzo added one outside the city, a farmhouse near Benevento. Might be useful soon."

Fred took the satchel and weighed it in his hands. "Anything else?"

Luciano gave Fred one last look, half amusement, half warning. "Go on. Get back to your café. Before someone else starts serving her coffee."

Fred chuckled. "She doesn't let anyone else near the machine."

As he walked away, bag slung over his shoulder, Fred glanced up at the Naples sky, blue, with clouds like torn muslin, and thought of Isabella, her eyes, the press of her hand in the dark. War remained, but beneath it now pulsed something new.

A reason.

A heartbeat.

Nineteen

Naples, Italy - September 1941

With the smell of fish in the air, Fred made his way down to the docks of Naples. Somewhere metal clanged against metal, and the tide slapped at the pilings in a restless rhythm.

It was a bustling scene, filled with fishermen mending nets, merchants haggling over the day's catch, and sailors going about their work. The clamour of voices and the cries of gulls created a cacophony that seemed to pulse with the life of the city. But beneath this normalcy lay a tension, a palpable unease that Fred could feel in his bones. The docks were heavily patrolled, and the presence of Nazi soldiers, ever-increasing, was a constant reminder of the war. Their grey uniforms and harsh voices cut through the noise like a knife, making Fred's skin prickle.

Fred kept his head down, his cap pulled low over his eyes as he moved through the crowd. He navigated his way past crates of fish and barrels of supplies, his eyes scanning the throng for any sign of his contact. A dockhand in a frayed cap muttered something about the weather as Fred passed. He nodded, neither slowing nor meeting the man's eyes, just another shadow in the crowd.

The docks were a critical point for the war effort, and the Italians had tightened their grip on the area, knowing of its strategic importance. The sight of German patrol boats and armoured vehicles was increasingly common, their presence a looming threat over the fishermen and dockworkers trying to go about their daily lives.

Across the quay, a man in a battered coat adjusted his cap. Once, twice, then turned away. Fred altered course without hesitation.

As he neared the rendezvous point, Fred's eyes flickered to a group of men fishing off the side of the pier, their faces lined with worry. Fishing had once been a simple livelihood, but now it was fraught with the dangers of occupying forces, curfews, and the constant threat of arrest. Fred could see the anxiety in their eyes as they cast their lines, their glances darting nervously toward the soldiers who roamed the docks.

Fred moved past them, heading towards a row of warehouses that loomed over the water. He pulled his collar up against the chill, his eyes narrowing as he spotted a familiar figure standing near a stack of crates. It was Paolo, a local dockworker and a member of the resistance, a man who had, according to Enzo, proven reliable in past encounters. Today,

Paolo would be the bearer of news that could change the course of the conflict in Naples.

Paolo's face was shadowed under his cap, his eyes constantly shifting, watching for anyone who might be paying too much attention. Fred approached him with the casual ease of someone who had been here many times before, his posture relaxed, but every nerve in his body alert. He stopped next to Paolo, his gaze directed out to sea, watching the waves lap against the hulls of moored boats.

"Busy day," Fred said, his voice low, casual.

Paolo nodded, his eyes still scanning the docks. "Always is," he replied. "More boats are coming in every day. Supplies, troops. It's a never-ending stream."

Fred glanced sideways at him. "You have something for me?"

Paolo nodded, reaching into his coat. He pulled out a small piece of paper, folded tightly, and handed it to Fred, his hand trembling slightly. "It's all there," Paolo said, his voice barely above a whisper. "The time, the place. You'll have to be careful. The patrols are tighter than ever, and Scholl's not a fool. He knows people want him dead."

Fred took the paper, slipping it into his pocket without looking at it. He kept his eyes on the horizon, giving nothing away. "Anything else I should know?" he asked.

Paolo hesitated, then shook his head. "Just…be careful. This is risky. If you get caught…"

"I won't get caught," Fred said, his voice firm. "Just make sure the escape route is clear. I'll handle the rest. What is a high-ranking General like Scholl doing in Naples?"

Paolo nodded, but the worry in his eyes didn't fade. "The city's different now, the Germans are increasingly turning their attention to Southern Italy," he said quietly. "More soldiers, more checkpoints. People are on edge. Scholl is the military attaché coming to check on things." Paolo looked over his shoulder and then grabbed Fred's arm, "If you do this, it's going to stir things up. There's going to be a backlash."

Fred looked at him, his expression unreadable. "There's already a backlash," he said. "People are suffering. This has to end. And if taking out Scholl makes things difficult for the fascists, then it's worth it."

Paolo didn't argue. He knew as well as Fred did that the stakes were high, that the assassination of Walter Scholl, a high-ranking Nazi, would send shockwaves through the German ranks. Scholl was a key figure, a man with the power to make life hell for the people of Naples. His removal would be a blow to the Nazis and a blow to the fascists in charge of Italy, a chance for the resistance to gain the upper hand, even if only temporarily.

Fred nodded to Paolo, his jaw set in determination. "I'll do what needs to be done," he said, his voice steady. "And when it's over, we'll be one step closer to taking back this city."

He turned and walked away, his mind already turning over the details of the mission. As he moved through the crowded docks, past the soldiers and the fishermen, he felt the impact of the assignment settle on his shoulders. The time and location of the assassination were set; now, it was up to him to execute it.

As Fred made his way back through the maze of warehouses, he couldn't help but feel a thrill of anticipation. The mission was dangerous, the stakes high. The city of Naples lay before him, a sprawling, chaotic landscape of possibility and peril. And in the midst of it all, Fred knew he would find a way to succeed.

The sun dipped lower in the sky, etching silhouettes across the docks, and Fred quickened his pace. The streets of Naples were a labyrinth of intrigue and danger, but Fred was ready to navigate them. A gull screamed overhead as he stepped onto the gangway, its shadow flickering over the water like a blade.

Twenty

The villa sat high above the city, its pale stone walls catching the last light. From a distance, it looked serene, almost beautiful, but Fred knew better. The air here, heavy with the scent of damp earth and crushed wild herbs, was a deception. Behind those walls were rifles, patrols, and Walter Scholl himself, a man who never travelled without layers of protection.

From the villa drifted the faint, sweet smell of gardenias from a hidden terrace, a cloying perfume that did little to mask the stench of military power.

Fred had climbed halfway up the terraced hillside, weaving through olive groves until he found a vantage point above the road. The long grass, dry and bristling, scratched at his face as he crouched, notebook balanced on his knee. He felt the dust in his mouth and took a small sip from his water flask, his tongue still tasting of the long, dry climb.
Below, a distant church bell pealed across the bay, its sound thin and mournful in the twilight.

He watched the two guards at the front gate, their dark uniforms stark against the bruised, pearlescent stone of the villa. Another pair walked the perimeter at regular intervals. Their paths overlapped every seven minutes. He wrote it down, quick sketches of routes and timings. A cypress tree partially shielded the rear courtyard, providing good cover if one knew when to move; its dark silhouette was a solid promise of concealment.

From the villa, faint noises drifted up the hillside: a burst of loud laughter, the scrape of chairs across marble, the tinny, upbeat melody of a German march from a gramophone. Scholl liked his comfort; that much was clear. Comfort dulled men's vigilance. Fred made a note of that, too, as a cloud of rich cigar smoke hung for a moment in the air from a balcony before dissipating.

The longer he watched, the heavier the mission weighed on him. This wasn't a dockside patrol to be avoided or a fuel depot to be sabotaged. This was different. He was planning the removal of a man whose absence would shake Naples like an earthquake. With every patrol he timed, with every window he sketched, he felt the cost rising higher. He had a sudden, sharp memory of a Naples morning, of the vibrant hum of a bustling market, the salty smell of the sea, the rich aroma of espresso, all things that would be swept away in the chaos his actions would unleash.

He shifted his position, brushing dirt from his sleeve, and forced himself to breathe steadily. His hands, gripping the notebook, felt cold and clammy. A single mistake here, even a snapped twig, and he'd be another nameless prisoner dragged through the villa gates. He couldn't afford carelessness. Not this time.

Fred closed the notebook and slipped it back into his coat. The pattern was clear enough for now; he would return tomorrow. Patience was his only weapon before the strike.

As he descended the hillside path, the city lights flickered awake below, golden veins in the dark. The sound of a ship's horn, long and low, echoed from the port. He thought of Isabella then, her voice, her stubborn gaze, the way she looked at him as if she saw straight through his false name. The thought of her brought a knot of fear to his stomach. He would have to speak to her before this was done. Not with whole truths perhaps, but with enough. Enough to let her know that tomorrow night might be the most dangerous of his life.

The villa remained behind him, quiet and watchful on the hill. But Fred felt its shadow following him back into the city, a cold, oppressive presence that seeped into the humid night air, a constant reminder of what was to come.

Twenty One

The bustle of the city, vendors shouting, carts rattling, radios humming with static, had all but faded, replaced by the quiet lapping of water. The sea was strewn with late afternoon light, its surface gently rippling as if breathing beneath the sun. Boats bobbed in the harbour, their hulls casting soft shadows on the worn stone walls of the docks.

Fred walked beside Isabella, their steps unhurried, their arms brushing now and then, not quite holding hands, not quite apart. She wore a faded blue linen dress, her hair loose for once, caught by the breeze as they strolled past moored fishing boats. He called himself Luca still, to her. But the name felt thinner each day, like a mask worn too long in the rain.

"I used to come here as a girl," Isabella said, nodding toward a row of battered crates and weather-stained barrels. "My father and I would watch the fishermen clean their nets. He'd smoke, and I'd pester him with questions about where the boats went at night."

Fred smiled softly. "And what did he say?"

She shrugged. "That they chased the stars. That sometimes, if you were fortunate, you could pull up the moon with your net."

He chuckled, but there was sadness in his eyes. "He sounds like a man who saw magic in the world."

"He was," she said. "Even when there wasn't much to believe in." She looked up at Fred. "You remind me of him sometimes. The way you look out across the water, it's like you're waiting for something to come back."

Fred glanced away, toward the horizon where the sun dipped closer to the sea. "Maybe I am," he murmured.

They walked in silence for a while. A boy sprinted past, barefoot and laughing, chasing a dog with a scrap of paper in its mouth. The breeze tugged at Isabella's dress and curled around Fred's collar. He felt the strain of the revolver back in his apartment. The folded map. The instructions he had memorised. He could almost feel the ticking of a clock inside him, loud and inevitable.

"Izzy," he said at last, his voice quieter than the wind. "There's something I need to tell you." She stilled, cloth in hand, the quiet hum of the café suddenly loud in the absence of words. Her brow furrowed, the corners of her mouth tightening as if she already knew this wasn't a confession about bread or wine. "What is it, Luca?" she asked again, softer now.

He hesitated, chewing the inside of his cheek. He wanted to tell her everything. Wanted to explain who he was, what he was fighting for, why tomorrow might be the last time he saw the sky.

He rolled the cup between his hands, watching the way the light caught the steam. The words were already on his tongue, heavy as lead, but for a moment, he listened to the clink of cups and the murmur of voices around them.

"There's something I have to do," he said instead. "Tomorrow night."

She didn't flinch, but her fingers tightened around the handle of her cup. "That sounds dangerous," she said, the words light, the tone anything but.

He nodded once. "Very."

Her eyes darkened. "Is it… because of the Germans?"

Fred gave a soft laugh, more breath than voice. "What in this city isn't these days?"

She reached for his hand, and this time he didn't resist. Her fingers were warm, firm. Grounding.

"You're not just a barman from the North," she said quietly. "I've known that from the beginning."

Fred stiffened, but she held his hand tighter.

"You don't have to tell me," she continued, "but I need you to promise something."

"What?"

"That you'll come back. That you'll try. Even if it's impossible."

He looked at her then, her freckles just visible across her cheekbones, at the defiance and softness tangled in her gaze. At the weight she carried, and how she never complained about it.

"I can't promise I'll come back," Fred said. "But I promise I'll try. I promise I won't stop trying."

She nodded, her throat working as she swallowed. "Then that's enough."

They sat for a while at the end of the dock, legs dangling over the edge, the sea lapping at the stone below. A small boat passed, its hull green with peeling paint, the older man steering it nodding once in their direction. The sun was setting, casting the sky in burnt orange and bruised purple. Fred wanted to stop time, just for a minute.

"I wish we had met before all this," he said softly.

Nearby, a delivery cart rattled past, its wheels thudding over cobblestones. The sound marked the moment, carrying it away into the street.

"I'm not sure we would have noticed each other," Isabella replied, leaning her head against his shoulder. "Sometimes it takes a broken world to make people see clearly."

They stayed like that until the lamps began to flicker on across the port and the stars blinked, one by one, into the darkening sky.

Twenty Two

The warm evening glow of Naples did nothing to soothe the sharp edge in Fred's gut. Naples may have been winding down for the night, but he wasn't. As he left the apartment, he looked up to see the sky over Naples had bled into a deep orange as the sun moved behind the horizon. Shadows were stretched long across the harbour, swallowing the narrow alleys in patches of dark.

The further he moved from the bustle of the inner city, the quieter the streets became, more peaceful and darker. Cracks echoed in the distance: a slammed shutter, a bottle broken underfoot, a dog barking once and falling silent. The silence pressed in like a weight.

Tucked beneath his worn coat, Fred could feel the revolver nestled tight against his ribs. Cold metal. Cold purpose. His fingers had brushed the weapon ten times in the past twenty minutes, not to draw it, but to remind himself it was there. A failsafe. A last resort.

The uniform Paolo had given him clung to him like a curse. Italian army surplus, sun-faded olive drab, a little too short at the wrists. He'd removed the insignias, but they had left ghost marks on the sleeves.

A keen eye might notice. That was the gamble. Everything tonight was a gamble.

The villa was on the outskirts of Naples, a grand estate that rose from the earth like a fortress wrapped in white stone and iron gates. It belonged to a wealthy sympathiser, an industrialist who'd thrown in with the Nazis early, ensuring his power stayed intact while his countrymen starved. Fred had studied the place through a cracked pair of opera glasses earlier that week. One entrance. Two outer guards. Possibly more inside. The meeting was private. There was no public fanfare, no extra patrols. But that didn't make it safer. It made it harder to predict.

Walter Scholl would be there. The man had a reputation that curdled the stomach. Ruthless, brilliant, and loyal to the Reich to his dying breath. The thought of getting that close to him made Fred's fingers twitch. Assassinate him, and the Nazi support in Naples would fracture; it would give people the belief that we can beat the fascists. But it had to be done clean. Quiet. One shot. No arrests. No witnesses.

Fred ducked into the shadows of a crumbling stone wall as the villa came into view. A pair of guards leaned lazily against the gateposts, their rifles slung low, laughing about something Fred couldn't hear. From this distance, they looked bored. But boredom could snap into suspicion in a heartbeat.

He closed his eyes for a moment and let the city fall away. He pictured the estate map. The uniform. The steps. The words he would say.

Infiltrate. Eliminate. Escape.

His breath caught, shallow in his chest. This wasn't like the lighthouse. That had been messy. Brutal. This had to be precise.

He stepped from the shadows.

The gravel crunched beneath his boots. Each footfall landed like a drumbeat in his ears. He kept his chin up, stride brisk but not rushed. One of the guards straightened slightly.

"*Chi sei?*" the guard asked. Who are you?

Fred didn't falter. "*Turno di riserva. Il capitano mi ha mandato.*" Relief duty. The captain sent me.

He kept his tone level, just bored enough to sound believable. The guard squinted at him for a beat too long. Fred felt a trickle of sweat run down the back of his neck. The grip on his pistol was slick with it. If they asked for papers, he'd have to shoot them. He couldn't risk being taken.

But the second guard just shrugged. "*Entra. Stai attento al cane.*" Go ahead. Watch for the dog.

The gate groaned open.

For half a heartbeat, he considered turning back, inventing a reason, walking away into the dark. But the gatekeeper's eyes were on him, and the path behind was no safer than the one ahead.

Fred stepped through.

The moment the gates closed behind him, the silence returned. Different now. More menacing. The villa loomed above him, tall and white like bone in the moonlight. Staff bustled in and out of side doors, servants, porters, maybe even local collaborators. Two of them muttered in low Neapolitan about the price of bread, their words clipped short when an officer strode past. Nobody looked twice at Fred as he moved toward the rear entrance. He didn't belong, not really, but that was the trick: to act like he did.

Inside, the contrast hit like a slap. Naples had been starved. Here, opulence bled from the walls. Crystal chandeliers, polished marble floors, fresh flowers in vases that cost more than a dockworker's wage.

Fred forced himself not to linger. He moved down the hall, copying the gait of the staff, pausing to wipe invisible dust from a sideboard. His eyes flicked constantly, always calculating.

He passed a pair of officers in a side hallway. They didn't look at him. That was both good and dangerous. Good because he wasn't challenged. Dangerous because it meant he was truly inside now. One wrong move, one misplaced glance, and he would die here, in this house, in borrowed clothes.

From the far side of the hallway came muffled voices. Fred crept to the edge of the corridor and peered around the corner to see a dining room or perhaps a conference room. A long polished table, a map of southern Italy spread across it. Men gathered around, uniforms bristling with medals, cigarettes smouldering in ashtrays.

And there, standing at the head of the table, was Walter Scholl. His posture was ramrod straight, one hand resting on the map, the other curled loosely at his side like it could close into a fist at any second.

Fred felt the shift immediately. Not fear exactly, but a cold focus. The kind he'd felt before missions in North Africa, before boarding ships under fire. It slowed time. Sharpened sound. The tick of a clock. The scratch of a pen. Scholl's voice was clipped and commanding.

Fred exhaled slowly.

There were officers between them; Scholl wasn't exposed. Not yet. Fred would have to wait. Drift closer. Choose the moment.

He felt the revolver again. So close. So fragile.

Then a sound behind him, a door.

Fred's blood turned to ice.

He froze.

Leather soles whispered on marble, steady and unhurried, and the faint scent of cigar smoke reached him before the shadow did.

Someone had entered the hallway behind him.

Twenty Three

The door behind him clicked shut with a sound that echoed like a gunshot in Fred's ears.

He didn't move. Didn't even breathe.

Footsteps. Slow. Methodical. Approaching from behind.

Each step sounded too measured, too deliberate. Not the careless shuffle of a servant, these were a predator's steps, each one closing the gap like a tightening noose.

Fred's pulse thundered in his ears. His mind raced, too fast to be useful. If it were an officer, he couldn't run. If it were a servant, they might scream. If it were a soldier…

A shadow crossed the marble floor beside him. The figure was almost level with him now.

Fred acted.

He straightened, turned on his heel, and walked. Not too fast, not too slow. Just another soldier on an errand. His gaze didn't waver. He didn't look at the figure.

But the man stopped. Fred's gut twisted.

"*Tu!*" the voice barked. You!

Fred turned, heart pounding.

It was a young Italian officer. His uniform was too clean, his boots polished to a mirror shine, and a cap tucked beneath one arm.

Arrogant, curious. A trace of sharp cologne lingered on him, foreign and out of place in a city scraping to survive.

"*Cosa ci fai qui?*" What are you doing here?

Fred's mouth went dry. He had two seconds to respond, three at most. He drew on everything Enzo and Luciano had drilled into him.

"*Il tenente Conti mi ha chiesto di portare i documenti dal portico.*" Lieutenant Conti asked me to bring documents from the porch.

The officer frowned slightly, clearly trying to place the name. Fred knew it was a gamble; the name had appeared briefly in a file Enzo intercepted. If this man didn't know Conti…

But then the officer just nodded, suspicious but not enough to challenge him further. "*Sbrigati. Non dovresti stare qui.*" Hurry up. You shouldn't be here.

Fred gave a curt nod and turned away, his lungs aching from the breath he'd been holding.

He moved back down the corridor and ducked into a narrow service passage before exhaling shakily. Sweat beaded at the back of his neck. That had been close. Too close.

Through a narrow vent in the wall, Fred could make out the voices beyond. Officers. One of them, precise, unhurried, chillingly calm, could only be Scholl.

He leaned closer, straining to hear.

"...*Lieferung verzögert... Widerstandsaktivität in Salerno nimmt zu...*"

...Shipment delayed... resistance activity in Salerno is increasing...

Scholl spoke again, his tone sharpened like a blade drawn across glass.

"*Wir werden sie zerschlagen. Stück für Stück. Italien darf nicht zu einem Nest für Verräter verkommen.*"

We will crush them. Piece by piece. Italy must not become a nest for traitors.

There was a pause. The following words were quieter. More dangerous.

"*Wenn Neapel fällt, fällt auch Rom.*"

If Naples falls, Rome falls too.

Another voice murmured assent, then silence, until Scholl spoke again, with a note of steel finality.

"*Ich will Namen. Jeden einzelnen. Wir fangen mit den Bars und Cafés an. Dort reden die Zungen am leichtesten.*"

I want names. Every single one. We begin with the bars and cafés, that's where tongues loosen first.

Fred stepped back, breath shallow.

The café. Isabella. The words hit like ice water down his spine. Her face, the quiet hum of the café, the sound of her laugh, all of it could vanish with a single name passed to the wrong ear.

He had to move. Fast.

140

He slipped back into the hallway, but something had shifted. There were more voices now, guards talking, boots echoing on stone.

His window was closing.

But he wasn't done. He still hadn't had a clear shot.

And that meant getting even closer.

Fred pulled the cap lower over his eyes and moved with purpose down the main corridor toward the rear chamber, where Scholl and his inner circle were now settling into armchairs for drinks. The atmosphere had shifted from strategy to leisure. That was both good and bad. Fewer people standing. Easier targets. But also more relaxed. Less tolerance for strangers.

He paused outside a servant's supply room. Inside, cloaks, dusters, linen, there was enough to change his silhouette slightly. He quickly pulled on a heavier coat and tucked his sidearm higher into his waistband, hidden but accessible.

Then he moved again.

Just past the chamber, he found the service door that led into the rear sitting room.

It was unlocked.

Fred cracked the door open an inch.

There he was.

Scholl.

Seated in a high-backed leather chair beside a bar cart glinting with half-drained decanters, laughing at something an older officer had said in German. His posture was relaxed, legs crossed, a cigar burning between two fingers. No sidearm. No guard within arm's reach. Only the low murmur of conversation and the soft clink of ice against glass.

Fred's hand hovered over his coat. His fingers brushed the grip of the pistol.

He steadied his breathing. Counted the steps. One shot. Centre mass. Then again, to be sure. Fast, efficient. No hesitation.

The plan was set.

But then, Isabella.

Her face flashed across his mind like a warning flare. The café. The life she'd rebuilt from ruins. If he were caught... if he failed... they would burn it all to the ground. She would be nothing but collateral in a storm he'd unleashed.

And Enzo. Luciano. Every contact he'd used. Every hand that had helped him.

He mouth went dry.

No mistakes.

His thumb slid the safety off.

Fred pushed the door open with the toe of his boot. Smooth. Quiet.

The sound of laughter didn't stop until it did.

Scholl looked up. A flicker of recognition crossed his face.

Fred raised the pistol. A heartbeat.

The room seemed to contract, all sound drowned beneath the thud of his pulse.

CRACK.

The first shot hit Scholl just below the eye, snapping his head back in a violent, jerking motion. Blood sprayed the wall behind him.

CRACK.

The second buried itself in his chest. The officer beside him leapt to his feet, shouting, reaching for a weapon.

Fred didn't wait.

He turned and ran, footsteps pounding down the corridor. Shouts erupted behind him. Alarm bells. Barked German and Italian. Boots thundered after him.

His pulse was a storm. His ears rang. Every nerve was alive. Somewhere behind him, a heavy door slammed, the sound echoing like the final nail in a coffin.

Scholl was dead.

Twenty Four

The gunshots still echoed in his skull.

Fred sprinted through the corridor, boots slamming the polished marble. Behind him, a storm had broken. Shouts, panic, the clatter of overturned chairs. The heavy tread of soldiers pounding after him.

He skidded around a corner, one boot scraping the marble as he caught himself. The villa's hallways blurred, gold-framed portraits, silk wallpaper, dark wood doors. He needed to vanish. Fast.

He ducked into a side room, some drawing chamber. Empty. Fred's eyes flicked to the harp, its strings silent, untouched. The chaos swallowed a fragile remnant of peace. Above it, a long curtain flapped near an open window, letting in the night air. He locked the door behind him and bought himself ten seconds, maybe less.

His chest heaved. Sweat stung his eyes. He yanked a linen runner from a side table, stuffed it into the hearth, and pulled the nearest oil lamp from the wall.

The glass smashed. The fire snapped and crackled as it devoured the linen runner. Heat flared, licking his skin, while sparks floated upwards like angry fireflies. The sharp smell of burning oil filled the cramped room.

Fred backed away, watching as the fire caught the curtain, then the chair, then the polished panelling. Smoke thickened quickly, curling black fingers along the ceiling. He yanked his coat over his mouth, choking back the acrid smoke, lungs burning, every step a fight.

Shouts rose outside the door. The handle rattled. A boot kicked it hard. Another.

He was out the window before the third kick landed.

The terrace was narrow, barely a foot of ledge beneath the shuttered glass. Below him, a drop into hedges. Above, a gutter.

Voices barked. One of them was giving orders.

"Das Feuer! Schnell!"

Perfect.

Fred dropped from the ledge, crashing through the manicured hedgerow with a grunt. Twigs snapped. Thorns clawed at his skin. Pain lanced through his arms and face where the thorns had caught, but he swallowed the sting and pushed forward. He hit the dirt hard, rolled, and came up running. His chest heaved. The cool night air hit his burning lungs like a shock, but there was no time to slow.

Behind him, the villa was waking into chaos. Firelight flickered across the stone. A plume of smoke curled up into the starlit sky.

He dashed behind a line of topiary, eyes darting, heart hammering. There, he saw a service path. Gravel crunched beneath his boots as he ran, keeping to the shadows.

But as he reached the edge of the garden, two guards stepped into view, rifles slung, drawn by the smoke.

"*Halt!*"

Fred didn't wait. He raised his pistol and fired twice.

No time for mercy.

The first guard fell backwards, a shocked grunt escaping him. The second ducked and fired blindly. The shot rang past Fred's arm.

He dove, rolled, and came up behind a low stone wall, more shouting. Footsteps converging. No time to think.

Fred turned and sprinted through a break in the hedge, across the orchard. His lungs burned. His ankle twisted painfully with every step. He couldn't stop. Couldn't even limp.

The outer wall loomed ahead. Not the main gate, too obvious. But there, near the edge, there was a narrow gap where ivy choked the masonry.

He ran for it,

And nearly slammed into a figure in the shadows, the pistol was up before he registered the familiar voice. Fred's voice rattled in his chest, "I almost shot you!"

"Fred!" Enzo hissed. "You did it?"

Fred nodded, breath ragged. "Scholl's dead. The whole place is on fire. They're swarming."

Enzo grabbed his arm. "Come on. This way."

They ducked into the gap, squeezed through the crumbling stone and out into the fields beyond the estate.

Behind them, flames now reached the upper windows. Smoke billowed into the sky like a signal flare. Sirens wailed in the city below. The villa was alight, both in fire and fury.

They ran.

Fred didn't look back.

The night fields stretched wide and dark, a patchwork of olive groves and stone walls broken by sloping terraces. Every breath was knives in his chest, the acrid smoke of the villa still lodged in his lungs. Enzo ran just ahead, his silhouette cutting a ragged shape against the glow of the fire.

Shouts carried faintly over the wind. A dog barked. Then another. The estate was in uproar, and soon the hunt would spill into the countryside.

"Faster," Enzo hissed over his shoulder.

Fred's ankle screamed, every step sending a jolt up his leg, but he bit it back and forced himself on. They vaulted a low wall, boots crunching against gravel before plunging into a vineyard, the vines clawing at their coats. Leaves slapped Fred's face as they crashed through, his pistol heavy in his hand, slick with sweat.

A sudden flare of lantern-light swept across the field.

"Down!" Enzo dragged him hard, and the two men fell into the shadows of the vines.

Two German soldiers trudged along the row barely twenty yards away, rifles slung, voices low and sharp. One swept his beam of light in lazy arcs, catching dust motes, and the other muttered about the fire. Fred pressed his face into the dirt, the earth damp and metallic against his lips. His lungs begged for air, but he didn't dare move.

The lantern beam passed, swung back, lingered. Fred's fingers tensed on the pistol grip.

Then a shout from the direction of the villa split the air. The soldiers turned, muttering, and their footsteps crunched away toward the noise.

Enzo exhaled, barely audible. "Come."

They crawled between the vines until the vineyard gave way to an irrigation ditch, the smell of stagnant water thick in the air. Fred slid down the bank, cold mud clinging to his hands, and crouched low until they were swallowed by reeds. He wanted to gag from the stench, but the cover was good.

For long minutes they waited, shoulders hunched, listening. Boots passed once on the road above, voices barking in German. Then silence, save for the wind in the reeds and the distant, hollow wail of sirens.

When the footsteps faded, Enzo stirred. "We move. Slowly now."

They followed the ditch until it spilt onto a dirt track leading down toward the city. The glow of the burning villa still painted the horizon behind them, a beacon of their handiwork and their danger. Fred's ankle throbbed, his face stung from scratches, his throat raw, but the adrenaline kept him upright.

As the first outlines of Naples appeared, rooftops jagged against the starlight, Vesuvius brooding in the distance, Enzo led him off the road, weaving through back lanes that smelled of damp stone and fish guts. Stray cats slunk across their path, eyes glinting in the dark. Laundry lines sagged between shuttered balconies, the sheets like pale ghosts in the wind.

Finally, Enzo stopped before a squat building pressed tight between two taller houses. Its wooden shutters were closed, its plaster cracked and flaking. To anyone else, it looked abandoned. Enzo tapped a rhythm on the side door, two short, one long, one short. A bolt scraped, and the door opened a sliver.

A woman's tired eyes blinked out at them, then widened. She said something quick in Italian.

"It's all right," Enzo answered softly. "Amici."

The door opened fully, revealing a narrow stairwell. Fred ducked inside, the sudden quiet almost deafening after the night's chaos.

The safe house was a single low-ceilinged room, lit by the stub of a candle on a crate. Straw was piled in one corner, a threadbare blanket folded on top. The air was thick with the smell of dust and old wood.

Fred sank onto the straw, chest heaving, every muscle trembling. Enzo crouched opposite him, running a hand through sweat-soaked hair.

"You can't go out again for a few days," Enzo said finally, his voice flat but firm. "They'll have roadblocks, patrols, papers checked at every corner. Even the rats will be questioned."

Fred rubbed his eyes with dirty hands. "And in a few days?"

"We move you back to the shop. You have to stay there for weeks if needed."

Fred shook his head, restless. "Weeks? We don't have weeks."

Enzo's eyes hardened. "Alive, we have weeks. Dead, we have nothing. You lit a fire in the heart of Naples tonight. You must let it burn without you."

The words hit harder than Fred expected. He pressed his face into his hands, replaying the villa in jagged flashes, the fire leaping up the curtains, the screams, the soldiers falling under his shots. His stomach twisted.

"I killed two men," he muttered.

Enzo didn't flinch. "They would have killed you. You did what was needed."

Fred lowered his hands. "That doesn't make it easier."

"No," Enzo agreed. "It never does. But remember, the more you feel it, the less you become like them."

Silence thickened. Outside, a cart rattled over cobblestones, and a drunk shouted in the distance. The war seemed far away for a fleeting moment, but Fred knew it was closer than ever, in every patrol, every informer, every shadowed street.

Enzo pulled the blanket from the corner and tossed it over. "Rest. Tomorrow we think. Tonight we breathe."

Fred lay back on the straw, staring at the low beams above. Every creak of the old house sounded like boots on the stairs, every gust of wind like a knock at the door. Sleep didn't come easily, but exhaustion finally dragged him under.

When he woke, pale light leaked through the cracks in the shutters. His body ached, his ankle swollen, his throat raw. Enzo was already up, standing at the window with a cigarette, the smoke curling faintly in the dimness.

"They'll search all day," Enzo said without turning. "Better if we don't move. By night, it will calm."

Fred pushed himself upright, grimacing. "And then?"

"Then you disappear into the tailor's. You'll be a ghost for a while. And ghosts are harder to catch."

Fred nodded, though impatience gnawed at him. He wanted to move, to act, to strike again. But for now, he was trapped in silence, the hardest prison of all.

Twenty Five

Naples, Italy - December 1941

Fred sat on the edge of the narrow bed, staring at the cracks in the ceiling. The room was dark, the shutters closed tight against the outside world: footsteps on the cobblestones, the distant rumble of a tram, the occasional shout in the street. But to Fred, it felt like he was a thousand miles away from it all, hidden in the shadows, his presence a secret that had to be guarded at all costs.

Outside, somewhere below his shuttered window, laughter spilt from a doorway, and the clink of glasses echoed down the alley. The smell of roasting chestnuts and wood smoke drifted in like faint ghosts. It felt close enough to touch, yet impossible to reach, a warm world sealed away by four cold walls and a bolted door.

The air in the room was stale, carrying the faint scent of chalk dust from the tailor's workshop below. Somewhere outside, a street vendor called out the day's final offers: chestnuts and roasted figs. Fred closed his eyes, letting the noises drift in, taunting him with the reminder that life outside still moves, still breathes, while he sits imprisoned by caution.

After the assassination, the city had become dangerous ground. The Gestapo had increased their numbers in Naples and were on high alert, searching for the man who had killed Walter Scholl. Fred had barely escaped with his life, thanks to Enzo's quick thinking. Now, he had to stay hidden, lying low until the heat died down. The risk was too significant. Even a single step outside could mean discovery, capture, or death.

Fred sighed, running a hand through his hair. He knew he couldn't afford to be reckless. He had to be patient, to wait for the right moment. He had to survive.

The door creaked open, and Fred tensed, his hand moving to the knife he kept under the pillow. His fingers gripped the knife's worn handle, the familiar weight a cold reassurance. In his mind, the next sound would be boots hammering the stairs, the metallic clack of a rifle bolt being drawn. He could almost feel the rush of cold air as the door burst open, hear the barked German commands.

Instead, a pause, then the softer rhythm of familiar steps. The tension didn't release until Enzo's face appeared.

He had a cloth bag slung over his shoulder, his face tired but calm. He closed the door behind him, setting the bag on the table.

"How are you holding up?" Enzo asked, his voice low.

Fred shrugged, trying to mask the restlessness that gnawed at him. "I'm managing," he said. "What's happening outside?"

"The city's still crawling with Germans asking questions," Enzo said, unpacking the bag. "They're questioning everyone, looking for any sign of you. You can't go out, not even for a moment."

"Any news on Scholl?" Fred already knew the answer, but needed to hear it.

Enzo nodded his head. "He's dead, there doesn't seem to have been any casualties from the fire, and they've doubled the patrols. We need to be careful."

"How did you do it?" Enzo asked, his tone firm. "You're still alive, and you did it. We've got to keep you safe."

Fred watched as Enzo pulled out a thermos and a small loaf of bread from the bag. The rich, savoury smell of minestrone filled the room, and Fred's stomach growled. Enzo handed him the thermos, a faint smile on his lips.

"Mama's minestrone," he said. "She makes the best in Naples. Eat, you need your strength."

Fred chuckled weakly. "If I'd known you were delivering this, I'd have staged that assassination months ago."

"Glory's nice," Fred said, eyeing the thermos, "but it doesn't come with garlic and tomatoes."

Fred took the thermos, unscrewing the cap and taking a deep breath of the steam. The aroma was intoxicating, the sweetness of the tomato hit first, then the peppery bite of fresh basil, followed by the soft, earthy depth of beans. The crunch of the bread in his hand felt almost alien after weeks of stale rations. Every mouthful was a reminder of kitchens, family tables, and things war had no right to take.

"This is amazing," Fred said, his voice thick with gratitude. "Thank you."

Enzo nodded, tearing off a piece of bread and handing it to Fred. "My mama worries about all of the resistance fighters," he said. "She says we must eat to stay strong."

Fred couldn't help but smile, despite the danger that surrounded them. "Your mother's right. This is just what I needed."

As they ate, Fred felt his body relaxing. The food, the warmth of the room, the quiet companionship of Enzo, it was a welcome reprieve from the constant tension, the fear of being caught. But their moment of peace was shattered by a knock on the door below, the sound echoing sharply through the building. Fred froze, his eyes darting to Enzo, who held up a hand, signalling him to stay quiet. They listened to the faint creak of floorboards as a woman's voice drifted up.

"Luca! Are you there? I need a word!"

Enzo sighed, setting down his bread. "It's Signora Greco, the landlady," he said quietly. "She's suspicious. Very... thorough."

Fred felt his throat. "How suspicious?"

Enzo shrugged, though his taut face betrayed him. "Enough to notice when my bag feels heavier. Enough to ask why a tall man with a Northern accent is visiting."

"They came by the market this morning," Enzo added quietly. "Two in grey coats, asking questions. People talk, Fred, and she listens more than most."

Fred's heart skipped. "What does she know?"

"Nothing yet," Enzo said. "But she has a knack for reading people. And she's clever. You'll see."

Fred strained to listen as Enzo made his way down the stairs, muffled murmurs drifting upward. Then Signora Greco's voice rang out, sharp and playful:

"So, Enzo... why hasn't your guest left his room? Are you hiding a secret mission? Coded messages? Or maybe... a spy in disguise?"

Enzo stifled a laugh. "Ah, Signora, if I were a spy, would I really be caught carrying bread?"

There was a pause. Then she continued, teasing, but with that underlying seriousness.

"Bread, you say? And yet, I've noticed the Northern accent, the way he moves, the timing of

156

his… errands. Tell me, Enzo, are you involved in something dangerous? Something for the other side?"

Enzo smiled, shaking his head. "Me? Dangerous? I only risk my life to make sure my guests get soup instead of bullets."

Signora Greco laughed, a warm, conspiratorial sound. "Ah, Enzo, you flatter me. But this city is no place for secrets, even clever ones like yours."

"Yes, Signora. I'll make sure he's well looked after," Enzo said, bowing slightly as if to a superior officer.

Footsteps receded. Then, quieter, Enzo muttered, "For now, she's gone."

Fred let out a thin smile.

"That woman could interrogate Mussolini himself," Enzo said, shaking his head. "And enjoy it."

Fred allowed himself a small laugh. "Good thing he's not upstairs with a fake fever, then."

Enzo nodded, coming back up the stairs. "Too close. We need to be more careful. I'll bring your food at night, when no one can see. And you can't make any noise. Not until this blows over."

Fred kept eye contact, understanding the gravity of the situation. "Thank you, Enzo. For everything."

Enzo waved a hand, dismissing the gratitude. "Just stay safe, Fred. We need you. The resistance needs you. And Mama, well, she's planning on making her Margherita pizza tomorrow. You'll want to be around for that."

Fred smiled, feeling a flicker of warmth amid the darkness. "I wouldn't miss it," he said, his voice filled with genuine appreciation.

When the door clicked shut, Fred let out a breath he hadn't realised he'd been holding. Somewhere below, the tailor's scissors snipped in steady rhythm, an ordinary sound in an extraordinary cage. He leaned back against the wall, cradling the thermos like a relic. Outside, war clawed at the city, but up here, for now, there was warmth, bread, and the promise of Margherita pizza. He would hold onto that, because sometimes survival was about small pledges.

Fred looked at the closed door and murmured to himself, "One day, I'll pay this back."

Fred leaned back against the wall, the taste of minestrone still on his tongue. He would lie low, and when the time came, he would strike back. For now, though, he would savour the simple pleasures: a bowl of soup and a piece of bread

Twenty Six

Luciano cursed under his breath, weaving through the thinning evening crowd near Via Donizetti, the narrow side street that Gianni had chosen for their meeting. A bakery's shutters were just being drawn; a cat darted under a stoop. The city held its breath.

Gianni was 27 years old. A quiet man with soft eyes and hands stained from factory grease, he had joined the resistance not out of ideology, but out of love. Love for his city, for justice and most of all, for Alessia. His wife was six months pregnant, their first child expected just after Christmas. He often joked during meetings that he hoped the baby wouldn't inherit his crooked nose.

Luciano's recovered hand still ached in the cold. He shoved it into his coat pocket and scanned the alley ahead.

Gianni wasn't there.

Instead, there was movement. A shadow shifted, too sharp, too stiff.

Luciano froze. The world seemed to narrow, the laughter and chatter from the street behind him dropping into a cold, brittle silence. The shadows ahead moved with precision, boots scuffing lightly

159

against the cobbles. His good hand twitched, itching for the pistol he knew he couldn't draw without sealing both their fates.

Two men stepped from either side of a doorway; they were Gestapo.

Gianni appeared between them, arms twisted behind his back, blood on his temple. He stumbled as one of the officers shoved him forward.

Luciano's mouth went dry.

No... not here. Not now.

Gianni saw him.

Only for a second.

In that heartbeat, Gianni's gaze locked onto his. Not panicked, but weighed down by everything unsaid. It was the look of a man who had already decided what would happen next. Luciano's chest ached with the instinct to move, to shout, to throw himself between them, but the knowledge slammed back just as hard: if he did, they would both die before sundown.

Their eyes met across the narrow street. Luciano half-concealed behind a stack of crates, his heart pounding so hard it made his vision blur.

Gianni didn't speak. But something passed between them in that instant. His lips barely moved, but Luciano caught it, two syllables, maybe a name, or perhaps just "*Vai*." Go. It rooted him to the spot for a fraction too long before his body obeyed.

Gianni wasn't a fighter by nature. But when he saw what Mussolini was doing to his beloved country, and his wife had subsequently fallen pregnant, he chose to resist. Not for the glory, but so that his child might be born in a country that could still call itself free.

Luciano backed away slowly, then turned and disappeared into the dark. Behind him, the sharp stamp of boots on wet stone echoed like a clock ticking down. Somewhere in the shuffle, a muffled groan, Gianni's, carried through the narrow walls. The metallic scrape of handcuffs caught against his ear and followed him long after the alley had swallowed the scene. Every instinct was screaming for Luciano to do something, but he didn't. He couldn't draw attention.

He made it two blocks before he leaned against a cold brick wall, retching into the gutter.

The hanging came with cold efficiency, without announcement or trial.

Luciano stood on the edge of the square, his eyes shaded by his hat, his coat collar turned up. The morning fog had barely lifted, and yet a crowd had already gathered. The enemy soldiers had ensured that, rounding up shopkeepers, students, and older women with heavy baskets.

"*Che cosa succede?*" murmured a man clutching his cap in both hands.

A mother dragged her son closer, whispering in his ear until his head disappeared against her skirts. No one spoke above a breath. Even the pigeons on the fountain rim seemed to hold still.

A small wooden platform had been erected beside the fountain. The rope swung gently, as if stirred by some unseen breeze.

Gianni was forced across the cobbled courtyard between two soldiers, each step dragging him further from freedom. He didn't resist. His hands were bound, his shoulders squared, and though a black eye had nearly swollen shut and blood dried at the corner of his mouth, he walked with the quiet dignity of a man who had already made peace with death.

The courtyard was silent.

"*Chi e?*" someone whispered in front. "*Dicono che ha ucciso un ufficiale tedesco,*" a different voice replied, sharp with fear. They say he killed a German officer.

Luciano watched from the shadows behind the window's broken slats, his breath caught in his throat. Rain slicked the flagstones, and every step Gianni took echoed like a drumbeat through the still air. Somewhere beyond, a bell tolled the hour, too slow, too solemn.

Gianni stumbled once. One of the soldiers jerked him upright. He said nothing.

His lip quivered, but not from fear. If anything, it was defiance, the stubborn flicker of a smile tugging at the corner of his mouth like the last act of rebellion he had left. He turned his head slightly, eyes scanning the courtyard as if trying to commit it to memory, the final thing he would ever see.

A small figure stood at the far edge of the crowd, her face half-hidden by a curtain of rain. Luciano squinted through the haze, following the trembling shape of her hands clutched around something. Then it hit him. Alessia.

Her coat clung, soaked dark through to the lining; her knuckles were white against the fabric she gripped, a scarf, maybe his.

She stood near the back of the forced crowd, small in the shadow of the guards, her coat soaked through with rain. Her hands were clenched tightly around something, a scarf, perhaps his, crumpled in her grip like she could wring the grief from it. Her lips were pressed together, trembling, and though she made no sound, a single tear traced a slow, deliberate path down her cheek.

Gianni's knees nearly gave out.

His breath hitched. The noose tightened just slightly with the motion. He forced himself to look at her, really look, drawing strength from her presence even as it threatened to unmake him. She shouldn't have come. And yet, she was here.

He gave her the faintest nod. A private farewell. An apology.

Memories crashed over him like waves: her laugh in the kitchen as she scolded him for stealing bites of bread, the way she always hummed under her breath when nervous, the scent of rosemary in her hair after working in the garden. The quiet warmth of her fingers resting against his cheek on the night before his arrest.

He wanted to call out to her. Just once. Her name.

But he didn't.

He stood straighter. His face grew still. He held it all, the pain, the love, the fear, and buried it in his chest like a secret he'd carry into death.

The officer barked the final words of the sentence, but Gianni didn't hear them. The only thing he saw in that last, eternal moment was Alessia.

The trapdoor dropped.

A cry tore from the crowd, a woman's sob, raw and sharp. This was quickly swallowed by silence. No one moved. No one dared. Luciano gripped the prayer beads in his pocket.

The officer stepped forward, boots clacking against the wooden platform. He surveyed the crowd with cold precision, then turned toward Gianni, who was swinging in silence, chin limp.

The officer's voice rang out in crisp, harsh German:

"*Dieser Mann hat einen Offizier des Dritten Reichs ermordet! Ein Angriff auf die Ordnung! Ein Angriff auf das Reich selbst!*"

"This man murdered an officer of the Third Reich! An attack on order! An attack on the Reich itself!"

Then he switched, clumsily, into loud, deliberate Italian:

"*Questo uomo… ha ucciso un comandante tedesco! Traditore! Spia! Il prezzo del tradimento… è la morte.*"

"This man… has killed a German commander! Traitor! Spy! The price of treason… is death."

He raised a gloved hand, voice booming across the square:

"*La giustizia del Reich… è veloce. È forte. Ricordatelo!*"

"The justice of the Reich… is swift. It is strong. Remember that!"

"*Siehst du? Keine Fragen,*" a soldier muttered to the man beside him. See? No questions.

The warning had been delivered.

And it had landed.

The crowd's heads dropped in near-unison, as though a sudden wind had bent them. No one spoke. A few shuffled backwards, their shoes skidding on the slick stones. One man coughed, the sound of jarring in the hush, and earned a sharp glance from a guard.

Luciano still did not move. His breath came thin and shallow as he stood watching until the body was cut down, bundled in burlap, and tossed without care onto a waiting cart like refuse. He stayed until it jolted away over the courtyard, the sound grinding into him as if to etch the moment into memory.

"*Addio, amico mio,*" Luciano whispered, low enough that only the rain could carry it away.

Then, slowly, silently, he turned and walked the long route home, every step heavier than the last.

Scholl was dead. A symbol of Nazi order and fear, removed in the blink of an eye. It had rattled them and made them nervous. Wasted time and resources in the wrong places.

But as Luciano walked the long route home, he couldn't feel the victory. Not with Gianni's face, Alessia's face, still in his mind. Not with the sound of that lever dropping still echoing in his ears.

One less monster.

One less comrade.

That was the burden of war.

Twenty Seven

"Luciano was there, he saw everything," Enzo said.

Fred sat on the edge of his bed, his head in his hands, the responsibility washing over him in waves. An innocent man had paid the price for his actions. Another life lost in the brutal, unforgiving tides of war. Even now, behind his closed eyes, he saw the image he'd built from Enzo's description. The platform, the rope, a man standing straighter than fear should allow, the bell tolling. The crowd's silence was like a held breath. His stomach churned; the minestrone he'd eaten earlier now was a heavy, unwelcome weight.

"I'm sorry, Fred," Enzo said quietly, standing by the door. "There was nothing we could do. They grabbed him in broad daylight, no trial, no chance to intervene. It was over before anyone could stop it."

The words brought the sound of a lever dropping into his mind, a wooden crack that seemed to echo through his skull. He swallowed hard, forcing the thought away.

Fred kept his head low for a moment longer, the words singing like stones. He could hear the imagined crack of a trapdoor, the murmur of a cowed crowd, things he hadn't seen but could picture with cruel precision.

Fred looked up, his eyes hollow, his face drawn. "Who was he?"

The name meant nothing to him at first, just a word in the air, until Enzo kept talking. Then it hit: someone's son, someone's husband, someone who had risked his life without ever having the comfort of being known.

"Gianni," Enzo said, his voice heavy. "He wasn't directly involved with us, but he'd done work for the resistance before. They found some leaflets in his room, and someone must have talked. They were looking for a scapegoat, and they found one."

Fred clenched his fists, anger and grief battling for control. "I should have handed myself in," he muttered. "This is my fault."

"If I hadn't…" Fred began, but his voice died in the stale air. He pressed his fists into his knees, as though force alone might keep the guilt from spilling over.

Enzo shook his head, his expression firm. "No, Fred. This is the fault of the Nazis and the Italians who stand with them, not you. You did what you had to do. Gianni understood the risks, just like the rest of us. He wouldn't want you to blame yourself."

"Do you ever stop blaming yourself?" Fred asked quietly, not quite meeting his eyes.

Enzo gave a faint, humourless laugh. "Not once. But I've learned to keep moving anyway."

Fred knew Enzo was right, but the knowledge did little to ease the weight on his conscience. He stood, pacing the small room, his thoughts a whirlwind. "Does this mean they've stopped looking for me?"

"For now," Enzo said. "With Gianni dead, they think they've caught the assassin. They're still on edge, but we should be able to continue our work now."

Fred nodded, the prospect of continuing with his mission a small, bitter comfort. The price had been too high.

Enzo poured out a glass of red wine and offered it to Fred, who took the chipped glass, the bitter red stinging his tongue. He noticed his hand was shaking, and he curled his fingers tighter, unwilling to let Enzo see just how unsteady he felt.

The deep red caught the light like blood on wet stone. He blinked, and the thought was gone, replaced by the simple warmth of Enzo's gesture.

"I'm off to the café later," Fred said, his voice flat.

Enzo gave him a tight smile. "She'll be glad to see you. But Fred, she doesn't know about... everything."

"Good," Fred said. "It's better that way. The less she knows, the safer she'll be."

Enzo nodded, understanding the unspoken concern. "Be careful, Fred. The Gestapo may think they've found their man, but we can't afford to take any chances."

Enzo reached for the door first, then stopped himself. "One more thing, if anyone so much as looks at you wrong, you walk away. Promise me."

"You sound like my father," Fred said, the faintest curve at the corner of his mouth.

"Then take it as fatherly advice," Enzo replied, deadpan.

"I will," Fred promised, pulling on his coat. As he stepped out into the cool evening air, he felt a mix of relief and sorrow. But at what cost? Somewhere nearby, a hammer struck wood, ordinary work, but for a heartbeat, he thought of the execution scaffold. He kept walking.

The face of the man who had been executed haunted him, a reminder of the harsh realities of war. But he couldn't dwell on it. He had to keep moving, to keep fighting. It was the only way to honour the sacrifices that had been made.

The streets of Naples were quiet, the sun sinking towards the horizon, as the night crept closer. His eyes scanned the faces of passersby, alert for any sign of danger. A shopkeeper swept his doorway in slow, distracted strokes, eyes flicking to every passing pair of boots. Two men leaned in to speak, their conversation clipped short as a soldier strode past.

Even the gulls seemed to keep their distance from the square.

The city felt tense, the recent events casting a pall over the usual bustle of activity. Fred's senses were on high alert, every sound and movement amplified in his mind.

When he reached 'Café Rossi', he paused outside, taking a deep breath to steady himself. The glow of the lights inside spilt out onto the street, a beacon of warmth in a world gone mad. He pushed open the door, the familiar chime of the bell announcing his arrival.

Isabella was behind the counter, her dark hair pulled back in a neat bun, her hands busy cleaning a glass. When she saw Fred, her eyes widened in surprise, then softened with relief. She set down the glass, her hands trembling slightly.

For a moment, she just stared, as if making sure he was real. The glass in her hand tilted, a bead of water sliding down the side and falling onto the counter with a soft pat.

"Luca," she said, with a mixture of joy and concern. "You're here. Enzo told me you were sick."

Fred managed a small smile, the sight of her easing some of the tension in his chest. "I'm better now," he said. "It was just a bad flu. I didn't want to risk getting anyone else sick. Then I had to go away for a while, visit some family." Fred hated to lie to

Isabella, but, for the sake of his mission and the sake of her safety, he didn't have a choice.

Isabella stepped out from behind the counter, closing the distance between them. Without a word, she wrapped her arms around him, pulling him into a tight embrace. Fred closed his eyes, letting himself relax in her warmth, the simple human contact a balm to his frayed nerves.

The rope. The rain. He forced the images down, focusing instead on the press of her arms and the faint perfume of soap in her hair.

"I'm so glad you're okay," Isabella said, her voice muffled against his shoulder. "You had me worried, Luca. You shouldn't have stayed away for so long."

"I didn't think you'd notice," he said, knowing full well how false it sounded.

"Don't be stupid," she replied, though the smile pulling at her mouth softened the sting.

"I'm sorry," Fred said, his voice thick. "I didn't mean to scare you. I just needed to be careful."

Isabella pulled back, looking up at him with a serious expression. "You don't have to face everything alone, you know. I'm here, Luca. You can talk to me."

"Some things…" he began, then stopped. Her gaze didn't waver. "Some things, talking about them would only make them more dangerous."

"Then tell me about the things you can," she said.

Fred nodded, the truth of her words striking a chord in him. He had been so focused on his mission, on surviving, that he had forgotten the importance of connection, of trust. He didn't have to carry the burden alone.

"Thank you, Isabella," he said, his voice sincere. "I don't know what I'd do without you."

She smiled, her eyes shining with warmth. "You don't have to find out. Now, sit down. Let me get you something to eat. You look like you could use a good meal. But there's no coffee, we are completely out, it'll have to be wine."

Fred let her lead him to a table, the tension in his shoulders easing as he sat down. As Isabella moved around the café, preparing a plate of food, Fred watched her, feeling a sense of peace he hadn't known in weeks. But even here, the image of a rope swinging in the rain pressed at the edges of his thoughts, a reminder that every quiet moment was borrowed time.

Twenty Eight

Naples, Italy - March 1942

The bells of Santa Chiara chimed six times, long and solemn. Enzo Moretti stood in the shadows of a crumbling tenement doorway, the edges of his coat damp with seawater and the dust of Naples. The city lay in fading amber light. He didn't trust it.

Somewhere in the maze of streets, a dog barked once, then fell silent. The smell of frying anchovies drifted from a window above. Enzo let his gaze move, not too quickly, from one shadowed doorway to the next, marking which ones had changed since he'd last passed this way. A shutter open where it had been closed yesterday. A new poster plastered crooked over an old one, Mussolini's face glaring above a tear in the paper. He noted it all. Change meant risk.

A boy played with a stick down the alley, drawing lines in the mud while his grandmother swept the steps behind him. The boy looked up as an Italian staff car passed, its black gloss paint glinting beneath a haze of cigarette smoke. The sweep of tension that followed, eyes averted, backs stiffened, was as familiar to Enzo now as the rhythm of his breath. He'd seen it so often it no longer needed uniforms to trigger it; the echo of regimented steps was enough to make backs straighten and words die in the throat. A city that once greeted strangers with a wave now kept its head down and its doors shut.

Enzo remained in the doorway a moment longer than necessary, letting the silence after the car passed seep into him. His instinct urged him to wait. Too many times, he'd seen men lifted from corners by soldiers who seemed to appear out of thin air. A cough, the strike of a match, a loose boot scuffing stone, the smallest sounds could betray you. He glanced behind him once more before finally moving.

His boots clicked softly against the uneven stones as he headed toward the water. The Porto di Napoli was quieter in the evenings, and that suited him. Fewer prying eyes. Fewer risks. Fewer names to remember if things went wrong. Still, he found himself cataloguing details: the figure leaning against a doorway too long, the curtain shifting in a window, the soldier smoking with his cap low. Maybe harmless. Maybe not.

Tucked inside his coat was a folded slip of paper written in Fred's tidy English hand. Coordinates. Times. Codenames. The Allies were planning a supply drop, and Enzo was expected to receive it. Trusting a foreigner with this task should have rattled him, but it didn't. What unsettled him was how much he wanted to trust.

He reached the seawall and leaned into the wind. The salt stung his eyes. The black water churned below, carrying secrets as easily as it carried driftwood. He unfolded the paper again, even though he'd read it four times already, and forced himself to commit every word to memory. If he lost it, he would lose more than ink on paper.

Later, in the empty back room of his home, the lights off, blinds drawn, he crouched over his notebook. The chipped radio crackled low, BBC Italian Service murmuring through the static. His pen hovered. He did not write names. He never wrote names. He had watched too many men vanish after a single careless word.

Instead, he wrote in fragments.

If the drop fails, evacuate through tunnel route C.

If Fred falls, burn all contact records. Do not go after him.

He paused, the ink dark on the page, his chest tightening. He wanted to write: If Isabella is taken… but he stopped. He couldn't set her name down, couldn't curse her with black ink. He underlined his last sentence instead:

Trust is a risk we no longer afford, but hope demands it.

He stared at it until it began to blur. He wasn't sure which would run out first, the hope or the people willing to spend themselves on it.

The bells of Santa Chiara rang again for the evening service. Enzo slid the notebook back into its hiding place beneath the floorboards. He lit a cigarette and stood at the window, watching shadows slip through the street. For a long moment, he considered staying there, safe in the dark, letting the city move without him. But Isabella's face pushed through the smoke, steady and insistent. He stubbed out the cigarette, took his coat, and stepped into the night.

The streets were narrow, their walls leaning inward as if listening. Laundry sagged overhead. He kept his pace casual, but his hand brushed the knife at his belt more than once. He passed a bookshop shuttered for the night, the smell of stale bread lingering in the air, a man pushing a coal cart toward the convent. Normal sights, ordinary lives. Yet every glance, every sound, made him wonder if the Gestapo were already two steps ahead, waiting for him to falter.

Ahead, Isabella waited beneath a broken streetlamp. Her posture was poised and elegant, even here in the decay.

"*Sei in ritardo,*" she said softly. You're late.

"I stopped for poetry," he replied dryly.

Her lips twitched, barely. "You shouldn't walk alone. They've doubled patrols near the docks."

"They always double the patrols when they suspect something," Enzo murmured. "What are they suspecting me of doing? Eating too much of Ma's minestrone?"

Isabella cast a glance down the alley before stepping closer, her voice dropping. "They came to the café. Asking about customers. Especially the Italian from the North."

Enzo's gaze sharpened. "They? Soldiers? What did you tell them?"

"That depends." She folded her arms, eyes narrowing. "Is it safer to tell the truth, or to lie for a man I barely know?"

A muscle twitched at the corner of Enzo's mouth. He didn't answer, and the silence stretched between them.

"Nothing," she said at last. Then, after a pause, "Not yet."

She shifted her weight, and the scarf at her neck loosened. Lamplight caught a shadow along her jawline: not dirt, not shadow. A bruise. Her fingers flew to the scarf, tugging it back into place, but too late for Enzo not to see.

His voice dropped to a quieter, colder tone. "They questioned you."

"They made suggestions. Asked questions. What is Luca a part of? What are you a part of?"

"Nothing you need to worry about, Isabella."

A bitter laugh slipped out. "You think?" She stepped closer, chin lifting. "Do you think I don't see? Customers who vanish. Families who stop coming because they're too afraid to be seen. Do you think I don't notice when men with clean boots sit at the corner table for hours and order nothing?"

Enzo stiffened. He wanted to tell her everything, but the words clung to his throat. The more she knew, the greater the danger she carried.

"Who is Luca?" she pressed. Her eyes searched his.

Enzo drew his coat tighter. "Go home. Find Luca. Have a hot drink. The Gestapo are fishing for anything and everything."

She trembled, not with fear but with frustration. "Do you think I don't see the way people vanish, Enzo? One day they're in the café, the next their family is selling their shoes in the market."

Her voice broke, and she dropped her gaze. "Fine. I'll just serve customers and try not to get people I care about killed."

Enzo studied her, guilt biting at the edges of his resolve. He wanted to reach for her hand, to say something that would ease the hurt, but the words stayed buried. Sometimes silence was the only shield he had left.

"Sometimes," he said at last, voice quiet as the night, "that's all it takes, doing nothing in the wrong moments."

Twenty Nine

Naples, Italy - May 1942

The morning air was brittle and cold, carrying the sharp scent of the sea and diesel fumes from the nearby docks. Naples had a stillness that day, a deceptive quiet Fred had learned to distrust. It was the kind of silence that lingered before something went wrong.

He adjusted the collar of his overcoat and checked his watch: 06:42. Enzo was late, again.

Fred leaned against a rusted bollard near the edge of the canal, one hand resting on the concealed pistol beneath his coat. He scanned the shadows between buildings, the slow trundle of a cart in the distance, the occasional bark of a stray dog. Nothing out of the ordinary... but something felt off.

Enzo finally appeared, emerging from a narrow side street with his usual swagger. He looked like a man walking home from a night of cards. His shirt untucked, cigarette dangling, that ever-present glint of mischief in his eye.

"You look like a man who hasn't slept," Enzo said, offering Fred a smirk. "Or kissed anyone good morning."

Fred gave a tight nod. "You're late."

"I'm always late. That's how I stay alive. If the fascists ever start counting on me to be punctual, I'm dead."

Despite himself, Fred cracked a half-smile. Enzo had that effect on people, light in the darkest places.

They moved quickly down a cobbled path between shuttered warehouses. The mission was simple: intercept a courier near the old shipyard, confiscate the briefcase, and disappear. It was meant to be quiet. No weapons drawn unless necessary.

Their contact had given them precise information: a single officer delivering documents to a German sub-lieutenant, unescorted, timed for just after sunrise.

"You trust the man who gave us this?" Enzo asked without looking at him.

"I trust the paper," Fred said. "Not the hands it passed through."

Enzo gave a low chuckle. "You're learning."

Enzo crouched beside a row of stacked crates, peering around the corner toward the canal lock.

"No one," he murmured. "Maybe our friend overslept."

Fred scanned the rooftops, then the street behind them. "Or we've been fed bad intelligence."

Enzo turned to him, eyes narrowing. "You think someone talked?"

"I don't know. But I don't like this."

181

A minute later, boots clattered.

Not one pair.

Three.

Then five.

The echo of military heels on stone.

"Shit," Fred hissed, ducking behind the crates. Enzo joined him, breath tight in his throat.

An Italian patrol rounded the bend, their rifles slung, heads alert. An officer barked something unintelligible, his voice sharp. They weren't just passing through. They were looking for someone.

Fred and Enzo exchanged a glance.

Move. Now.

They took the alley, sprinting over the slippery cobbles. Fred led the way. Shouts rang out behind them, *'Férmete, mo!'*, then the crack of a rifle. A splinter of wood grazed Fred's cheek.

More bullets splintered wood beside Fred's head.

They burst through an old gate into a crumbling courtyard, breath ragged, the stone walls echoing with gunfire. Fred darted behind the well, but when he glanced back, he saw Enzo stagger, a red bloom spreading across his shirt.

"No!" Fred lunged toward him.

Enzo dropped to one knee beside a broken cart, clutching his side. His fingers came away slick with blood. A bullet had torn through his lower ribs, just above the hip. He tried to rise, stumbled, and half-fell against the cart, teeth bared against the pain.

Fred slid to his side, pressing down on the wound. "Stay with me…"

Enzo shoved him away, gasping, "I can still move." With a burst of will, he dragged himself into the shadow of a back alley, forcing one foot in front of the other. His face had turned the colour of ash, but still he pushed on.

Boots pounded closer. Shouts rattled through the courtyard. They had seconds, maybe less.

"You have to go," Enzo said, his breath ragged. "Fred… go."

"I'm not leaving you here," Fred growled.

Enzo's hand shot out, gripping Fred's collar, dragging him close. His voice was raw but steady.

"If you die here, it means nothing. But you… you have work left. You understand me?"

Fred pressed his palm hard against the wound, feeling hot blood pulse between his fingers.

Enzo's gaze softened for a fraction of a second. "Tell Lucia… tell her I was laughing at the end. You promise me."

Fred's chest ached as he forced the words out. "I promise."

Enzo shoved something into Fred's hand, a folded note, already damp from his blood. Then he pulled in a breath, steadying himself.

"You'll hear two shots," he murmured. "That's your moment. Don't waste it."

Fred shook his head, but Enzo's grip tightened once, then let go. He turned toward the corner of the cart, leaned out just far enough to fire into the air. The cracks of the pistol echoed like thunder in the narrow space, drawing the soldiers' attention.

Fred didn't watch the rest. He was already moving, vaulting the low wall at the courtyard's edge, the sound of Enzo's final cry following him into the streets.

He didn't stop running until the sun was high above the rooftops.

Fred arrived at the safe house, sweating and out of breath. As he pushed open the door, the floorboards creaked beneath his boots, the air inside stale with dust and disuse. A draught tugged at the candle flame, casting tall, trembling shadows on the walls.

He'd checked the alley twice before unlocking the door, certain he'd heard footsteps shadowing his own. Even inside, he kept the curtains drawn and the pistol within arm's reach. The city felt smaller without Enzo in it, every street darker, every shadow longer.

That night, Fred sat alone, Enzo's note unopened beside a cup of untouched coffee. The silence was unbearable.

Enzo had been more than a comrade. He had been a brother in all but blood. Funny, loyal, reckless, brave.

And now he was gone.

All for a mission that had meant nothing.

Thirty

Luciano didn't remember how many drinks he'd had, only that his glass was never empty.

The bar was dim and reeking of sweat, tobacco, and something sour beneath it all. The kind of place that kept no names, where the piano was missing half its keys, and nobody asked about bandages.

He sat alone in a corner booth.

The low wheeze of the piano drifted across the room, half the notes flat, the rhythm staggering like a drunk looking for the door. A man at the following table coughed into a handkerchief and didn't bother hiding the red stains. Luciano stared into the rim of his glass, the rum's oily surface catching the yellow lamp light, and for a moment, he almost saw Enzo's grin reflected there; that quick, lopsided smirk he'd wear after bluffing his way through a checkpoint. The memory hit hard enough to make him blink.

Enzo was gone.

The thought repeated like a drunk man's mantra. Enzo. Gone. Enzo. Gone. Every time Luciano closed his eyes, he could see Enzo smiling, hear him laughing, but it all faded away when he opened his eyes again.

He'd heard how it had happened. He couldn't get the image out of his mind.

The Resistance had sent word to scatter, but Luciano hadn't scattered. He'd spiralled.

Now, a bottle of bitter Sicilian rum sat beside him, and the bar's owner had stopped making eye contact.

Two German soldiers entered the tavern.

Their boots struck the floor like punctuation. Their voices were too loud, their laughter too sharp. Everyone noticed. No one acknowledged them.

Luciano's gaze locked onto them through the glass of his drink. His jaw clenched. One of the soldiers leaned against the bar and said something about "Neapolitan rats."

Luciano stood.

He didn't remember crossing the floor. Only the taste of bile. The sting in his shoulder.

Then suddenly, a hand on his chest.

Pietro, the barkeep. Shaking his head, eyes wide.

"Don't," he whispered. "Not here. Not now. Don't give them a reason."

Luciano hesitated. His breath was a snarl. "They don't need one." His bandaged hand trembled with rage.

Pietro gestured towards the exit, "Then don't make it easy."

The soldiers didn't see the exchange. Or if they did, they dismissed him. He was nobody. A limping local with drink in his gut and smoke in his eyes.

He turned and left before he could do something fatal.

The wind off the bay knifed through his coat and into the wound like it knew where to hurt him. He walked with no direction. Past shuttered homes, past watchful windows. Past the alley where he and Enzo had once lit a fire to warm children on a winter night. He passed the bakery where Enzo had once talked the owner into giving them a sack of stale bread "for the cause", then eaten half of it himself before they reached the safe house. A cracked plaster wall still bore the faded chalk mark Enzo had drawn to signal a clear street during the last curfew. It was nothing now, just dust on stone, but Luciano's eyes lingered on it until the wind stung them dry.

By the time he reached Isabella's flat, the bottle was nearly empty.

She answered the door with wary eyes, ushering him inside before questions could be asked by neighbours.

He stood in the centre of her kitchen like a fisherman in a storm.

"Enzo's gone," he said.

"I know."

She offered him water. He waved it away.

"I thought I could hold this together," he said, voice hoarse. "That we'd just regroup. But I was wrong."

She didn't speak, only watched him.

"I wanted to kill them tonight," he said. "Two soldiers. Laughing like they owned this city. I would've done it if Pietro hadn't stopped me."

His chair scraped back across the tiles as he stood and paced, the cramped kitchen too small to hold the storm building in him. His knuckles rapped the table edge before he caught himself. "They drink in our bars, eat our food, and laugh like they've already won. They think this city's theirs, and maybe it is, because all we do is keep our heads down and serve them." His voice cracked, rage and grief wrestling for control.

He slumped into the chair. His body shook, from rage or cold or grief, he didn't know.

"I want to burn something, Isa. I want to tear down every checkpoint and drown every boot in the Bay of Naples."

She reached for his good hand. He didn't pull away.

"There's nothing left to lose," he said.

"Yes," she replied quietly. "There is. There always is."

He looked at her then. Eyes hollow. Face drawn.

"They took him. And now we don't just fight with secrets. We fight with fire. You understand?"

She didn't answer.

But she didn't let go of his hand, either.

Luciano's eyes dropped to their joined hands, the warmth of her fingers at odds with the chill crawling through his bones. The city had just lost one of its best, and he needed the comfort.

Thirty One

Naples, Italy - August 1942

Months had passed since Enzo's death, but Fred still felt it pressing on him like a weight that refused to shift. Naples throbbed with life all around him, louder and brighter than any place he had known in wartime, and yet inside him stretched a hollow silence that nothing seemed to fill.

By day, the city shouted its defiance at the war. Market stalls spilt their colours into the streets: piles of ripe tomatoes like bursts of blood-red, lemons catching the sun, fish glistening silver on wet boards. Children ran between the stalls, shrieking with laughter, their voices cutting through the drone of traders calling out prices. Fishermen dragged their catches ashore, gulls wheeling overhead, the harbour air thick with brine and the chatter of survival.

Fred walked among them unnoticed, another face in the crowd, but the noise felt distant, as though the world was taking place behind a pane of glass. He saw the colours but felt only greys. Every laugh, every shouted bargain, only reminded him of what was gone: Enzo's quick smile in the shadows of Naples, the way he had spoken of freedom as though it were a tangible thing just waiting to be grasped.

191

At night, the silence came down heavier. He lay awake in his narrow rented room above the tailor's shop, staring at the cracked plaster ceiling, listening to the uneven tread of boots on the street below. His dreams were no kinder than his waking thoughts. Rose came often, her hair catching Worthing sunlight, her eyes turning away from him on the shingle beach. Then Enzo would be there, clutching his side, eyes clouded, lips moving in words Fred could never quite hear before the dark took him. Sometimes Luciano bled too, cursing through his pain. Faces blurred and returned, one loss feeding another, until Fred woke with sweat cooling on his chest and the certainty that he had failed them all.

Rose had been his first ghost. Enzo joined her now. Together, they haunted every step he took. Isabella, when she looked at him across a table with that careful curiosity of hers, only seemed to stir them more. He longed to tell her the truth, to strip away the mask of Luca and let her see Fred Bennett for who he was, but truth was the most dangerous possession he owned. He had guarded it longer than he could remember.

And yet, secrecy was beginning to rot him from within.

Luciano was the crack in the armour. One humid evening Fred found him sprawled outside the harbour tavern, wine staining his shirt, muttering Enzo's name like a prayer or a curse. He had said too much in the company of others, half-slurred stories about missions, about risks taken and friends buried. Fred dragged him back to his room, but the damage was done. If Luciano could slip, anyone could. And if Isabella had overheard even fragments, the danger would spread to her like fire through dry grass.

By August, the strain had become unbearable. Every time Fred looked at Isabella, he felt it, the truth swelling in his chest, pressing against his ribs until it hurt to breathe. She had given him more than kindness: a safe corner in her café, a smile that softened the world, a hand that lingered when she passed him bread. And he had given her only lies.

The war had already taken too much. He couldn't bear to let silence take this, too.

It was late one evening when the café had finally emptied. The air was thick with the scent of bread baked hours before, fading now into the shadows. The shutters were half drawn, muting the last rumbles of carts in the piazza. Isabella moved between tables with a cloth, her motions steady, her humming low and absent-minded.

Fred stood at the counter, watching her, the knot in his chest coiling tighter.

"Let me help you with that," he said, picking up a spare cloth and moving toward her.

She looked up in mild surprise, amusement lighting her face. "You're a guest here, Fred. I should be the one helping you."

"Maybe I just want an excuse to spend more time with you," he answered. The words left him without thought, too bare, too raw.

Colour touched her cheeks, though she smiled faintly. "You don't need an excuse."

They worked together in silence, the scrape of chairs stacking, the soft rhythm of cloths swiping over wood. Their nearness was both a comfort and a torment. Fred felt each second weigh heavier, as if the truth were building inside him like pressure in a boiler. He had lied long enough.

When the last chair was stacked and the hush of evening lay thick around them, he turned to her. His throat felt dry. "There's something I need to tell you."

Her cloth stilled. She looked up slowly, cautious but open. "What is it, Luca?"

The name hit him like a blow. Luca. The mask. The lie. He drew in a breath and forced the words out before he could stop himself. "I haven't been honest with you. I'm not just a traveller. I'm here on a mission for the Allies."

The silence after the admission was like a stone dropped into deep water.

"I gather intelligence," Fred went on, his voice hushed. "On Italian naval movements. Shipments. Loyalists and traitors. It's dangerous work. And I should never have involved you. But I couldn't keep lying. Not after Enzo. Not after everything."

Her eyes widened, then softened. Fear flickered there, but something else too, understanding, perhaps, or the relief of truth spoken aloud.

"Why are you telling me this, Luca?" she asked, her voice breaking on the false name.

"Because Luca isn't who I am." His chest ached with the admission. "My name is Fred. Fred Bennett. And you deserve to know the truth, however much it costs me."

She searched his face as though reading something written there. At last she whispered, "Fred." She let the word sit in the air a moment, tasting it. Then she nodded. "I knew something didn't fit. Luciano… he told me. Not everything, but enough. He was drunk, grieving. I guessed the rest."

Fred's breath caught. "Then you know the risk. If anyone suspects…"

"I know," she cut in, her voice rising sharp. "The Gestapo. The Fascists. I see them every day, lurking on corners, watching with their black eyes. And still you come here. What if they followed you one night? What if they came through that door with rifles? Would we both be lying in the street before dawn?"

Her fear lashed him harder than a whip. He wanted to deny it, to promise her the safety he couldn't give. "I won't let anything happen to you," he said instead, quiet and desperate. "That's a promise I'll keep for as long as I breathe."

Her eyes filled. One tear slipped, and Fred reached up to brush it away, his fingers trembling at the warmth of her skin. In that fragile stillness, their lips found each other. The kiss was brief, fierce, tasting of salt and fear and something far more dangerous than either.

The days that followed blurred into something Fred had never expected: relief and dread bound together. The relief was simple, Isabella no longer looked at him with questions in her eyes, no longer skirted the silence between them. She called him Fred, softly at first, then with growing ease. She poured his coffee with a smile that reached her eyes. Sometimes, when the café was quiet, her hand lingered in his as though it belonged there.

But the dread came just as swiftly. Now she knew, she bore the danger too. Fred saw it in the way she glanced at the windows when boots echoed outside, in the sharp flinch of her shoulders when a car door slammed in the piazza. He caught her once at the counter, her hands trembling as she stacked cups, and she forced a smile that didn't reach her eyes.

They clung to what moments they could steal. A walk by the harbour at dusk, when the air smelled of salt and frying fish and the gulls wheeled overhead. An evening spent mending one of the café's broken chairs, Fred holding the frame while Isabella steadied the nails with careful fingers.

Laughter, brief and sudden, when a fishmonger chased a gull from his stall with a broom.

But for every heartbeat of peace, the war pressed closer. Luciano drank harder, spoke sharper, his grief spilling over into bitterness. Fred noticed faces lingering too long near the piazza. Once, walking back to his lodgings, he thought he saw the same man twice on different streets, though when he turned to look, the figure melted into the alleys.

One evening, a car backfired outside. Isabella jerked so violently she dropped a tray of glasses, shards scattering across the tiles. Fred caught her hands, steadying her as she tried to laugh it off, but her eyes brimmed with unspilled tears. He wanted to gather her up, carry her away from Naples, from the war, from all of it.

That night, he walked home through narrow alleys smelling of smoke and fish, glancing over his shoulder at every corner. The city was alive, pulsing with its stubborn rhythm, but Fred knew beneath it ran a darker current, ready to pull them under.

The truth had been necessary. He no longer doubted that. But in giving it, he had drawn Isabella into the shadows with him. And now, for the first time, Fred Bennett was no longer sure he could protect her.

Thirty Two

The sun had just set over Naples, painting the sky in shades of pink and orange as Fred and Luciano sat in a shadowy corner of 'Café Rossi'. The café was empty, the door locked, and the shutters drawn to keep prying eyes away. Fred could feel the tension radiating from Luciano, the frustration simmering beneath the surface. They had been talking for nearly an hour, and Fred knew this wasn't just another routine meeting.

Luciano's eyes were dark, his voice low as he leaned across the table. "Fred, we've intercepted some new information," he began, urgent. "There's a palazzo near the centre of the city. The Germans are using it as a temporary command post to support the fascists here. They're planning something big, something that could change the course of the war here in Italy. There seems to be an increase in German presence here at the moment."

Fred leaned in, "What kind of information are we talking about?"

Luciano glanced around, as if checking one last time that they were truly alone. "Maps, orders, communication logs. Everything we need to understand their plans, their defences. It is meant to be proof that the Germans are moving more troops to Naples. If we can get our hands on it, we could finally give the Allies the upper hand."

Luciano sat back in his chair, lowering his voice further. "The palazzo sits on the edge of the old quarter. Iron gates, two sentries at the main entrance. You'll need to have your best acting skills for this one."

The plan was beginning to form in Fred's mind. This was the break they had been waiting for. Months of espionage and intelligence gathering, all leading to this moment. The weight pressed down on him. There could be no more mistakes.

"We'll need to plan this carefully; things haven't been as tight without…" Fred said, tapping the table. "I'll need blueprints of the palazzo, details of the guards' routines, entry points, anything you can find."

Luciano nodded. "It will be tight, I'll get what you need. But Fred…" He hesitated, his eyes narrowing as he looked at Fred. "We need to talk about Isabella."

Fred stiffened, knowing where this was going. "What about her?"

"You told her you're a British spy," Luciano said, his voice sharp with accusation. "Do you have any idea how dangerous that is? For you, for her, for all of us?"

Fred met Luciano's glare, his own frustration bubbling to the surface. "I know it was a risk, but I trust her. She's been nothing but loyal. And I couldn't keep lying to her, Luciano. Not after everything we've been through. Not that it matters, talking about trust, Luciano? When you can't keep your mouth shut after a drink! How many times have I had to drag you out of a bar to stop you getting us caught?"

"Trust?" Luciano spat, his voice rising. "This isn't about trust, Fred. It's about survival. Every word, every secret could mean the difference between life and death. You won't remember Maria, but she poured coffee for the same men every morning, smiled like she didn't understand a word. One day, a soldier asked her where her brother worked. She hesitated, hesitated, Fred, and two days later he was hanging from the pier. She didn't betray him, but they didn't care. Do you want that for Isabella? You English, you think you can just waltz in here, with your rules and your honour. But this is war. You can't afford to have a conscience. Think about Enzo."

Fred's temper flared, his fists clenching on the table. "I'm well aware of what's at stake, Luciano. I saw Enzo die, and I've lost friends. I know what war is. But I also know that living a lie can be worse than death. I couldn't keep pretending, not with her. Are you going to ignore that you had already told her whilst drunk?"

Luciano shook his head, his expression a mix of anger and resignation. "You're a fool, Fred. And me? I am a damned fool. But I can't change who you are or who I am. Just know that if anything goes wrong, if they come for you or me, they'll come for all of us."

Fred swallowed hard, Luciano's words settling heavily on his shoulders. He knew Luciano was right, that their actions had consequences beyond his own life. But he also knew that he couldn't live in fear, couldn't shut himself off from the connections that made him human. He had to believe that there was still room for trust, for honesty, even in the midst of war.

"I understand," Fred said quietly. "I'll be careful. And I'll make sure this mission goes off without a hitch. We can't afford to fail."

Luciano's gaze softened slightly, a grudging respect in his eyes. "Just promise me you'll keep your head down. You've already got enough blood on your hands. I was in a dark place; I've passed that now."

"I will, and I hope that's true," said Fred.

Luciano reached under the table and produced a small bottle of Limoncello, then poured two short measures.

Outside, a lone cart rolled over the cobbles, the sound fading into the distance. The shutters rattled softly in the evening breeze, a reminder of how thin the walls were between them and the city.

"To Fools," he said.

Fred raised his glass. "To fools who get the job done."

Luciano took his drink in one hit and swiftly poured himself another.

Fred looked out the window onto the city, his promise heavy in the air between them. "Oh, Luciano, who was Lucia? Enzo had never spoken of her before."

Luciano looked away; despite the months that had passed, the rawness of losing Enzo still cut deep. "Lucia, that was Enzo's sister."

He rubbed his thumb along the edge of his glass, not meeting Fred's eye. "She left Naples before the fascists took control. Smart girl. Enzo used to say she was the only one in the family with any sense." Luciano drew a slow breath, "Now she's the only one left."

Thirty Three

Naples, Italy - September 1942

In the weeks that followed, Fred immersed himself in the details of the mission. He pored over maps and blueprints until he could trace every corridor in his sleep. Luciano fed him guard schedules, watch changes, and quiet entry points. He rehearsed them until they became instinct.

Fred spent sleepless nights crafting plans, contingency plans, and backups to those. He paced the length of his room, the candle burning low as sketches of the palazzo sprawled across the table. Arrows marked guard patrols. Numbers noted timings. Every possibility, entry, exit, and failure was etched into his mind until he could see it even with his eyes closed.

He met the resistance in back rooms and shuttered cellars, the smell of damp stone and cigarette smoke clinging to his clothes long after. The mood was fractured. Some avoided his eyes when he spoke, fear bleeding through their silence. Others pressed forward, voices sharp, eager for vengeance.

"We should plant charges," Vittorio said one night, his hands twitching on the table. "Blow the whole place sky-high. That would cripple them more than a few scraps of paper."

Fred didn't raise his voice. He didn't need to. "Scraps of paper win wars, Vittorio. Orders, codes, maps. The Allies can use them. A fire leaves ashes. Information leaves them blind."

Across from him, Luisa tapped her fingers restlessly against her mug. "And if the information is worthless?" she challenged. "If it's just supply lists and requisition forms? We risk everything for nothing."

Fred leaned forward, his eyes hard. "Then we risked it and lived to try again. But what about troop movements, supply routes, and communications to Berlin? That could save thousands. That's worth a dozen risks."

The room fell quiet. Carlo, the youngest of them, shifted uneasily. His voice cracked when he spoke. "They'll shoot us if we're caught. No trial. No prison. Just the street and a wall."

"They'll shoot us anyway," Fred said, sharper than he meant. He forced a breath, softer now. "We're already at the wall. The difference is whether we leave something behind when we go."

The silence that followed was heavier than the stone walls around them.

Finally, he spread a map on the table, the palazzo and its surrounding streets sketched in ink. His finger tapped the side entrance. "Here. Delivery carts bring food and supplies each morning. I've watched them. The guards barely glance at the crates. That's one option."

He traced another path, along the rear garden wall. "Here, the patrols cross every ten minutes. If one is delayed, if the timing is right, we can slip through. But timing has to be perfect."

Some leaned in, others leaned away. Fear, eagerness, doubt, he read it in every pair of eyes. They carried their own reasons: vengeance for brothers shot, food stolen from children, rage at the boots on their streets. Fred had to bind them all into one plan, one strike.

"This isn't fire and fury," he said finally, his voice low but firm. "This is silence and shadows. We get in, we take what we need, and we leave no trace we were ever there."

Luisa smirked bitterly. "Like ghosts?"

Fred met her gaze. "Exactly like ghosts."

The lantern sputtered, throwing long shadows across the maps. Fred gathered the papers into a single neat pile, his fingers lingering on the edges as though order itself might hold back disaster. He couldn't afford another failure. Not now. Not with so much at stake.

During the day, he kept up appearances, visiting 'Café Rossi' and speaking with Isabella, his heart aching with the knowledge that he was drawing her deeper into his web of danger. She had sensed his preoccupation, asking gentle questions, her concern evident in the way she looked at him. Fred had reassured her as best he could, but the strain was beginning to show. He couldn't be sure if it was him, but something felt off for him.

"Fred, you've been so distant lately," Isabella said one afternoon, as they sat together in the café. "Is something wrong?"

Isabella's gaze lingered on the door every time a shadow passed outside. She was quieter than usual, her laughter slower to come. Fred wondered if she could sense the danger circling closer, even without knowing the details.

He forced a smile, reaching for her hand. "No, Isabella. I'm just busy. There's a lot going on right now. But I'm fine, really."

She studied his face, her eyes searching. "You don't have to carry everything alone."

Fred squeezed her hand, seeing the fear in her eyes. "I know. But right now, I just need you to trust me."

Isabella nodded, her concern not entirely eased, but she smiled, a small, sad smile. "I trust you, Fred. Just promise me you'll be careful."

"Careful is easy. Staying alive is the hard part." Fred replied.

"Then promise me both," said Isabella.

He gave her a faint smile. "You drive a hard bargain."

As the days passed, Fred's preparations continued, each step bringing him closer to the moment of truth. The palazzo loomed in his mind, a fortress of stone and secrets. It was a daunting task, but Fred was ready. He had to be. The fate of the Allies, the fate of Italy, rested on his shoulders.

That evening, Luciano found him in the back of the café. He didn't sit.

"When you go in there, remember, they will be expecting someone, even if they don't know it's you. Keep moving. Keep breathing. And if something feels wrong… leave it. Paper can't save lives, but you can."

After Luciano had left, Fred sat in his room with the dim light casting shadows on the walls. He checked his equipment one last time, his hands steady, his mind focused. He couldn't afford to think about the risks, about the consequences if he failed. All that mattered was the mission, the chance to strike a blow against the enemy, to change the course of the war.

As he lay down to sleep, his thoughts drifted to Isabella, to the warmth of her smile, the kindness in her eyes. There was a final look over her shoulder as he left her that night, but he couldn't work out the look she had on her face. He knew he was putting her in danger, that his actions could bring the wrath of the Gestapo down upon her. But he also knew that he couldn't turn back, couldn't walk away from the fight. He had made his choice, and now he had to see it through. He couldn't give Isabella any more thought.

Fred laid the pistol on the table beside his pack. "Let's hope we don't meet tonight," he muttered to the weapon, half in jest, half in prayer.

With a sigh, Fred closed his eyes, the impact of his decisions heavy on his chest. Tomorrow, he would face the palazzo.

Thirty Four

Fred Bennett moved through the alleys with the quiet confidence of a man who knew how to vanish into a city's shadows. His footsteps were silent, his body tense with anticipation. He had been planning this infiltration for weeks, gathering intelligence on the building's layout, the guards' routines, and the officers who worked there.

Tonight, everything would come to a head.

A patrol passed at the far end of the alley, their boots striking the cobbles in perfect rhythm. One of them laughed at a joke Fred couldn't catch. The sound was too loud in the narrow street. He pressed into a doorway, counting the steps until they faded. Only then did he move again.

The target was an old palazzo, nestled between two larger buildings near the harbour. It was used by the Italian military command to coordinate naval operations in the Mediterranean, and Fred had learned that crucial documents were stored there: documents that could turn the tide of the war. The building was heavily guarded, and getting inside would be no easy feat. But Fred had no choice. This information was invaluable to the Allies, and he was determined to obtain it. He was stationed in Naples for this exact reason.

A block away, he had left Vittorio and Carlo on watch. Vittorio would stage a commotion with a cart if patrols drew too near; Carlo's job was simpler, to run if soldiers appeared from the east. Neither would follow him inside; this part was Fred's alone, but their presence steadied him.

As for Luisa, she had pressed the forged delivery papers into his hand that morning with a look that lingered longer than words. "If they stop you," she'd said, "you have maybe two seconds to sell the lie."

Fred had no intention of being stopped. Still, the weight of her words sat with him now. He reached the back of the palazzo, where a high wall enclosed a small courtyard. Fred glanced around, ensuring no one was watching, then pulled a rope from his satchel. With practised ease, he threw it over the wall, the grappling hook catching in the edge. He tugged it to make sure it was secure and began to climb.

His muscles strained as he hauled himself up, the rough stone scraping against his palms. He reached the top and paused, listening. The sound of voices drifted up from the courtyard below. Two guards, their conversation casual, unaware of the danger lurking just above them. Fred peered over the edge, seeing the guards leaning against the wall, their rifles slung over their shoulders. One of them took a drag on his cigarette and said something about his cousin's wedding next week. The other laughed, stamping his feet against the chill. The mundanity of it only made Fred's pulse hammer harder.

He couldn't afford to be seen. Moving quickly, Fred swung a leg over the wall and dropped silently into the shadows. He crouched, his back pressed against the cold stone, his heart pounding in his chest. The guards were only a few feet away, their laughter grating on his nerves. He had to wait, to be patient.

He thought of Isabella then, of how her eyes had searched his when she asked him to promise he'd try to come back. He hadn't told her what this mission truly was, only that it was dangerous. She deserved more than silence. If this went wrong, she would never know why he hadn't returned.

Minutes passed, each one stretching into eternity. Finally, the guards moved away, their footsteps fading into the distance. Fred exhaled slowly, then moved on, keeping to the dark edges of the courtyard. He reached the door at the back of the building, his fingers closing around the handle. It was locked, as he had expected.

"Come on… come on…" he muttered under his breath, the tumblers resisting like stubborn teeth before finally clicking into place.

Fred slipped inside, the door clicking shut behind him. He found himself in a narrow hallway, dimly lit by a single bulb hanging from the ceiling.

The air was thick with the smell of old paper and musty wood. He moved quickly, his eyes scanning the hallway for any sign of movement. He knew he had to find the office where the documents were kept, and he had to do it fast.

He reached a staircase and paused, listening. Voices echoed from somewhere above, muffled by the walls. Fred ascended the stairs, his movements slow and deliberate. He reached the landing and saw a door slightly ajar, light spilling out into the hallway. He edged closer, peering through the gap.

Inside was a large room filled with filing cabinets and a desk cluttered with papers. Maps of the Mediterranean covered the walls, marked with red pins. This was it, the command office. Fred's pulse quickened as he scanned the room, his eyes falling on a locked cabinet in the corner. That had to be where the documents were stored.

He slipped into the room, his steps silent on the wooden floor. He crossed to the cabinet, his hands moving to pick the lock. It was a simple mechanism, and he had it open in seconds. Inside were files, neatly arranged, marked with the seal of the Italian Navy. Vittorio's voice echoed in his head: "Scraps of paper won't change anything." Fred's hands tightened on the folders. He had been wrong, every line, every cypher, every signature here mattered. The Allies would see the patterns, the routes, the weaknesses. Enzo had died for Naples, for hope. Fred would not leave empty-handed.

He pulled them out, his eyes skimming the pages. Naval movements, supply routes, communication codes, everything the Allies needed to gain the upper hand. He was about to stuff the documents into his satchel when he heard it, a soft creak, the sound of a door opening. Fred froze, his heart hammering in his chest. He turned slowly, his hand moving to the knife at his belt. A shadow fell across the floor, and a soldier stepped into the room, his eyes widening in surprise.

The soldier stepped fully into the light, squinting. "Capitano? You're not supposed to be…" His gaze dropped to Fred's satchel. "Wait… who…" "*Chi sei tu?*" he barked, his hand darting for the pistol at his belt.

Fred didn't hesitate. He lunged forward, his knife flashing in the dim light. He caught the soldier's arm, twisting it behind his back, the knife pressed to his throat. For a heartbeat, Fred's grip faltered. He could tie him, gag him, try to slip away. But the man's breath was fast and shallow, his eyes darting to the desk. Fred knew that one shout would end it all. The choice was no choice at all. The soldier struggled, his eyes wide with fear, but Fred held him tight, his grip unyielding.

"*Non muoverti,*" Fred hissed, his voice low and dangerous.

213

The soldier's breathing was ragged, his body trembling. Fred knew he couldn't let the man live. If Vittorio had been here, he might have argued for a cleaner, louder solution. If Carlo had been here, he might have panicked. But this was the reason Fred had insisted on going in alone. The responsibility, the blood, had to be his. He couldn't risk the alarm being raised. With a quick, practised motion, he slid the knife across the soldier's throat. The man gurgled, his eyes rolling back as blood spilt down his chest. Fred held him until the life drained from his body, then lowered him to the floor.

Fred's hands trembled as he wiped the blade clean. He hadn't wanted to kill the man, but he had no choice. He glanced down at the body, his stomach churning. He had to hide it, had to buy himself more time.

He dragged the body into a corner, covering it with a heavy curtain. It wasn't a perfect solution, but it would have to do. Fred returned to the cabinet, stuffing the documents into his satchel. He had to get out of here, had to escape before the body was discovered.

As he turned to leave, documents secure in his satchel, a sudden explosion split the night. The floor trembled beneath his boots, plaster drifting from the ceiling. Shouts rang out above him, sharp, frantic, half in German, half in Italian. Another blast followed, farther away but no less deafening, echoing down the narrow streets outside.

Fred's heart kicked. Vittorio. The diversion.

The timing was perfect, too perfect to be anything but planned. Guards thundered overhead, their boots rattling the floorboards, weapons clattering as orders were barked. But the rhythm of their movement wasn't toward him. It was outward, spilling into the streets, chasing the chaos Vittorio had lit like a fuse.

Fred darted from the office and down the stairwell, slipping through smoke-tinged shadows. A pair of soldiers charged past the lower landing, neither sparing him a glance, too intent on the roar of confusion outside. He reached the ground floor and pressed against the cold wall, waiting. When the shouts receded, he pushed through a side door into the courtyard.

The place was deserted. The two guards who should have been leaning on their rifles, bored and half-asleep, were gone, drawn into the storm. Only the echo of orders and the smell of cordite carried on the breeze.

Fred vaulted the wall and dropped into the alley beyond. His boots hit the cobbles hard, but he was moving before the pain reached his knees.

"*Nach ihm! Schnell!*" a voice suddenly barked from somewhere behind, too close. A rifle bolt snapped home. Fred swerved as a bullet sparked off stone near his shoulder, shards of masonry peppering his face.

He pushed harder, the labyrinth of alleys twisting ahead. Every corner was a gamble: wrong turn meant a dead end, a bullet in the back. He ran blind, lungs burning.

A hundred yards on, a shadow detached itself from a doorway. Vittorio. His face was grim, eyes bright in the dark. He jerked his head once, sharp and urgent.

"West alley's clear!" he hissed, before vanishing back into the night.

Fred didn't pause. He turned into the west alley, boots hammering, breath ragged.

Further down, Carlo appeared like a ghost, wide-eyed, darting across the street. "Patrols at the piazza, hurry!" he whispered hoarsely, then bolted the other way, disappearing into the dark.

Thirty Five

Fred's lungs burned as he navigated the labyrinthine streets of Naples, the satchel bumping against his side, the stolen documents inside a constant reminder of the risk he had taken. The fire he had set still lit up the night sky, a flickering glow in the distance. The sound of sirens and shouts echoed faintly through the alleys, the city coming alive in response to the chaos he had unleashed.

He couldn't stay on the main roads. With every turn, his eyes darted, scanning for signs of pursuit. He had made his way through the bustling markets earlier, slipping unnoticed among the throngs of locals and soldiers, but that route was out of the question now. The fascists would be looking for someone, anyone suspicious, and Fred's gut told him to avoid the well-lit paths.

His instincts, honed over years of surviving the front lines, screamed at him to stay vigilant. He slipped into a narrow alley, pausing to listen. The only sounds were the far-off clatter of a tram and its ragged breathing. He moved on, taking obscure backstreets that looped through the city before bringing him back toward his apartment.

Now and then, he glanced over his shoulder, his nerves on edge. Was that a shadow moving in the darkness? A glint of metal reflecting the moonlight? A voice barked somewhere behind him, too far to make out the words, but enough to quicken his pace. He ducked into a doorway, pressing flat against the damp wall as two Carabinieri passed, their boots clicking in step. They didn't glance his way, but Fred stayed in the shadows until their footsteps faded.

Paranoia was both an ally and an enemy in his line of work, keeping him alive but fraying his nerves to the breaking point.

"...*tutto bruciato*," a man's voice muttered from an open window above, the word *burned* carrying into the night. A woman replied sharply, "Zitto, do you want them to hear you?" The shutters slammed closed.

After what felt like hours, Fred finally approached the nondescript building that housed his apartment, a small, unassuming place. He paused across the street, taking in the scene. The façade was dark, the windows on the upper floors shuttered. A single bicycle leaned against the wall by the entrance, not his neighbour's. He hesitated, listening. No sound came from the stairwell, but the scent of cigarette smoke lingered in the air. There was no sign of movement, no indication that the enemy was lying in wait.

Still, Fred didn't trust it. He circled the block twice, checking every alley, every doorway. His heart hammered in his chest, the adrenaline of his escape still coursing through his veins. Satisfied that he hadn't been followed, he crossed the street and slipped through the door into the cool interior.

The entrance was empty as he headed for the stairs. He took them two at a time, his senses still on high alert, his hand resting on the knife at his belt. He reached his room on the second floor, the door a welcome sight after the harrowing journey.

He slipped inside, closing the door softly behind him. The room was dark, the curtains drawn. Fred stood for a moment, letting his eyes adjust to the dim light. He listened for any sound, any sign that he wasn't alone. Nothing. Just the soft ticking of the clock on the nightstand, the distant murmur of the city beyond the walls.

He let out a breath, his muscles relaxing slightly. He had made it. He was safe.

Fred crossed to the window, peering through a crack in the curtain. The street below was quiet, the flickering light of a gas lamp painting the ground in shifting shapes. There was no one there, no sign of pursuit. He had gotten away with it.

For now.

He moved to the small desk in the corner, pulling the stolen documents from his satchel. He spread them out, his eyes scanning the pages. Everything he was told it would be, everything he had risked his life for, right here in front of him. It was a victory, a hard-won prize in a war that had taken so much.

Fred's fingers traced the edges of the papers, his mind replaying the events of the night. The infiltration, the soldier, Vittorio's explosion. He had killed before, but this was different. It was cold, calculated. Necessary, but not easy. He pushed the thoughts aside, focusing on the task at hand.

He needed to get these documents to his contact, to get them out of Naples and into the hands of the Allied command. But that would have to wait until tomorrow. Tonight, he needed rest. His body ached, his mind exhausted from the tension and adrenaline. He folded the documents carefully, hiding them in the false bottom of his suitcase.

He sat for a moment on the edge of the bed, head in hands, the silence almost oppressive. In another life, he might have celebrated a job well done. Here, in occupied Naples, there was no one to raise a glass with.

The others were already gone. That had been the plan from the start: Vittorio, Carlo, Luisa, scattered to safe houses beyond the city before the smoke had even cleared. They had been assembled for one purpose, one night, and now the circle was broken again, swallowed by the war. Fred knew he might never see any of them again. That may be for the best. The fewer attachments, the fewer names for the enemy to carve out of you if you were caught.

220

Still, for a moment, he let himself remember their faces in the dark, quick nods, hurried whispers, shadows moving in step with his. Then he pushed the thought aside. Naples had a way of devouring people. Better to keep walking.

Fred moved to the small bathroom, splashing cold water on his face, the shock of it bringing him back to the present. He looked at himself in the mirror, his face pale, a thin line of dried blood under his chin. He wiped it away, his mind already moving to the next step, the next mission.

As he lay down on the narrow bed, the events of the night played over and over in his mind. He thought again of the fire, the way it had consumed the building, destroying everything in its path. It was a fitting metaphor for the war itself, a relentless force that consumed everything it touched.

Fred closed his eyes, his body sinking into the mattress. He had survived another day, another mission. But he knew the war was far from over.

For now, though, he allowed himself to listen to the quiet of the room, the distant sounds of the city lulling him into a restless sleep. The war would be waiting when he woke, but tonight, in the small, dark room of a hotel in Naples, Fred Bennett was safe.

Thirty Six

The next afternoon, the café was quiet; the usual hum of conversation had been replaced by a tense silence. Isabella moved around the empty tables, her movements mechanical, eyes unfocused. The sun was setting, washing the tiled floor in gold, but Isabella barely noticed. Her thoughts were consumed by the empty space where her children should be.

Marco and Sofia should have been home by now. Marco had gone to the market, and Sofia had been playing with the neighbour's children. Isabella had expected them back hours ago. She had gone out to look for them, asking neighbours, checking the square, but there was no sign of them.

On her way back, old Signora Bellini leaned out her window. "No sign of them yet?"

Isabella shook her head. "If you see them, send them straight home." "I will. But these days…" The old woman's voice trailed off, and she shut the shutters. Panic rose like bile as she returned to the café, her mind racing with terrible possibilities.

She was wiping down the counter for the third time when the door swung open. Isabella looked up, hope flaring in her chest, but it wasn't her children.

Instead, a man in a dark coat and hat stepped inside, his presence sending a chill down her spine. She recognised the insignia on his lapel; it was the mark of the Gestapo.

He closed the door behind him with deliberate slowness, removing his gloves finger by finger. The sound of leather against skin seemed loud in the empty café. Isabella gripped the cloth in her hand, her knuckles whitening, but she didn't move.

"Signora Rossi?" he asked, his voice cold and clipped.

Isabella's heart pounded. "Yes," she replied, forcing her voice to remain steady. "What do you want?"

The man's eyes were like ice, devoid of emotion. "Your children, Marco and Sofia, are in our custody. They will remain with us until you provide the information we require."

The ground seemed to shift beneath Isabella's feet. "What? No, that can't be true! Where are they? I want to see them!"

The Gestapo officer's expression remained impassive. "You will see them when you give us what we need. Information about the British spy, Fred Bennett. You know him, yes?"

Isabella felt the blood drain from her face. They knew. Somehow, they had found out about Fred. Fred's face came unbidden to her mind, the way he'd looked at her the night he told her the truth. Fear gripped her, but it was nothing compared to the terror that threatened to overwhelm her at the thought of losing her children.

"What... what do you want to know?" Isabella whispered, her voice trembling.

"Where is he staying? What are his plans? Anything that will help us capture him," the officer said. His voice was calm, as if he were discussing the weather. "Tell us what we want to know, and your children will be returned to you unharmed."

"And if it is not?" Isabella asked before she could stop herself.

The man's faint smile did not change. "Then we will speak again."

Isabella's mind raced. Fred had told her his true identity and had trusted her with his mission. He was staying in a small room above a tailor's shop, keeping a low profile as he gathered intelligence. She had kept his secret, even as her fear grew. But now, Marco and Sofia's lives were on the line.

She swallowed, forcing herself to meet the officer's gaze. "He's staying above the tailor's shop on Via Toledo," she said, her voice breaking. "He's alone. Please, just let my children go."

The officer nodded, a faint smile playing at his lips. "Good. You have made a wise choice, Signora. We will confirm your information, and if it proves accurate, your children will be returned to you."

224

Isabella's legs felt weak, her body shaking. She had done it. She had betrayed Fred. The man she loved, the man who had brought light into her life amid war. She had given him up without hesitation, driven by the fierce need to protect her children. A wave of guilt and shame washed over her, but she pushed it aside. There was no room for regret, not when Marco and Sofia's lives were at stake.

The officer turned to leave, his footsteps echoing in the quiet café. Isabella watched him go, her heart heavy with the significance of her decision. She sank into a chair, her head in her hands, tears streaming down her face. Outside, the street went on as though nothing had happened; a cart rattled over the stones, a boy whistled off-key.

The night dragged on, each moment filled with a tension that Isabella could barely stand. She kept glancing at the door, waiting for the knock that would signal the return of her children. The knock that would confirm that the Gestapo had found Fred, that they had captured him.

But the knock never came. The hours stretched into eternity, the silence pressing down on her like a weight. She loved him, but she had sacrificed him. And no matter what happened, no matter if Marco and Sofia were returned safely, she knew she would have to live with the consequences of her choice.

As the first light broke through the windows, Isabella sat alone in the quiet café, her heart heavy with the burden of her betrayal.

She had to open the cafe as normal.

Thirty Seven

Fred woke early, and for a moment, he lay still, letting the first light filter across the room. The events of the previous night felt distant, almost dreamlike, until he turned his head and saw the suitcase by the wall. Reality came rushing back, sharp and cold.

He sat up, rubbing his fingers through his hair. His apartment was quiet, the only sound the faint hum of the city waking up outside. Fred swung his legs over the side of the bed, his muscles protesting the movement. Every part of him ached, a reminder of fight, flight, and the constant strain of being hunted.

But there was no time for rest. Today was a critical day.

Fred dressed quickly, pulling on a plain shirt and trousers, the sort worn by dock workers and shop clerks. He checked the mirror, ensuring he looked like any other local, a weary man worn down by the trials of war. Satisfied, he moved to the suitcase, retrieving the stolen documents from their hiding place.

The papers felt heavy in his fingers, a tangible weight that signalled more than just the value of the information. These documents could change the course of the war, could turn the tide in the Allies' favour. But only if he got them into the right hands.

Fred tucked the papers into an inside pocket of his coat, securing them with a button. He took a deep breath, steeling himself for what lay ahead. The contact was reliable, someone Fred had worked with before, but the streets of Naples were more treacherous than ever. One wrong move, one moment of bad luck, and everything would be lost.

He left his apartment through the back door, avoiding the front entrance of the Tailor's shop. The narrow alley behind the building was empty, the brick walls still cool with the night's chill. Fred moved quickly, his footsteps echoing softly off the cobblestones. He slipped into the main street, blending with the small crowds of people starting their day.

The meeting point was a small piazza near the harbour, a place where fishermen sold their early morning catch and vendors set up stalls to sell bread and fruit. Halfway down Via Marina, he stopped to tie his bootlace, using the moment to scan the street. A delivery cart rattled by. A woman bargained loudly over a basket of anchovies. No shadows broke from the doorways, no hurried footsteps followed. Still, he kept to the edge of the crowd, never walking in a straight line for long.

As he walked, Fred kept his head down, his eyes scanning the street. German soldiers were becoming a common sight in Naples, their uniforms a grim reminder of the war. Today was no different. Fred spotted a pair of them on the corner, rifles slung over their shoulders, watching the passersby with bored eyes. He kept his pace steady, his face impassive, heart thudding as he passed.

The piazza emerged, carrying the heady mix of freshly baked bread and the crisp bite of sea salt. Fred relaxed slightly. The square was crowded, the noise of the market bringing him comfort. He moved through the throng, his eyes searching for the contact.

A man stood near a small stall, examining a display of fruit. He was tall, with dark hair and a moustache, his clothes neat but unremarkable. To anyone else, he was just another shopper, but Fred recognised him immediately.

Alberto.

As Fred reached the stall, Alberto glanced at a passing vendor hawking figs. Without looking at Fred, he shifted a single orange from one hand to the other, their agreed signal that it was safe to speak.

"The oranges are fresh today," Fred's voice was barely audible over the noise of the market.

Alberto didn't look up, his attention still on the fruit. "The oranges are always fresh," he replied, his tone equally soft.

Fred picked one up, weighing it in his palm. "Not like last winter. These have real juice."

"Winter will come again soon enough," Alberto murmured. "Best to take what's sweet while you can."

Fred reached into his coat, pretending to adjust his collar. His fingers brushed the edge of the documents, a silent promise of what was to come.

"Walk with me," Alberto said, turning away from the stall. Fred fell into step beside him, the two men blending into the flow of the crowd. They walked in silence, heading towards a quieter part of the piazza, away from the market's central hub.

Alberto led them to a small alley, the walls close enough to muffle the noise of the market. He turned to Fred, his eyes sharp. "You have them?"

Fred nodded, reaching into his coat. He pulled out the documents, handing them over without a word. Alberto took them, his fingers brushing Fred's briefly before he tucked the papers into his own coat.

For a moment, they stood in silence, the strain of the exchange heavy between them. Fred knew what those documents meant, not just for Naples, but for the entire war effort. It was information that could cripple Axis control, paving the way for Allied forces to claim the city.

Alberto broke the silence first. "These will help," he said, his voice low. "The Nazis have been tightening their grip, but this...this could change things. They've been too confident, thinking they're untouchable. This will show them they're not."

Fred nodded, relief flooding through him. It was done. The information was out of his hands, in the possession of someone who could use it to strike a blow against the enemy. It was a small victory, but a crucial one.

"Be careful, Fred," Alberto said, his tone serious. "The enemy is on high alert after last night. They'll be looking for someone. Keep your head down. They've already knocked on doors near the harbour," Alberto said. "In the early hours they pulled a man from his bed, and he hasn't been seen since. They're not just looking for you, they're making examples."

"I always do," Fred replied. He hesitated, then added, "Thank you, Alberto. For everything."

Alberto nodded, his expression unreadable. "We all have our parts to play." With that, he turned and walked away, disappearing into the crowd.

Fred watched him go, relief and tension coiling in his chest. He turned and walked back towards the market, blending once again into the flow of the city. As he moved, he kept his head down, his face impassive, just another man going about his day. But inside, his mind was already turning to the next mission, the next step in the fight.

Fred Bennett was a soldier, and his war was not yet over.

Later that day, Fred arrived at the café.

"It's quiet in here," Fred said, glancing at the empty tables.

"Mornings are for the market," Isabella replied, busying herself with a tray so he couldn't see her eyes. "And for those with rations left." Isabella could barely meet his gaze, the guilt gnawing at her insides.

"How are you?" Fred asked, concern in his voice. "You seem distracted."

Isabella shook her head, forcing a smile. "It's nothing," she said, her voice tight. "Just a long day."

Fred frowned, reaching out to take her hand. "If there's anything wrong, you can tell me, Isabella. You know that, right?"

She nodded, her throat tight. She wanted to tell him, wanted to confess everything, but she couldn't. If he knew what she had done, if he knew the truth, he would never forgive her. And more importantly, it would put him in even greater danger. No, it was better this way. Better that he didn't know.

"I'm fine," she said, squeezing his hand. "Really. I just need some rest."

Fred smiled, lifting her hand to his lips. "Then rest," he said softly. "I'll be here when you're ready."

Isabella nodded, tears stinging her eyes. She watched as Fred moved to the counter, pouring himself a cup of coffee, oblivious to the storm that had just passed through.

Thirty Eight

Fred knew something was wrong the moment he stepped out of the café. The late afternoon streets of Naples were unusually quiet, and there was a tension in the air, hushed, shadows pooling in the alleys like they were waiting for something. He pulled his coat tighter around him, his eyes scanning the empty alleyways. The war had a way of making everything feel dangerous.

He turned onto Via Toledo, the narrow street leading to the tailor's shop, which was below the room he rented. The sun was barely up, casting shadows that seemed to stretch and twist like reaching fingers. Fred quickened his pace, eager to be off the streets, to find the safety of his little room. But as he approached the door, he sensed movement. A shutter clicked shut above him. A man paused mid-conversation to watch him pass. Somewhere behind, a boot scraped stone, not quite in time with his steps.

Too late.

Figures emerged from the shadows, grim-faced Gestapo agents in dark coats. Fred's instincts kicked in, his fingers reaching for the knife he kept hidden in his belt, but strong arms seized him, twisting his arms behind his back. He struggled, lashing out with his feet, but the grip was iron, unbreakable. He was forced to his knees, the rough cobblestones digging into his skin.

A cold voice spoke, cutting through the chaos. "Fred Bennett, you are under arrest for espionage against the Reich."

"You've got the wrong man," Fred said, though they both knew it was pointless.

The man before him was tall, his face shadowed by the brim of his hat, but there was no mistaking the cruelty in his eyes. Fred's heart pounded, his mind racing. How had they found him? He had been careful, had taken every precaution. But even as he thought it, the answer came crashing down on him, a weight that drove the air from his lungs.

Isabella.

She had betrayed him. The realisation was like a physical blow, stealing his breath, leaving him stunned. He could see her now, her dark eyes filled with tears, her voice whispering promises of love and loyalty. Lies. All of it. Lies to gain his trust, to get close to him, to feed him to the wolves.

Anger surged through him, hot and blinding. He wanted to shout, to demand answers, but a hand clamped over his mouth, silencing him. They dragged him to his feet, shoving him into the back of a waiting car. The door slammed shut, plunging Fred into darkness as the sound of the engine roaring to life filled his ears.

As the car sped through the streets of Naples, Fred fought to keep his emotions in check. He couldn't afford to let his anger cloud his mind. He needed to think, to plan. There had to be a way out of this. He couldn't allow himself to be captured, to be used against the very people he was fighting to protect. He had to escape. He had to survive.

The car screeched to a halt, and Fred was yanked from the backseat, his feet barely touching the ground as they hauled him into a building. The air was thick with the smell of sweat and fear, the dim light casting eerie shadows on the stone walls. He was thrown into a small, windowless room, the door slamming shut behind him with a finality that sent a chill down his spine.

The beatings began immediately. They stripped him of his coat and his shirt, leaving him shivering in the cold stone cell. The harsh light stung his eyes. The men circled him like vultures, their voices low and menacing.

One of them slid a photograph across the floor, a grainy image of an Allied operative he didn't know. "She's dead because of you," the man said flatly. Fred knew it was a lie, but it still lodged in his gut.

"Where are your contacts?" another soldier growled in German, slamming a fist against the wall beside Fred's head.

"Who gave you orders?" another demanded in rough Italian, spitting the words like venom.

Fred clenched his jaw, biting down the pain that threatened to break him. He had been trained for this, endless hours in the cold, relentless drills where surrender was not an option. He heard his old sergeant's voice echoing in his mind, gruff and commanding: "Pain is weakness leaving the body. You hold. You do not break."

Fists landed hard on his ribs, knocking the air from his lungs. A boot crushed into his side. The cold steel of a gun barrel pressed against his temple, numbing his thoughts.

But he stayed silent.

His mind drifted to Enzo, his friend's warm laughter ringing in his ears, the way he'd clapped Fred on the shoulder before they set out on their last mission. "We do this together," Enzo had said, eyes bright with hope. That hope felt fragile now, like a candle flickering in the storm. Fred swallowed the lump in his throat and forced himself back to the present.

"London will forget you," another man said in halting English. "They always do." The interrogator leaned in close, his breath sour. "You will talk," he hissed. "Or your friends die."

Fred's gaze hardened. He could not, would not betray them. As the soldiers left, one of them left a final punch in the side of Fred. "You wait til Rehn gets here!"

Hours blended into days, each one marked by the steady rhythm of pain and silence. He learned to count time by the guard's meals; the smell of cabbage, the clink of enamel mugs. Twice a day, maybe three. Enough to keep him alive, not enough to keep him strong. His body screamed with every bruise and cut, but his mind clung to the training, to Enzo's face, to the promise that no matter what, he would endure.

But the betrayal festered, a wound that refused to heal. He thought of Isabella, of the look in her eyes when they were together, the way she had touched his face, kissed his lips. It had felt real, more real than anything he had known in years. And yet, she had given him up. She had sold him to the Gestapo without a moment's hesitation. The thought made him sick, a bile rising in his throat that he could barely swallow.

Why? The question burned in his mind, even as he tried to push it away. Why had she done it? Had she ever cared, or had he been her puppet all along?

Fred's fists clenched, his nails digging into his palms. It didn't matter. None of it mattered. He couldn't afford to dwell on it, to let it distract him. He had to survive, had to find a way out of this hell. He would not let her betrayal be the end of him.

He forced himself to focus, to push past the pain and the anger. He studied the room, the routine of the guards, searching for a weakness, an opportunity. He would find a way to escape, to return to his comrades. And when he did, he would close his heart to Isabella forever. He couldn't allow himself to be vulnerable, to be hurt like this again.

The door creaked open, a shaft of light cutting through the darkness. A guard entered, a sneer on his lips, a familiar sadistic glint in his eyes. Fred braced himself, his body tensing for the next round of interrogation. He met the guard's gaze, his own eyes cold, devoid of the warmth they once held.

"Ready to talk, Bennett?" the guard asked, his voice mocking.

"Not to you," Fred rasped.

Fred stared forward, his jaw set. He would not give them the satisfaction. He would not break. And as the guard approached, Fred made a silent vow, a promise to himself and to the memory of the man he had been before the war had torn his life apart.

He would survive this. He would find a way to fight back. And when he did, he would bury the past, the pain, and the betrayal deep inside, where it could never touch him again. The war had taken everything from him, but it would not take his spirit.

Not yet.

Not ever.

Thirty Nine

The children were asleep. Isabella wanted to cry, to scream, but instead she held them tighter.

Sofia curled against her shoulder, breathing in tiny puffs. Marco snored gently from the mattress on the floor, one arm flung across a threadbare toy rabbit that had somehow survived the chaos. Their cheeks were flushed from warmth and tears, but they were safe now. Safe and home.

Isabella sat in the dark, back against the doorframe of their bedroom, her shawl wrapped tightly around her. She hadn't slept since they'd been returned. She couldn't.

The Gestapo hadn't touched them, but they'd taken something worse. The belief that mothers could protect their children from monsters. And worse: they'd turned them into currency.

And I gave him away.

Her fingers squeezed around the chipped mug. The chicory inside had gone cold hours ago.

She had said Fred's name aloud only once since they were returned. Whispered it. Then swallowed it like poison. Her heart twisted when Sofia asked, "Will Fred come back soon?"

She hadn't answered. Couldn't.

A soft knock pulled her from the silence.

She froze. It was late. Too late for neighbours. She glanced at the children, then at the door. Slowly, she stood and moved to it, peering through the narrow gap.

Luciano.

He looked thinner. Pale beneath the olive of his skin. But his eyes still burned. She opened the door just enough for him to enter, saying nothing. Inside, he removed his cap, his expression unreadable. "So they gave them back," he said, nodding toward the bedroom. "That was the price?"

The words pulled her back to that moment, the dusty ribbon on the table, the officer's voice calm as he promised she'd never see her children again. The smell of his leather gloves lingered still, a phantom she couldn't shake.

Her mouth went dry.

She nodded once.

Luciano crossed to the table and sat, slowly. "They told us Fred was caught straight after the drop." His voice was low, even.

"I didn't tell them everything," she said quietly, defensively. "Only what they needed to hear. Only enough."

Luciano looked at her, eyes hard. "But enough to get him caught."

Tears stung her eyes, but she didn't let them fall. "They took my children, Luciano. They showed me Sofia's ribbon, the one she wears in her hair,

241

covered in dust, thrown on the floor like a trophy. They told me I had to or they would..." Isabella couldn't finish her sentence.

Silence stretched between them.

At last, he exhaled. Not forgiveness, not quite, but something less sharp than before.

"I don't blame you," he said. "But I hate that they've done this to you."

She lowered herself into the seat opposite him, hands trembling in her lap. "I didn't think they'd hurt him. I thought... maybe he'd slip away, like always. He's clever. Quiet. I thought he'd be a ghost to them."

She'd told herself that Fred was different: quick, untouchable. The sort of man who slipped past danger like smoke. Believing that had made it easier to speak the words they wanted.

"You don't understand," Luciano said. "They weren't looking for ghosts. They wanted a symbol. Something to shake what we're building. Fred was the heart of it, especially since losing Enzo."

She swallowed the lump rising in her throat. "Do you think they'll kill him?" Outside somewhere, a gramophone played a scratchy tango. Life went on, indifferent.

"I don't know."

The room fell still again, save for the creak of wood and the muffled sound of Marco stirring in sleep.

Luciano leaned forward slightly. "You loved him?"

She nodded.

"And he loved you?"

Another nod. This time, shakier.

"Then I hope," Luciano said, his voice quieter now, "you find a way to forgive yourself. Because he won't."

She blinked, wounded.

But he stood, pulling his coat around him.

He reached the door, then paused.

"They've poisoned enough of us, Isabella. Don't let them take more, even if it's just the part of you that still feels alive."

Then he was gone.

The door closed with a soft click that echoed louder than it should have in the still apartment. Isabella stood motionless, the cool night air curling in around her ankles like a whisper. Outside, the alley was quiet, no footsteps, no distant voices, just Naples breathing in the dark. Somewhere far off, a dog barked once, then fell silent. She felt the tremble in her legs only when the magnitude of Luciano's words began to settle.

The kitchen smelled faintly of burnt sugar and lemon peel, remnants of a pot she'd left boiling too long the day before. The scent mixed now with the metallic tang of fear and the salt of dried tears on her cheeks. Her stomach churned with hunger

243

and guilt in equal measure. She turned, slowly, and reached for the oil lamp on the counter, but her hand hovered over the matchbox, unsure.

The darkness felt more honest.

She stood at the threshold for a long time after, her fingers still clutching the doorframe like it might anchor her.

Behind her, Sofia murmured Fred's name in a dream.

Forty

Prison, Naples - January 1943

The room smelled of old tobacco, damp stone and sweat as Oberstleutnant Dieter Rehn stood by the window, arms folded behind his back, watching the last of the Neapolitan daylight fade. The sun nestling behind the clustered rooftops like a retreating enemy. Rehn preferred Berlin's steel skies to Naples' humidity, but orders were orders.

Behind him, two junior officers sat at the conference table, Untersturmführer Klaus Meissner, young and overeager, and Unterscharführer Vogel, quiet, methodical, and precise. Between them lay two open files, filled with notes, photographs, and cross-referenced reports.

Rehn turned and walked toward the table, the heels of his boots tapping out a measured rhythm on the stone floor.

"Let's begin," he said, his voice clipped. "Our subject, he's been here for a few months already and hasn't talked."

Vogel opened the top file. A photograph of Lieutenant Fred Bennett sat neatly clipped to the page, young, sharp-featured, British. The kind of face you wouldn't look at twice in a crowd, which made him perfect for covert work.

Meissner shifted on his heels, eyes darting to Rehn for approval. Vogel, stone-faced, traced the edges of the photographs with a fingertip, as if memorising every line before speaking.

"Captured near Via Toledo," Vogel began. "We found false documentation, coded fragments of intercepted wireless transmissions, and a concealed vial of microfilm sewn into his jacket lining."

"Amateur mistake," Meissner muttered.

"No," Rehn said. "He knew the area was compromised. Men like him don't blunder, they choose."

He tapped the photo with a gloved finger. "And now he's ours."

Rehn motioned to the second file. Vogel opened it with quiet efficiency.

"Bennett's recent movements show proximity to known sympathisers in the Quartieri Spagnoli. The café appears frequently, Café Rossi. We believe it serves as a communications hub."

"Was," Rehn corrected. "It was a communications hub. Until Enzo Moretti was killed."

At that, even Meissner fell silent.

"Moretti's death destabilised the local network," Rehn continued. "Now we have their point of contact. Bennett will know what cells remain, who

246

replaced Moretti, and, crucially, whether London still sees this city as operational."

He lifted a page. There, in faded surveillance photographs, was Isabella, leaving the café at dusk, her eyes hidden under the brim of her hat.

Rehn studied her a moment, then looked up. "He cared for her. That made her useful for us."

Vogel raised an eyebrow. "Did we release her children when she gave up his location?"

"Yes," Rehn replied calmly. "And we will let him know that she gave him up."

"Isn't that risky?" Meissner asked.

"He's trained to resist pain," Rehn interrupted. "But betrayal? That's harder. He trusted Moretti. And now Moretti is gone. The girl, what if she's gone too? A frightened man breaks differently from a proud one. But they all do break, in the end."

He paced slowly, deliberately. "No bruises. No screaming. That's for amateurs. We dismantle him quietly, starting with time. Twelve hours in isolation. No food, no voice, no sound."

Rehn pictured Bennett alone in the cell, hours stretching like lead, counting nothing, hearing nothing, imagining faces that no longer existed. He'd break not with pain, but with emptiness, hunger, silence and memory.

"A bit late for that," Vogel smirked.

"No more bruising. We offer him water. Ask his name. Tell him the girl has been beneficial. That

Moretti's death was swift. That London has abandoned this city."

Meissner nodded. "Psychological erosion."

"Exactly," Rehn said, "We're letting him erode quietly, without knowing it."

The room fell quiet again, just the soft shuffle of pages, the hum of a faulty wall lamp.

Rehn lit a cigarette and turned back to the window. Naples twinkled below in flickering shades of brownout. Lanterns behind drawn curtains. Shadows behind shutters. Rehn exhaled a stream of smoke and watched it curl toward the ceiling.

"We begin tonight," he said. "No theatrics. Just silence. We let him sit with the ghosts of those he trusted. When he breaks, we will be ready. But before we do, can one of you please explain to me why you hadn't arrested him before? Considering the detailed surveillance in this file?"

Meissner shifted his weight onto his right foot, "Well, after Scholl was killed…"

"And the fire, don't forget the fire…" chipped in Vogel.

"Yeah, and after the fire, lots of files were lost, forgotten. We had to start again with a lot of it."

"Right, wartime delays. Well, no more delays, let's go." Rehn stood up at the table and walked out.

Behind him, the officers stood and followed.

Rehn's fingers itched near the cuff of his sleeve, anticipation coiling tight. Somewhere down

248

the corridor, a lock slid back with a metallic echo, and the game began.

Forty One

The silence had no beginning. It might have been days. Time dissolved in the whitewashed box of a cell: no windows, no clock, no voice. Just the steady hum of the overhead light and the faint dripping of a leaky pipe behind the wall. His body had long since adapted to the cold. It was the quiet that scraped at his sanity.

He sat with his back straight against the chair, chained at the ankles but no longer at the wrists. That was part of the game. Give just enough back, a little movement, a mouthful of water, a few words, to keep hope alive, then retreat.

They wanted him to fill the void himself.

He had trained for this, but theory and practice were distant cousins. His instructors had warned that pain fades, but quiet gets sharper every hour. Here, the enemy wasn't a man in uniform; it was emptiness. The kind that makes you question if anyone still remembers you're alive.

Then, the door opened.

A tall man in a pristine Gestapo uniform stepped inside, gloved hands resting lightly behind his back.

Oberstleutnant Rehn.

Fred had heard his name muttered by guards. The one who didn't need to raise his voice. The one they feared.

Rehn didn't sit. He paced the cell like an appraiser circling a forgery, weighing the flaws. Then, with the faintest frown, he pulled out a chair and scraped it across the floor. The sound tore through the silence like a scream. Sweat trickled down Fred's spine as the room's stale air pressed in.

Rehn adjusted the chair with a surgeon's precision, as if testing the sound it would make before letting it scrape the floor, folding his gloves onto the table between them.

He didn't speak for a full minute.

Fred stared past him, fixing his eyes on the hairline crack in the wall.

Then Rehn said, in faultless English: "Lieutenant Fred Bennett. Royal Navy. Coastal operations division, Mediterranean theatre. Last assigned to Naples cell."

Fred blinked.

Rehn folded his arms. "That's what we know. What we need… is the missing frame around the picture."

Fred said nothing.

"You're not the first of your kind we've brought in," Rehn continued. "But you might be the first who thinks silence is a strategy."

Fred remained still.

Rehn reached into a leather folder and removed a photograph. He placed it on the table between them, face down.

Fred didn't look at it.

Rehn tapped the edge of the photo once. "Enzo Moretti. Shot three times. Your contact, if I'm not mistaken. Died quickly, which is more than we can say for most who've sat in that chair."

Fred's whole body tensed.

Rehn's voice softened. "Did you feel it, when it happened? That vacuum? When the anchor slips beneath the waves?"

Still, Fred said nothing.

Rehn glanced at the untouched photo. "We don't need the codes, Lieutenant. We already intercepted your last transmission. We're here to confirm what we know, nothing more."

Fred's silence cracked, not into speech, but into a dry, rasped breath.

Rehn studied him, calm and cold. "You see, men like you don't break with beatings. They break when you make them doubt. When you make them listen to their thoughts for too long."

He stood.

Fred thought that was it, the end of the session.

But then Rehn said, "She gave you up to protect herself. Did you expect loyalty from a woman you met in wartime?"

Fred looked up sharply.

Rehn gave a slight smile. "There it is. The fracture."

He left without another word, leaving the photograph where it lay. Fred stared at it. He didn't turn it over.   His hand hovered, but never touched it. He didn't want to know. Not yet. Not until he was strong enough to hear the truth, whatever it was. So he closed his eyes and whispered under his breath, the only voice in the room:

"You don't get to write my ending."

Forty Two

Prison, Naples - May 1943

They moved him without warning. Shackles, a blindfold, an engine rumble for minutes, a door slammed, and the air changed.

The air hit him first: damp, rot, and something sharper, like old blood. It was the stench of hopelessness, of lives pressed flat under fear. As the heavy metal door clanged shut behind him, Fred knew he had entered a new kind of hell.

They threw him into a cell barely large enough to stand in, the stone walls closing in like a tomb. The single high window offered no view of the outside world, just a thin beam of light that slanted through the bars, more a reminder of his imprisonment than a comfort. His ribs throbbed from the boots. Blood trickled from a cut on his forehead, spotting the cold stone.

Fred leaned back against the wall, every movement sending a jolt of pain through his bruised and battered body.

Questions filled his mind.

Days passed in a haze of pain and silence; his senses had dulled. The guards brought food twice a day, slop that barely passed as sustenance. Fred forced himself to eat, knowing he needed strength to survive, to think. He couldn't let them break him, couldn't let them see the despair that lurked at the edges of his mind. He was a soldier, and soldiers endured.

He curled tight against the cold wall, knees drawn in, eyes fixed on nothing. The silence was so complete it pressed against his eardrums like pressure from the deep. For a moment, uninvited, fragile, he remembered the letter from his mother. Her handwriting looping across blue paper. The smell of jasmine. The sound of her voice humming in the kitchen. He'd given it up without protest, and now he would have given anything to hold it again. To feel like he belonged to something softer than this.

The interrogations began again in the new prison. They dragged him from the cell, his wrists bound with rough rope that chafed his skin. The interrogation room was a stark contrast to the darkness of the cells. Bright, sterile, with a single table and two chairs. Rehn stood by the table, his uniform pristine, a cruel smile on his lips.

"Sit," he ordered, his voice cold. Fred obeyed, every muscle tensing as he lowered himself into the chair. The man circled him like a predator, his eyes gleaming with a sadistic delight.

The light bulb swung slightly above him, casting dizzying circles on the ceiling. Sweat pooled in the small of Fred's back, cold and itching.

"We know more than you think," the man began, his voice smooth, almost conversational. "We know you have information about Allied operations. You can make this easier on yourself by cooperating."

Fred said nothing, staring at a spot on the wall. Silence was his only weapon now, his only shield. He knew the man was lying; if they had known everything, he wouldn't still be alive. They wanted to break him, to force him to give up names, locations, plans. Fred knew he was an asset to them.

The first blow came without warning, a fist to his gut that knocked the breath from his lungs. Fred doubled over, gasping, but he didn't make a sound.

"We do know more than you think," Rehn smirked again from his chair.

"Then you don't need me," a defiant Fred replied. Another punch caught him in the side of the head, then another. The pain was a constant, blinding force, but Fred forced himself to stay silent, to keep his mind clear. He couldn't let them have the satisfaction.

Time lost meaning in the cell. Days bled into weeks, each one marked by the same routine of pain, hunger, and the constant, gnawing fear of what came next. The interrogations continued, each one more brutal than the last. They used fists, then batons, then the thin, biting lash of a whip. They left him chained to the wall for hours, his arms pulled taut above his head, his body screaming in agony.

Fred's world shrank to the small cell, to the brief moments of respite when the pain faded enough for him to think. He tried to remember his training, the techniques for withstanding torture, but it was hard to focus, hard to remember anything beyond the next breath, the next heartbeat.

The nights were the worst. Alone in the darkness, with only the sound of his breathing for company. He thought of England, of the rolling hills of Sussex, of the sound of the sea crashing against the cliffs. He thought of his parents, his mother's gentle smile, his father's steady hand on his shoulder.

And he thought of Isabella. Her face haunted his dreams, her eyes filled with the pain of betrayal. He replayed their last moments together, searching for some sign, some hint that she had been forced, that she hadn't meant to betray him. But all he could see was her face, pale and drawn, her eyes wide with fear.

And then, unexpectedly, he thought of the children. Marco was chasing a red ball across the cracked courtyard, his laughter echoing off the stone; Sofia perched on the windowsill, plaiting her doll's hair with a seriousness that made Fred smile. They had trusted him and adored him, even. In those rare, quiet afternoons, he had almost believed he could belong in their lives. The small, golden, unspoiled memory pierced through the fog of anger. He pressed his forehead to the wall, and for the first time in days, he didn't think of Isabella's betrayal, but of something warm.

Fred's body grew weaker with each passing day, the constant pain and lack of food taking their toll. His whole body shook, his vision blurred, but still he held on. He couldn't give up, couldn't let the Gestapo win, even if the odds were impossible.

Months passed, though Fred lost track of time. His beard grew long and ragged, and his clothes hung off his emaciated frame. The interrogations became less frequent, the guards seeming to lose interest in him. They still beat him, still left him chained to the wall, but it was more out of habit than purpose. To them, he was no longer a man. Just a shape in the dark that breathed.

Forty Three

Prison, Naples - June 1943

Somewhere between beatings and the endless days of hunger, Fred found a strange rhythm. The guards came less, and when they did, they barely looked at him. He was no longer their project, just another ghost in uniform. That suited him fine. With neglect came freedom, enough to trade for a cigarette, enough to hear another man's story. In the dust-mottled light of the cell, voices rose and fell, and Fred realised he had not heard laughter in months. It felt almost indecent, but he welcomed it.

"So, why do German soldiers go into battle with their hands up??" Tom said, grinning. "Saves time!"

The men in the cell chuckled, their laughter a brief escape from their surroundings. Fred took a long drag on his cigarette, savouring the taste. Weeks of quiet words and smuggled chocolate had won him a reluctant ally, Günter, a young German with tired eyes and no stomach for cruelty."

"Günter's not so bad," Fred had explained to Tom one evening. "He's just a kid, drafted into a war he doesn't care for. Doesn't have the stomach for it, I reckon. He told me yesterday that the Germans are losing faith in Mussolini."

Tom had nodded, his eyes thoughtful. "Hell, Fred, if you can get him to sneak in some whiskey next, we might survive this place with our sanity intact."

A noise from the corridor caught their attention, and Fred turned to see a new group of prisoners being led in. His heart skipped a beat when he recognised a familiar face among them. "Jonesy!" Fred hissed, moving to the bars of his cell.

Jonesy, an old friend from Fred's training days, looked up, his eyes lighting up with surprise. "Fred? Bloody hell, "Fred's grip tightening on the bars, "What are you doing here?"

"Long story," Fred replied, a wry smile tugging at his lips. "You look like hell, mate."

Jonesy grinned, his face pale and gaunt. "Yeah, well, it's not exactly a holiday camp, is it? When was the last time you saw a mirror?"

Fred laughed. He couldn't remember the last time he laughed out loud.

Over the following days, Fred and Jonesy fell into a quiet rhythm of whispered conversations through the rusted bars that separated their cells. The prison stank of mildew and sweat, its walls thick with damp and silence, broken only by the shuffle of boots or the distant clang of metal doors. Most of the men kept their heads down, conserving energy, clinging to slivers of hope. But not Jonesy. He leaned against the stone like a man rehearsing his exit.

"Do you remember Portsmouth?" he asked one night, his voice just above a breath.

Fred glanced toward the bars, eyes adjusting to the dark. "Course I do. You nearly got us both court-martialled for stealing that motorbike."

Jonesy chuckled softly. "Worth it, though. That speed… God, I felt alive for the first time in months."

"We were meant to be learning how to dismantle mines, not break the bloody speed limit."

"Yeah, well. Mines kill you slower."

Fred didn't reply, but a smile tugged at the corner of his mouth. He remembered Jonesy as reckless but magnetic, one of the few men who could laugh in the face of danger without sounding like a fool. During training, they'd shared late-night cigarettes, bruises from sparring drills, and the unspoken knowledge that most of them wouldn't survive what came next.

But this, this prison, wasn't what either of them had imagined. And it was starting to show in Jonesy's voice.

"They change shifts at midnight," Jonesy said a few days later, crouched by the bars again. "Only two on patrol. One of 'em's got a limp. Right leg."

Fred's stomach turned. "You're planning something."

Jonesy didn't deny it. "Been watching. Timing the steps. There's a window, Fred. A gap."

"There's also a fifty-fifty chance they shoot you in the back before you even reach the gate."

Jonesy's eyes flicked toward him. "Fifty-fifty's better odds than sitting here rotting."

Fred shifted on the thin bed, the iron frame creaking beneath him. "You try it and they'll double down on the rest of us. We're already on borrowed time."

"I know," Jonesy said, his voice quieter now. "But you've still got a shot. You're useful to them. Me? They've seen my file. They know I was caught trying to blow a fuel dump. I'm not coming out of this place alive, Fred, not unless I make it happen myself."

Fred swallowed the lump rising in his throat. "You've got nothing left?"

Jonesy leaned back, looking up at the cracked ceiling. "I've got a sister. Back home in Hastings. I keep her photo in my boot. I won't let them break me in here. I'd rather die on my feet."

Fred was silent for a long time. The walls around them breathed cold and stone. He understood that look in Jonesy's eyes now, something between defiance and desperation. The same look he'd seen in men before a charge, or just before a storming raid.

"When?" Fred asked finally.

"Tonight. Midnight. When the corridor's quiet."

Fred leaned his head against the bars, eyes closing. "Then promise me one thing."

"What's that?"

"If you make it out… don't stop running."

Jonesy grinned in the dark. "Was never very good at standing still."

"It's now or never, Fred," Jonesy had insisted, his voice low and intense.

They slipped out with a makeshift key, Jonesy's hand shaking as he turned it in the rusty lock. For a heartbeat, it looked possible. The hinges groaned like a warning, but the door gave way, spilling two shadows into the corridor. Fred caught a glimpse through the bars, Jonesy in front, teeth clenched, another prisoner close behind, both moving with desperate, jerky steps, like men running on borrowed time.

The corridor swallowed them. Silence pressed down on the cellblock, every man holding his breath, listening. A single clatter of boots echoed, then hushed voices, German, sharp and suspicious.

Fred gripped the bars. Come on…

For a moment, it worked. A corner turned, no alarm raised. Then a shout split the air, guttural and certain. The rattle of a rifle bolt being worked. A barked command.

Gunfire. Deafening in the stone halls.

Fred flinched. The others ducked instinctively, the cellblock alive with sudden whispers, prayers, curses. He pressed his face against the iron, straining for a glimpse. Shadows tangled in the torchlight. One figure stumbled, crashed to the ground. Another tried to drag him up, but more shots rang out, echoing like hammers on anvils.

Then silence.

Boots approached. Guards came back first, rifles still smoking. Then Jonesy. Or what was left of him, dragged by his arms, heels leaving two long smears of blood across the flagstones. His face was pale, slack, mouth half-open as if trying to form one last wisecrack. The other prisoner never returned.

Fred backed from the bars, the copper stench of blood thick in the air. Around him, no one spoke. There was nothing to say.

It was war, Fred thought. Life came and went in a moment.

Without pause.

Without thought.

Just death.

The next morning, Günter handed Fred a cigarette without a word, his eyes avoiding Fred's. Fred lit it, the smoke burning his throat, the bitter taste doing nothing to dull the ache inside. He exhaled slowly, watching the smoke swirl in the air.

"We're all just waiting for the end, aren't we?" Fred said quietly.

The young guard glanced at him, a shadow of understanding passing across his face. "Ja, Fred," Günter replied softly. "One way or another."

Forty Four

Prison, Naples - July 1943

The night was cold, a bitter wind howling through the cracks in the ancient stone walls of the prison. Fred lay on his bunk, staring up at the ceiling, the echo of gunfire still ringing in his ears. Jonesy's death replayed in his mind, the desperate scramble, the sharp crack of rifles, the spray of blood on the stones. Fred squeezed his eyes shut, but it did nothing to banish the images. The memory was etched in vivid detail, a reminder of how close freedom had been for his friend, and how quickly it had been snatched away.

Fred's mind drifted back to Jonesy, to the desperate scramble and the crack of rifles. He had known the plan was reckless, but hope had flared anyway, a knife now twisting in his gut.

He rolled over, trying to push the thoughts away, but they clung to him like a second skin. The guards were more alert now, their eyes sharper, their patrols more frequent. The prison was a taut wire; everyone was on edge after the failed escape. Fred knew he should let it go, bury the thought of freedom deep where it couldn't torment him, but the idea gnawed at him, refusing to be silenced.

The hours dragged by, the silence of the prison broken only by the occasional cough or muttered curse from the other cells. Fred knew the rhythm of the night shift, the clink of keys, the shuffle of boots, the brief lapses in vigilance, every sound memorised from long hours in the dark. The thought came unbidden: if only Jonesy had waited.

The sound of approaching footsteps pulled Fred from his thoughts. He lay still, eyes half-closed, watching the shadow stretch across the floor. It was Günter, his slight frame outlined in the dim light. The young guard paused, glancing into Fred's cell. Their eyes met for a brief moment, and Fred saw the same haunted look in Günter's eyes that he'd seen in his reflection.

"Mussolini's gone," Günter whispered, glancing down the corridor. "Our army is moving in fast, trying to keep control before the Italians give up." A boot scrape from the distance distracted Günter, who moved on without another word.

Fred knew Günter wasn't like the other guards. There was a quietness to him, a softness that hadn't been hardened by years of cruelty. Fred had seen Günter flinch when the other guards beat the prisoners, had noticed the way he'd slip extra food to those who looked like they were on the edge of starvation. Fred wondered if there might be a way to use that to his advantage.

He waited until the footsteps faded, then slid silently from his bunk. His heart pounded in his chest as he moved to the bars, his eyes scanning the corridor. It was empty, the shadows deepening in the corners. Fred had a makeshift key, one Jonesy had given him in the event of a second chance. His fingers fumbled as he pulled it from its hiding place, his breath coming in shallow gasps.

For a moment, Fred hesitated, this was impulsive, something he had avoided being since arriving in Naples. He could almost hear Jonesy's voice, urging him on, the echo of his last words still hanging in the air. Fred closed his eyes, steeling himself, then slid the key into the lock. The soft click of the tumblers sent a shiver down his spine, the sound too loud in the stillness of the night.

The door swung open with a faint creak, and Fred slipped into the corridor, moving quickly and silently. His heart was a drumbeat in his ears, each step a risk. He knew the patrol routes, the blind spots, and had memorised them in the long hours of confinement. He crept along the wall, his eyes darting to every shadow, every flicker of movement. The plan was simple: reach the storeroom, slip through the window, disappear into the night. It was madness, but it was all he had.

He was almost at the corner when he heard it, a low murmur of voices, the scrape of a chair. Fred froze, pressing himself against the wall, his breath catching in his throat. The guardroom was just around the corner, the glow of a lantern spilling into the corridor. Fred risked a glance, his pulse quickening. Two guards sat at a table, their backs to him, one of them laughing softly. Fred's hand gripped the key, his mind racing. There was no way past without being seen.

He was about to turn back when he heard footsteps approaching from the opposite direction. Panic surged, but before he could move, Günter appeared at the end of the corridor. Their eyes met, and for a heartbeat, time seemed to freeze. Fred saw the surprise flicker across Günter's face, followed by something else, something that looked like understanding.

Günter hesitated, his hand dropping to the sidearm at his waist. Fred held his breath, waiting for the shout, the alarm, the end. But instead, Günter nodded, a barely perceptible movement, and turned away. Fred didn't wait to see if it was a trick. He pushed off the wall, slipping into a side corridor, his heart hammering. He could still hear the murmur of voices, but they were fading, drowned out by the blood rushing in his ears.

The storeroom was just ahead, the door slightly ajar. Fred slipped inside, his hands shaking as he fumbled with the latch on the window. It gave with a soft pop, the cold night air rushing in. Fred swung his leg over the sill, his body tense with anticipation. For a moment, he hung there, caught between the safety of the prison and the uncertainty of freedom.

There was a sudden shout, the sharp crack of a door slamming open behind him. Fred didn't wait to see who it was. He dropped to the ground, landing hard, the impact jarring his bones. He rolled, coming up in a crouch, his eyes scanning the darkness. The yard was empty, the gate a dark silhouette against the night sky. Fred took a deep breath, then sprinted, his legs pumping, the cold air burning his lungs. He wasn't as strong as he used to be.

He was halfway across when the first shot rang out. Fred stumbled, his foot catching on a loose stone, sending him sprawling. He scrambled to his feet, the sound of shouting growing louder, closer. The gate was a few yards away, but it could have been miles. Fred could feel the air hum with tension; every muscle in his body screamed for him to move.

Another shot, then another. Fred threw himself to the ground, rolling into the shadow of a wall. The bullets hit the stone behind him, sending chips of rock flying. Fred lay still, his heart pounding, his breath coming in ragged gasps. He could see the guards now, their silhouettes moving against the light. He knew he was caught, knew there was no escape, but still, he couldn't make himself move.

A figure appeared above him, blocking out the light. Fred looked up, expecting to see the barrel of a rifle, but instead, it was Günter. The young guard's face was pale, his eyes wide with fear. For a moment, neither of them moved, the air thick with tension. Then, Günter reached down, grabbing Fred's arm, pulling him to his feet.

"Go!" Günter hissed, his voice urgent. "Now, before they see you!"

Fred hesitated, but Günter shoved him towards the gate, his eyes darting to the shadows. Fred stumbled, then ran, his legs weak, his body aching. He reached the gate, his hands fumbling with the latch. Behind him, he heard the shouts, the pounding of feet. Fred's fingers slipped.

Then, Günter was there, his hands steadying Fred's, the gate swinging open. Fred looked at him, his mind reeling, trying to understand. But there was no time, no chance for questions. He nodded once, then slipped through the gate, the cold night air swallowing him whole.

Fred ran, his feet pounding against the earth, his breath coming in ragged gasps. He didn't stop, didn't look back, the memory of Jonesy's body driving him forward. He didn't know where he was going, didn't care, as long as it was away. The forest loomed ahead, a dark mass against the sky, and Fred plunged into it, the branches clawing at his skin.

He ran until his legs gave out, until he couldn't breathe, until the world spun around him. Fred collapsed, his body shaking, the cold ground pressing against his skin. He lay there, gasping for air, his mind numb, his thoughts a chaotic whirl. He had done it. He had escaped. But as the adrenaline faded, a new feeling took its place: fear.

Fred knew he couldn't stay, knew he couldn't go back. He was a fugitive now, a hunted man. And he knew, with a sinking certainty, that he wouldn't get a second chance.

Günter's face flashed in his mind, the look in his eyes, the quiet understanding. Fred knew he owed his life to the young guard.

Out of nowhere, a bullet came zipping past his head, then another. Fred threw himself to the ground, rolling into the shadow of a wall. The bullets hit the stone behind him.

"Stop right there!" The beam of a flashlight swung towards them, blinding Fred. The clatter of boots echoed in the night, more guards closing in.

Fred's heart sank as the guards aimed their rifles. Günter's face was tense, conflicted. He didn't resist, couldn't, but he watched the young guard, searching for understanding.

Fred raised his arms slowly, defeat washing over him. The guards grabbed him, forcing his arms behind his back, the cold metal of handcuffs biting into his wrists. Fred didn't resist. He felt numb, his body and mind exhausted.

"Thought you could escape, did you?" one of the guards sneered, shoving Fred forward. Fred stumbled but kept his balance, his eyes flicking to Günter. The young guard stood to the side, his gaze fixed on the ground. Fred wanted to say something, anything, but the words wouldn't come. There was nothing left to say.

They dragged Fred back through the prison gates, the door slamming shut behind them with a finality that made Fred flinch. The sound echoed in the courtyard, a grim reminder of the walls that would never let him go. They led him down the corridor, past the cells where other prisoners watched in silence, their eyes following him, their faces set with pity and resignation.

The guards shoved Fred into an empty cell, the door clanging shut behind him. Fred sank to the floor, his back against the cold stone wall. He could still feel the sting of the gunfire flying past him, the chill of the night air, the fleeting hope that had been so close he could taste it.

Hours passed, or maybe it was minutes. Fred couldn't tell. The cell was dark, the air thick with the smell of decay. His thoughts were a jumble, his mind replaying the escape, the close call, the way Günter had hesitated. The guard had helped him. But why? And why had he stopped? Fred rubbed his wrists, the pain a welcome distraction from the chaos in his head.

The cell door creaked open, and Fred looked up, expecting more guards, more punishment.

Instead, it was Günter. The young guard stepped inside, his expression guarded, his eyes searching Fred's. They stood in silence for a moment, the tension between them heavy and unspoken.

"You shouldn't have tried," Günter said finally, his voice low. There was no accusation in his tone, only a weary acceptance. "They'll be watching you now, more than ever."

Fred nodded, his throat tight. "I had to," he replied, his voice hoarse. "I couldn't stay here, not after Jonesy…" He stopped, the name catching in his throat.

Günter's gaze softened, a shadow of understanding passing over his face. He stepped closer, his voice barely above a whisper. "I'm sorry about Jonesy. But you need to be careful. They won't be so lenient next time."

"There won't be a next time," Fred said, the words heavy. He knew he had come too close to losing everything, too close to ending up like Jonesy. The risk wasn't worth it, not anymore. He looked up at Günter, searching the young guard's face for answers. "Why did you help me?" he asked.

Günter hesitated, his eyes flicking to the door, then back to Fred. "Because I know what it's like to feel trapped… to want out at any cost. But you have to survive, Fred. This place breaks people, don't let it break you."

Fred nodded slowly, Günter's words sinking in. He understood now the silent bond between them, forged in the shared misery of their existence. They were both prisoners, in different ways, both caught in a place that would never let them go.

Günter turned to leave, pausing at the door. "Stay out of trouble, Fred," he said, his voice a mix of warning and hope. "There's more to life than this place. You have to find a way to hold on."

The door closed behind him, the sound echoing in the small cell. Fred sat back against the wall, eyes closing. He would survive, he would endure, and one day, he would find a way to truly be free. Until then, he would wait, bide his time, and hold on to the thin edge of hope that remained.

But the next night, a fever took hold. A deep, rasping cough tore through his chest, burning with each breath. Sweat soaked his shirt, then chilled him to the bone as the damp air gnawed at his skin. When he begged the guard for water, for a doctor, he was met with laughter and a slammed door.

The pain only worsened. His stomach cramped, his vision blurred, and every cough left him doubled over, gasping, the taste of iron in his mouth. He pressed his forehead to the stone wall, trying to anchor himself, but the world tilted and slipped away.

Darkness surged in, thick and merciless. Fred's body gave out. He fell, weightless, into black.

Forty Five

Prison, Naples - October 1943

There was no light.

No sound.

No time.

Fred floated, fever burning away the last edges of reality. Thought was like swimming against a tide, each movement dragging him deeper. His body was gone; he couldn't tell where breath began or ended. Only the cold remained, seeping through marrow and dream alike.

Then, a flicker.

A soft warmth bloomed in the distance, as if someone had struck a match in a vast cavern. Shapes formed. Shadows layered over light. He strained to see through the haze.

Rose stood beneath a willow tree. She beckoned, her mouth moving soundlessly. She looked just as she had the last day he saw her, standing beneath a tree at the edge of Leigh Road, hair in a loose plait, arms folded against the chill, a grin tugging at the corner of her lips. The hem of her dress fluttered in a breeze he could not feel. She didn't speak, but her eyes said everything: joy, surprise, heartbreak.

Then came his father, bent over the workbench, smiling. But Fred couldn't quite reach them. His legs wouldn't move. His feet sank through the floor like smoke through wood. Rose took a step back, lifting her hand, and then…

She vanished.

The light pulsed again, a golden shimmer now turning colder, thinner. Another figure emerged through it.

His mother. She was sitting in her old floral chair by the fire, knitting in her lap. But her hands were still, fingers paused mid-stitch. She looked up at him slowly, her face lined, older than he remembered, but the same warmth in her eyes that no time could erode. Her mouth moved, a whisper forming.

He moved closer.

But no words came. Only the sound of wind brushing past his ears, low and steady.

Behind her, in the doorway of memory, stood his father again, one hand in his pocket, watching the sea beyond the prom. He turned just enough to meet Fred's gaze, solemn, proud. A nod. A quiet gesture between men. Between generations. And then he faded into grey.

Fred tried to follow, shouting for them, but his voice made no sound.

Shapes continued to swirl.

Enzo appeared next. His overcoat was torn at the shoulder, his face tired but defiant. He was leaning against a crumbling stone wall holding a cigarette with no smoke. He gave a small, crooked smile, the kind he used to offer before a mission.

"Enzo!" Fred called, but again, no voice came.

Enzo lifted his chin, pointing behind Fred with two fingers, then tipped the cigarette toward the sky and vanished like a mirage in wind.

Another figure now, closer, Luciano, bruised and battered, his lip split and jacket torn. His eyes burned with grief, or rage, or both. He walked straight up to Fred, fists clenched at his sides. Fred reached out.

This time, their arms almost touched.

But Luciano stopped just short, looking past Fred. He opened his mouth, trying to say something, a single word. Fred could almost read his lips.

"Run."

Then he, too, dissolved into mist.

Fred was alone again.

But not for long.

The fog twisted, began to pulse like a beating heart. There were footsteps, fast, panicked. He turned,

Isabella.

Her voice shattered the silence.

"Fred! Get up! You have to get up!"

She ran to him, dress torn, face streaked with dust and tears. Her hands gripped either side of his face, her touch warm and trembling.

"Please," she begged, shaking him. "This isn't where it ends. Not for you. Not yet. Now get up!"

Fred opened his mouth to ask why she was here, but the world fractured. Her face dissolved into light, her voice scattering into the void.

The dream burned away like paper to flame.

Forty Six

Fred woke to fire.

He jolted upright, his heart hammering, the room shuddering with violence. It wasn't a dream. Somewhere beyond the prison walls, a battle was raging. Not an air raid; this was closer, chaotic. Gunfire cracked like whips. The smell of smoke seeped through the stone.

Somewhere beyond the walls, a battle raged. The stone seemed to hum with each explosion. Fred's ribs ached with every breath. His mouth tasted of rust and grit. Dust drifted from the ceiling, and the floor trembled beneath him.

A moment later, the cell door burst open, not by a key, but by force.

A figure staggered into view, half-hidden by smoke. A young man in civilian clothes, a rifle slung over one shoulder, his face streaked with ash and sweat.

"Fred?" the man rasped, stepping forward.

Fred blinked. "Luciano…?"

It was him, battered, older somehow, eyes bloodshot, darting as if counting every second. He grabbed Fred by the arm. "We don't have time. There's been an uprising. Germans are pulling back, burning everything as they go."

Fred tried to stand. His legs failed him, fever weakening what little strength remained.

Luciano threw Fred's arm over his shoulder. Together they moved, one limping, the other dragging. Gunshots cracked down the corridor. Somewhere nearby, someone screamed.

They barely made it two turns before a grenade exploded ahead of them.

"Go!" Luciano shouted, shoving Fred through a side door as a blast shook the hallway. Rubble rained from the ceiling with a deafening clatter, shards biting at his skin. Fred stumbled into a narrow stairwell, falling down the last steps into the half-ruined kitchen of the prison.

When he looked back up, the door was caved in, and Luciano was gone.

The next thing he knew, he was outside: coughing, choking. Maybe someone pulled him. Maybe he crawled. But suddenly he was in the street, in the open air, the sky above him bleeding fire and black clouds.

Buildings blazed around him. Civilians: men, women and even children, fought in the streets with whatever they could grab: stolen rifles, bottles of burning fuel, fist-sized stones. The Germans were in retreat, but they made the rebels pay for every step.

Fred stumbled into a shattered alleyway, smoke burning his throat. He didn't know where he was going. His entire body throbbed with pain, his shoulder aflame, his ears ringing from the close blasts.

A cry cut through the haze: "British soldiers! Down the road!"

Fred followed it, limping, blood dripping down his side. He reached the end of the alley to see them: khaki uniforms, helmets and Sten guns. Allied troops were carefully moving through the outer districts, their boots crunching over glass and debris.

Relief hit him like a breaking wave. His knees buckled, and he dropped into the rubble. Smoke clung to his skin, sweat and blood mingling at his temple. His breath came in ragged gasps.

He raised one hand, trembling and barely steady.
"Help…" he croaked.

They saw him.

"Hold on, MEDIC!"

Boots thundered against the broken stones. Shadows moved through the smoke. In the blur, a soldier dropped beside him, young, sharp-eyed, breathing hard. Fred flinched as hands reached for him, instinct warning of pain or another blow.

But these hands were careful.

"Easy now," the soldier said, voice calm and clipped, English. He had missed it. "You're alright. We've got you."

Fred felt himself lowered to the ground, gently this time. His head rested against something soft. A gentle hand pressed against his forehead. The touch was cool, firm, grounding.

"He's one of ours, wounded, but alive," the soldier called out.

A second pair of boots arrived. Another voice, lower, slower, joined the first. "Chest wound. Burned, exhausted. Fever. But he's lucid."

Fred wanted to speak, to ask where Luciano was. Instead, a weak cough escaped him. Dust clung to the back of his throat.

"Water," he rasped.

A gloved hand touched his throat, then his forehead, cool against the heat in his skin. The medic eased a canteen to his lips. The first sip made him gag, metallic and warm, but he drank anyway, desperate. The second sip steadied him.

"You're safe now, soldier," the first man repeated, kneeling beside him. "You're out. You made it."

Fred blinked up at him, his vision still fractured at the edges. Tears formed unexpectedly in his eyes, not from pain, but from the shock of hearing those words. Safe. Out. Words he'd almost stopped believing in.

He reached out, fingers finding the sleeve of the soldier's jacket, gripping it weakly.

"Luciano," he managed. "There was… someone with me. Italian resistance. He pulled me out."

The medic's face changed. Subtle, but Fred caught it.

"Is he... here?" Fred whispered.

The man looked back and shook his head. "No sign of him. Many didn't make it."

Fred's grip slackened.

Missing.

That meant dead. Or captured.

The ache in his chest was sharp and deep. The sudden hope he'd felt began to unravel. It had all happened so fast: Luciano's face, his voice, his arm under Fred's shoulder. And now... nothing.

Fred closed his eyes.

His body was done. His mind tried to hold on, to fight against the tide of sleep pulling him under, but it was no use.

Orders barked around him; gunfire rattled in the distance. But in his ears, there was only the beat of his heart and the last whisper of Luciano's name.

He let go.

Darkness closed in, not cold this time, but numb and quiet. As he drifted, the pain softened, fading under the noise of his thoughts.

Rose. Luciano. Enzo.

So many names, so many faces he couldn't save.

Forty Seven

Allied Camp, Naples - October 1943

He remembered lights, yellow, then white. Faces. Voices without the German bark. Someone pressed water to his lips. He drifted, floated, sank, while subconsciously listening to the muffled sounds of distant movement in the camp.

And then, silence.

A clean silence, like snow.

When he next opened his eyes, he was in a bed. White sheets, thinner than regulation. The air smelled of antiseptic, blood, and damp canvas that had been stretched too long in the sun. He turned his head just enough to see a figure slumped in the chair beside him; a young nurse, auburn hair tucked beneath her cap. Her brow was furrowed in concentration over a dog-eared book, eyelids heavy, with faint perfume and antiseptic lingering in the air.

She was surprised by his movement, dropping her notes. "You're awake," she said gently, her voice edged with surprise as she bent down to pick them up. "We weren't sure you'd come round today."

Fred tried to speak but found only air.

"Don't try yet," she added quickly. She poured water into a chipped metal cup and helped him sip. "You've been through hell."

She checked his pulse with a practised hand. "They brought you in three days ago. You're lucky they got you out when they did. My brother's in the Navy too, haven't seen him in two years."

Fred tried to sit, but pain flared sharp and white-hot beneath his ribs. He hissed and fell back.

The flap of the tent lifted, and a thin man in a sweat-streaked uniform entered: a doctor, collar askew, sleeves rolled. He didn't waste time with niceties. No yelling, no threats, just the steady command of someone used to saving lives rather than taking them.

"Lie still," he said. "You've got two cracked ribs, bruised lungs, severely dehydrated. You're stable now, but you won't be sprinting anytime soon. You'll be discharged from here in a few more days. Command wants you back in Britain."

Fred blinked slowly, the fog still thick in his mind. "How...?"

"Resistance got you out. You were half-dead when they found you. Then one of ours picked you up." The doctor paused, studied his face. "You remember anything about the escape? The chaos?"

Fred's lips twitched, but words stuck. Fire, rubble, Luciano's shouts. Only the sky.

"Nothing… just flashes," he rasped. Fred's lips twitched, but the words never came. Fire. A tunnel. Gunter screaming. Then sky. Real sky.

The nurse changed his bandages. Days passed. His strength returned in slivers, first standing, then walking the edge of the tent. He ate, sparingly. Slept in fits. Each time he woke, he expected the clang of a cell door, but it never came.

Then, one morning, the tent flap pulled back and Sergeant O'Malley ducked inside.

Fred stared.

O'Malley grinned. "You look like you've been dragged backwards through hell."

Fred rasped a laugh. "Feels about right."

O'Malley moved to the cot, eyeing the nurse who nodded and left them alone. He dropped into the chair with a groan, slinging his pack beside him.

"They told me you were dead," Fred said.

"They told me the same about you," O'Malley replied. "I nearly punched the officer who said it." He leaned forward, voice lower. "You made it out on your own?" O'Malley's eyes searched Fred's face.

"Not alone… Gunter helped, and Luciano. Kept me moving."

O'Malley nodded, the hint of relief breaking through his stern mask.

"You're heading home," he said after a moment. "Orders came through. They're shipping you back to Portsmouth next week. A slow vessel, safer that way. Command wants you debriefed, and frankly, you need rest. Proper rest."

Fred didn't reply. The thought of England felt unreal.

"You'll be all right," O'Malley added, standing. He clapped Fred lightly on the shoulder. "See you back there."

Fred sat back on the edge of the cot after O'Malley left, listening to the soft rustle of the canvas tent. The nurse had returned quietly, carrying a small kit bag: a folded uniform, a toothbrush, a tin of soap, and a pair of socks. She laid it on the cot beside him, her eyes meeting his with an unspoken encouragement.

He ran his fingers over the worn fabric, noting the significance of it in his hands, the faint smell of disinfectant lingering. Nearby, a clerk shuffled papers. Fred watched as he scribbled signatures across forms, stamping them with a precise, mechanical rhythm. Fred's own name seemed foreign on the page, almost like a promise he wasn't sure he could keep.

Outside the tent flap, voices drifted in. Two soldiers argued quietly about a skirmish on the outskirts of Naples. One swore the resistance had sabotaged a German fuel depot; the other grumbled about lost supplies. The fighting was still raging, still alive, still dangerous. Fred closed his eyes briefly, letting the distant sounds of boots and shouting fade into the hum of his pulse.

He packed the kit slowly, folding each item with care. Each movement felt deliberate, grounding him. When he finally slung the bag over his shoulder, it was as if he carried a piece of this place with him; its antiseptic smell, its quiet urgency, the shadow of lives half-lived while the war raged on. He lingered for a moment at the tent flap, staring at the fading light, before stepping away, ready to face the next stretch of the journey.

The journey began at dawn a week later.

Fred stood on the dock in a borrowed uniform, thinner than he remembered being, his ribs still wrapped tight beneath his shirt. The sea air was cool, laced with diesel and salt. The ship loomed in front of him, an old escort vessel converted for transport, no frills, no comforts.

The nurse had slipped a note into his pocket before he left. He hadn't read it yet.

He boarded in silence, boots echoing on the gangplank, and didn't look back.

The slow crossing blurred into days. He slept in a shared bunk, wrote nothing, spoke little. He stood at the rails most evenings, staring west. The sea was iron-grey, sometimes choppy, sometimes calm. Once, a pod of dolphins raced beside the ship, their fins slicing water like blades. Fred watched them, unmoving, as the others cheered.

That night, in his bunk, Fred reached into his pocket and felt the folded paper again. He'd nearly forgotten it was there. For a long time, he turned it between his fingers, rough from salt and rope. Finally, he opened it.

The handwriting was neat, practical, with just a hint of haste in the strokes:

You're alive. That's what matters. Don't waste the chance. Go home, and when you breathe free air again, remember those who cannot. That's how you win.

There was no signature, only a small cross drawn at the bottom, as if to ward him on his way. Fred folded it carefully and slipped it back into his pocket, staring at the dark ceiling. He didn't sleep for hours.

He thought of Naples. The uneven stone steps slick with evening dew, voices calling across alleys, and laughter spilling from open windows. He remembered the warm brush of a woman's hand on his face, and the echo of children chasing each other up narrow stairways. Even in sleep, he could feel the sun-warmed stones under his palms.

And then, one morning, they docked.

The sky was a bright overcast, the kind unique to England; pale, soft light and no shadows. Fred stepped off the ship with his duffel over his shoulder. The dock in Portsmouth was busy with voices, carts, and officers barking names.

And just like that, he was back home.

Forty Eight

Portsmouth, England - November 1943

Fred stepped off the ship onto British soil for the first time in years. The air felt heavier here than at sea, close against the skin rather than rushing wide and salt-scoured. It carried the greasy haze of engine oil drifting from the cranes and cargo trucks along the quay. Fresh paint on the dockside bollards left a faint, stinging trace that mingled with the earthy damp of rope and timber. Every breath seemed to draw in the layered life of the harbour: work, repair, salt, and motion.

But this wasn't the triumphant return he had once imagined. The prison had left its mark, in bruises that hadn't yet faded, and in shadows that no sunlight could shift. Dark circles now shadowed his once bright eyes, and the hard lines of his face spoke of pain and endurance.

A naval officer greeted him at the port, his crisp uniform contrasting sharply with Fred's dishevelled appearance. "Lieutenant Bennett," he said, extending a hand. "Welcome home. I'll be overseeing your recovery here in Portsmouth."

Fred managed a tired nod. "Thank you, sir." He studied the man for a moment; the sharp brow, precise tone, until memory fell into place. "Hargrove. I wasn't expecting to see you here."

Hargrove led him to a waiting car, its engine humming quietly. As they drove through the narrow streets of Portsmouth, Fred couldn't help but notice the changes. They passed a grocer's with boards nailed over its blasted windows, and a laundry line strung across the shell of a terrace, white shirts flapping like surrender flags in the wind. A woman cycled by with a wicker basket of ration tins strapped to her handlebars, her scarf pulled tight against the cold. In the next street, a boy kicked a dented football between piles of rubble, his laughter oddly bright against the muted city.

The city bore the scars of conflict; there were bombed-out buildings and hastily constructed shelters dotting the landscape. Civilians bustled about, their faces showing a weary determination. Despite the destruction, life went on.

"How are you feeling, Lieutenant?" Hargrove asked, breaking the silence.

Fred shifted uncomfortably in his seat, the stiff bandages around his torso reminding him of the beatings he'd endured. "I'm alive," he replied, his voice hoarse.

Hargrove nodded, sensing Fred's reluctance to speak. "We have a place set up for you at the naval base. You'll have everything you need there: a bed, medical care, and… some peace. You'll need time to heal, both physically and mentally."

Fred stared out the window, watching the blurred faces of the people outside. He wondered if quiet would ever truly be his again. The memories of his time in prison were relentless, invading his thoughts day and night.

The interrogations, the pain, the sound of his own screams, it was all still too vivid.

The car eventually pulled into the gates of the naval base, a sprawling complex of red-brick buildings and steel structures. Sailors and officers moved about with purpose, a small piece of order amidst the chaos of the fight. Hargrove led Fred to a small, nondescript building on the edge of the base. Inside, a nurse greeted them, her kind eyes filled with sympathy.

"Lieutenant Bennett, I'm Nurse Collins," she said, taking his arm gently. "Let's get you settled in."

Fred was shown to a modest room with a single bed, a small desk, and a window overlooking the sea. It was simple, but it was more than he had expected. Nurse Collins helped him out of his worn uniform, revealing the extent of his injuries. His ribs were bruised and a jagged cut ran down his side. The nurse cleaned and re-bandaged his wounds, her touch gentle.

"You've been through a lot," she said softly, her voice laced with concern. "But you're safe now. You'll recover, I promise."

Fred nodded, not trusting himself to speak. The physical pain was nothing compared to the weight of betrayal and loss that he carried.

When she left, Fred sat for a long while, tracing the room with his eyes: the scuffed floorboards, the chipped enamel mug on the desk, the faded curtain lifting in the sea breeze. He ran a hand over the blanket, surprised by its warmth. In the prison, there had been nothing soft; even the air had been stiff and cold. Here, every small comfort felt strange, almost unearned.

He lay back on the bed, exhaustion overtaking him. As he closed his eyes, the sounds of the sea outside mingled with his thoughts, lulling him into a restless sleep.

Days turned into weeks as Fred settled into a routine at the naval base. Each morning, Nurse Collins would check his wounds, administering medicine and changing bandages. The pain slowly began to fade, replaced by a dull ache. Physically, he was healing, but his mind was another matter. Nightmares plagued his sleep, dragging him back to the prison cell, to the moments when he thought he wouldn't survive.

Lieutenant Commander Hargrove visited him regularly, providing updates on the war and offering words of encouragement. "We've got the Axis forces on the run," he said one day, a hint of satisfaction in his voice. "Your work in Naples was vital. The information you obtained helped us plan the bombing raids that crippled their supply lines."

Fred nodded, but the sense of accomplishment felt hollow. Hargrove's voice dropped slightly, as if the walls might be listening. "There were a few raised eyebrows at how you got that intel out. But it worked. Command doesn't forget results like that." He straightened, tapping the papers on his knee. "Truth be told, Naples is in a better place; you lit the fuse down there."

He had done his duty, but at what cost? He thought of Isabella; her image haunted him, her eyes filled with love and sorrow.

Forty Nine

Hospital, Portsmouth - December 1943

The knock on the door was soft, muffled slightly by the howling wind outside. Fred turned his head, expecting Nurse Collins or perhaps Lieutenant Commander Hargrove with more war updates. But instead, the door creaked open and a voice, warm, familiar, and entirely unexpected, broke through the quiet.

"Well, would you look at that. Thought I'd find you in a Santa hat surrounded by adoring nurses."

Fred blinked, then blinked again. For a moment, the face didn't quite fit the name; the years apart had sharpened the jawline and deepened the lines at the corners of the eyes. Then the tilt of the grin, the stubborn set of the shoulders, struck like a flare in the dark. Tommy Lake, his oldest friend, was standing in the doorway, wearing a heavy coat dusted with sea salt and snowflakes, a half-grin on his wind-reddened face.

"Tommy?" Fred said, his voice hoarse with disbelief.

"In the flesh." Tommy stepped in, pulling off his gloves and clapping his hands together to warm up. "Had to bribe a petty officer with a bottle of brandy and my mother's best mince pies to get in here. Reckon that makes me the most determined visitor on base."

Fred gave a weary smile, the slightest flicker of warmth surfacing in his chest. "Your mum's mince pies? You trying to kill people?"

Tommy let out a bark of laughter. "They've survived three air raids and a kitchen fire. Indestructible."

He dragged the chair closer to the bed and sat, his eyes flicking over Fred's pale face and the bandages peeking from under his shirt. "Bloody hell, mate. You look like you've been through a meat grinder."

Fred shrugged, the movement stiff. "Close enough."

Tommy didn't press. He just sat there for a moment, watching him, then said, "Come on. Let's get some air. Harbour's quiet this time of year, and I've had enough of hospital corridors."

Fred hesitated, glancing at the orderly who hovered by the desk. A nod from the man and a scrawl on a clipboard set them free. The corridor smelled faintly of boiled cabbage and disinfectant, its linoleum floors gleaming under the yellow bulbs. They passed a pair of young sailors in slings, swapping cigarettes outside the ward doors, and the muted thud of a distant typewriter followed them all the way to the exit.

As they stepped outside, the frost crackled underfoot. The harbour sat still, mirroring the heavy, grey sky above. Fred's breath rose in soft plumes, ghosting into the air before vanishing.

The December wind sliced in off the sea, sharp and bracing. Across the water, cranes stood like skeletons against the grey, their arms frozen in mid-swing. A lone tug chugged past, its deck crew hunched in greatcoats, breath trailing like smoke from chimney stacks. Somewhere deeper in the dockyard, a ship's whistle sounded: long, low, mournful.

Snow clung to the edges of rooftops and railings, and the lamps along the quay burned soft golden halos in the gathering dusk. The scent of salt mingled with woodsmoke and the faintest trace of mulled wine from the officers' mess behind them. It was a distinct difference from that of the harbour in Naples.

Fred pulled his coat tighter around himself, his breath misting in front of him. He ambled, stiff from his injuries, and Tommy matched his pace without comment.

"Place hasn't changed much," Tommy said, his voice carrying in the cold. "Even with Christmas round the corner. Got a few wreaths tacked up in the mess, a sorry-looking tree in the canteen. I think someone tried to decorate it with rifle casings."

Fred gave a soft grunt. "Festive."

They walked in silence for a while, the crunch of boots on frost-covered stone the only sound.

"Your parents," Tommy said gently, "they're doing well. Your mum sends love. She's taken to knitting scarves for the Home Guard, says it keeps her hands busy and her heart steady."

Fred pictured her, head bent over a length of khaki wool, lips moving silently in the half-light of the sitting room. Knitting had been her way of waiting during the last war, too. The thought struck him like a bruise: she'd been younger than he was now when she first learned to fill the silence with the click of needles.

Fred didn't reply, eyes fixed on the dark water.

"Your dad, though…" Tommy gave a short laugh. "You should see him in that blasted Home Guard uniform. Looks like an angry badger in khaki. Swears blind he stopped a German saboteur last week. Turned out to be the postman's nephew visiting from Bognor."

A faint smile tugged at Fred's mouth.

"He carries that walking stick like it's a bayonet," Tommy added. "Your Mum says he does patrols around the garden after dark, just in case the cat's a spy."

Fred let out a short breath, close to a laugh, or maybe a sigh. The ache in his ribs throbbed, but it was the ache behind his sternum that truly gnawed at him.

Tommy stopped beside a rusted old bollard, hands in his coat pockets. "They miss you, you know. Properly. Mum said the house feels colder without you in it. Even with the fireplace roaring."

Fred stared out at the grey water, the lights of distant ships flickering like stars caught in the tide. "I don't know if I'll ever be able to go back," he said quietly. "Not the same way."

The thought of walking up the front path felt impossible, as if the man who'd left Worthing had been buried somewhere far away, under rubble only he could see.

Tommy didn't answer right away. The wind picked up, tugging at their coats.

"You don't have to be the same, Fred," he said finally. "You just have to come home. That's enough for them. It's enough for me."

Fred turned his face slightly. "You don't know what I've done."

"I don't need to." Tommy met his eyes. "I know who you are."

Fred's throat tightened. He wanted to speak, to spill everything, the pain, the betrayal, the haunting image of Isabella's eyes the night she gave him up. But the words tangled. He shook his head. "It's all just… too much. Feels like if I start talking, I won't stop."

Tommy didn't press. He reached into his coat pocket and pulled out a small, wrapped parcel, neatly folded in brown paper tied with a string.

"Your mum made this up. Said it's not Christmas without you opening something under a tree, even if that tree's a broomstick in a metal bucket."

Fred took the parcel with shaking hands, brushing snow off the top. The paper was crisp under his fingers, faintly scented with the lavender drawer-liners his mother had used since he was a boy. The string was knotted tight, as if she'd wanted to be certain it wouldn't come undone before it reached him. He held it as though it might vanish if he let go. He didn't open it. Just held it, allowing the feel of home to settle against his chest.

As they turned back toward the infirmary, the snow began to fall in earnest, soft and steady, blanketing the harbour in silence.

The snow fell thicker now, softening every edge until harbour, rooftops, and sky blurred into one. Fred let the quiet seep into him, and for the first time in weeks, the weight he carried felt just a fraction lighter.

Fred closed his eyes, listening to the hush of falling snow. He had told himself he wouldn't go, that he couldn't bear his parent's eyes on him, not after everything.

Fifty

Worthing, England - December 1943

The wind coming off the Channel was sharp enough to sting Tommy's cheeks as he stepped off the coastal train and adjusted the worn duffel bag over his shoulder. Worthing hadn't changed: sleepy rows of pebble-strewn gardens, chalky salt air, the low murmur of waves pressing against the shore.

But he had changed. And so had Fred.

The last time they'd both been here, they were chasing footballs down the beach and shouting over the wind, not a care in the world. Now Fred was lying wounded in a naval hospital, and Tommy had the scars to prove how close they'd all come to never coming back.

He made his way down the familiar lane that led to the Bennett house. The windows were glowing softly with amber light. A modest wreath hung on the door. Even in wartime, Mrs. Bennett kept the place warm and welcoming, like nothing could ever break through her resolve.

He paused at the gate before knocking, his hand resting on the cold iron latch. For a moment, he was sixteen again, standing there after a muddy football match, hoping Mrs. Bennett had baked something. This house had always been more than Fred's; it had been a second home.

It opened within seconds.

Mrs. Bennett, still wearing her apron, gasped. "Tommy!"

He barely had time to respond before her arms wrapped around him, as though she could squeeze the relief straight out of her bones. Behind her, Mr. Bennett appeared, tall and wiry, his greying hair combed back, pipe in hand.

"I'll be damned," he said, a grin spreading. "I told her you'd come for Christmas."

"I couldn't stay away," Tommy said, smiling. "And I thought you'd like an update from someone who's seen him."

They sat him down at once, Mrs. Bennett tucking a warm blanket over his knees as though he were still ten years old. A kettle boiled. A plate of scones appeared from nowhere. The fireplace crackled.

"He's safe," Tommy began quietly. "He's alive. A bit worse for wear, but he's in good hands now. They've got him resting up at the base."

Mrs. Bennett's eyes shimmered, but she blinked them away. "They wrote to us, the Admiralty. Said he'd been hurt, but not much else. You're the first to tell us anything."

Tommy nodded. "He's…" He paused, choosing his words. "He's not himself. Not fully. The sort of things he went through, it'll take time. But he's still got that stubborn streak."

Mrs. Bennett's fingers wrapped around her teacup. "What do you mean, not himself?"

Tommy hesitated. He could still see Fred's eyes in the hospital bed, hollowed by something no medicine could touch. "The war changes people," he said finally. "But he's fighting his way back. Still Fred underneath."

Mr. Bennett chuckled. "Gets that from his mother."

Mrs. Bennett swatted him gently with the tea towel.

Tommy took a sip of tea and exhaled slowly. "He still asks about you both. Not out loud, maybe, but… you can tell. He'll be back when they let him. Just needs time to find his footing again. He holds onto home like it's a lifeline."

There was a quiet pause as the fire popped. Mr. Bennett stood and crossed to the mantle, taking a framed photo of Fred down from the shelf. It was one from before the war, Fred in a cricket jumper, squinting at the sun, grinning.

"You know what's funny?" he said, holding the frame. "He's out there running missions for the Navy, risking his bloody life. And I'm here in Worthing… leading the Home Guard."

He gave Tommy a mock-serious look. "We drill in the church hall, you know. Once a week. Except when there's bingo."

Tommy laughed, the sound unexpectedly full.

"Real terror to the Luftwaffe, are you?" he said.

"Absolutely," Mr. Bennett replied. "I've got a broom handle painted black. That'll give any parachuting Jerry a fright."

Mrs. Bennett sighed quietly, but Tommy could see the way her shoulders relaxed. The humour softened the worry behind her eyes.

They talked late into the night. About Fred, about the war, about the neighbours. Tommy shared stories he could about the barracks, the food, the feeling of sand in your boots for days, and held back the parts that weren't meant for parents.

Later, as Tommy stepped outside to head to his own parents' house, Mr. Bennett followed him to the gate.

"Thank you," he said quietly. "For looking out for him."

Tommy nodded. "I'll keep doing it. Until he's home."

They shook hands, firm and wordless. The wind was colder now, and Christmas lights from windows up and down the street blinked through the darkness. Somewhere in the distance, a radio crackled with a wartime carol.

As Tommy walked down the road, he looked back once, just once, to see Mrs. Bennett in the window, holding Fred's photograph to her chest.

Fifty One

Hospital, Portsmouth - January 1944

As further weeks passed, Fred began to venture outside, first with the aid of a walking stick, then without. His strength returned slowly, like a tide creeping back over sand, imperceptible at first, but steady. The first steps had felt almost insulting; every muscle weak, his balance faltering as though his own body no longer trusted him. Each corner of the base seemed farther than he remembered, every stair an effort.

The cold January air bit at his face and caught in his lungs, but he welcomed it. After the suffocating heat of the prison cell and the stale infirmary air, it was proof that he was alive.

Most afternoons, he would take slow walks along the edge of the naval base, coat buttoned tight, collar turned up, his breath hanging in the air like smoke. The base was quieter this time of year: fewer drills, more letters from home. Outside the mess hall stood a drooping tinsel-strewn fir, its needles nearly gone.

But it was the sea that drew him. Always the sea.

He stood by the docks often, watching the water lap at the pilings, the sky overhead bruised with winter dusk. The salt air cleared his thoughts in ways nothing else could. It didn't ask questions. It didn't offer comfort. It just was. He imagined the same water washing into Naples. Here it was quiet, the tide lazy, unhurried. The contrast unsettled him more than he cared to admit.

It was during one of these moments, late in the afternoon, when the light had begun to bleed gold across the water, that he heard footsteps behind him. A voice followed, crisp and low.

"Lieutenant."

Fred didn't turn at first. He recognised the voice, Lieutenant Commander Hargrove, his superior, and in some ways, a steady hand through the chaos of recent months.

"Sir," Fred said, finally glancing sideways.

Hargrove came to stand beside him, gloved hands behind his back, eyes fixed on the horizon where a pair of destroyers sat silhouetted against the sinking sun.

"How are you holding up?"

Fred hesitated. The question was routine, but the tone behind it wasn't.

He gave a slight shrug. "As well as can be expected, I suppose. The ribs are mending. The mind... slower going."

Hargrove nodded slowly, as if he'd been expecting that. "The body often knows how to heal without asking. The mind… needs permission."

Fred didn't reply, but something about the phrasing lodged in him.

They stood there for a time, not speaking. The sea rolled in and out with a restless rhythm, gulls calling overhead, a buoy clanging in the distance. The cold wind cut across the docks, and Fred pulled his coat tighter around his frame.

"You've been through hell," Hargrove said finally, his voice low. "More than most men your age will ever see. I read the report. Naples. The prison. The informant. The…" He stopped himself. "You don't have to say anything."

Fred looked down at his boots. "I wouldn't know where to start if I tried."

"I don't need the story. I've seen the aftermath. That's enough."

Fred swallowed hard. "It wasn't clean. None of it was."

"It rarely is," Hargrove replied. "But even in the mess, you got us what we needed. That intelligence helped cripple two major Axis supply routes. Bombing runs were adjusted. Lives were saved."

Fred looked out at the darkening sea. "And others lost."

There was silence again.

"I'm not here to make speeches," Hargrove said eventually. "We need men like you. Field-tested. Smart. Adaptable. This isn't over, not even close, and what's coming next may be harder still. When you're ready, I want you back out there."

Fred didn't answer straight away. The gulls had gone quiet, and the wind had shifted direction. He felt the old weight of duty stir in his chest, familiar and heavy.

"I don't know if I'm ready," he said, voice low. "But I will be."

He turned then, looked at Hargrove thoroughly for the first time. There was no fear in his eyes, just the flicker of something more profound, reluctance, perhaps. Or memory.

Hargrove nodded. "That's all I needed to hear."

He left him then, boots clicking softly on the dock until the sound faded into the distance. The silence left in Hargrove's wake pressed heavier than his words. Only the wind filled it, worrying at the mooring ropes and setting the flag above the dock, shuddering.

Fred remained, watching as the sun dipped lower behind the ships, bleeding orange and violet across the horizon. The sea glowed for a moment, then dimmed to steel.

His breath came slower now, more even. His heart didn't race. The nightmares still came, but less frequently. He still saw her eyes, Isabella's, full of sorrow and betrayal, but they no longer stole the breath from his chest.

The conflict had taken almost all of him. But not all.

Not yet.

The past could wait.

The future, uncertain, unforgiving, was still his to walk toward.

Fifty Two

Hospital, Portsmouth - May 1944

Fred awoke to the sound of seagulls squawking overhead and the soft murmur of waves crashing against the shore. It was a sound he had grown used to during his recovery in Portsmouth, a constant reminder of the sea and the battles that awaited beyond its horizon. The steady routine of life at the naval base had done him good; his wounds had healed. Yet, the restlessness inside him grew. He was a man of action, and the thought of sitting idly while the battles raged on was unbearable.

One crisp morning, as Fred sat in the small mess hall, sipping his tea, Lieutenant Commander Hargrove approached him, a serious expression on his face.

"Lieutenant Bennett," Hargrove said, sliding into the seat across from Fred. "How are you feeling?"

Fred straightened, sensing something in Hargrove's tone. "I'm ready, sir. Just waiting for orders."

A faint smile tugged at Hargrove's lips. "Good. Because we have a new assignment for you.

You'll be rejoining the fleet aboard the HMS Belfast."

Fred's heart skipped a beat at the mention of the ship's name. The Belfast was a Town-class light cruiser, one of the most formidable ships in the Royal Navy. He had heard rumours of its involvement in upcoming operations, but he hadn't dared to hope he'd be assigned there.

"The Belfast?" Fred echoed, his voice betraying his surprise.

Hargrove nodded. "Yes. We're forming a task force for a major offensive. The Belfast will be part of a fleet preparing for the invasion of France. Operation Overlord." He paused, letting his words sink in. "It's the beginning of the end, Fred. We're taking the fight to Hitler's doorstep."

Fred leaned forward, lowering his voice. "Will we be covering the landings directly?"

Hargrove's eyes narrowed, weighing how much to reveal. "Fire support. Coastal batteries. Protecting the transports. And keeping the Channel lanes clear. Every ship will matter."

Fred felt a surge of adrenaline. The invasion of France was the operation that everyone had been waiting for. This was history in the making.

"When do I leave?" Fred asked, his voice steady, betraying none of the excitement that simmered beneath the surface.

"Tomorrow," Hargrove replied. "You'll take a transport to Belfast's current position. There's a lot of planning and preparation to be done, and the fleet is already moving into position."

Fred nodded, a sense of purpose filling him. He was returning to the sea, to the fight, where he belonged. As Hargrove stood to leave, Fred couldn't help but ask, "Why me, sir? Why assign me to the Belfast?"

Hargrove looked at him, his gaze steady. "Because you've proven yourself time and time again. You've shown courage, resilience, and loyalty. We need officers we can count on, and I can think of no one better suited for this mission than you."

Fred felt a swell of pride at Hargrove's words. He stood, saluting. "Thank you, sir. I won't let you down."

"I know you won't," Hargrove replied, returning the salute. "Good luck, Lieutenant. And Godspeed."

The following day, Fred stood on the docks, a duffel bag slung over his shoulder, watching as the transport ship prepared to depart. Fred felt the chill of the sea breeze on his face, the water churning below hinting at journeys yet to come. He boarded the ship, finding a spot on the deck where he could watch the receding shoreline. As Portsmouth faded into the distance, Fred's thoughts turned to the mission ahead.

Operation Overlord. The invasion would be the largest amphibious assault in history, a massive undertaking that required precise coordination and timing. Fred knew the risks were high. The German defences along the French coast were formidable, and the fighting would be fierce. But he also knew that this was their best chance to break through, to push the Nazis back and liberate Europe.

The transport sailed through the choppy waters of the English Channel, and Fred's mind drifted to the men he would soon be commanding. The crew of the HMS Belfast was a seasoned group, veterans of many battles. They would be ready, but Fred knew that leadership was crucial. He would need to inspire confidence, to lead by example. The lives of his men depended on it.

A pair of stokers leaned on the rail nearby, smoking and talking in low voices. One swore the Germans knew everything already, that the beaches would be deathtraps. The other laughed it off, saying the Yanks had brought enough kit to build a new London on French soil. Fred listened without joining in, staring out at the grey swell, the Channel rough and slate-coloured beneath the wind.

After several hours, the outline of the HMS Belfast appeared on the horizon, its grey hull cutting through the water with quiet power. As the transport drew closer, Fred could see the crew bustling about, preparing for the upcoming operation. The ship was a hive of activity, sailors moving with purpose, the air charged with anticipation.

Fred disembarked, his boots thudding on the metal deck of the Belfast. He was greeted by the ship's captain, a tall, broad-shouldered man with a stern expression and a clipped moustache.

"Lieutenant Bennett, I presume?" the captain said, extending a hand.

"Yes, sir," Fred replied, shaking the captain's hand.

"Welcome aboard. I'm Captain Stuart. I've heard good things about you, Bennett. I trust you're ready for what's to come?"

"Fred straightened. "Yes, sir. Ready as I'll ever be."

Stuart studied him for a beat, as though testing the seriousness of the reply. "We'll see soon enough. The sea has a way of stripping men down to the truth. I'll have one of the men show you to your quarters. We'll be conducting a briefing at first light."

"Understood, sir," Fred said, saluting.

As he was led to his quarters, Fred couldn't help but feel a sense of deja vu. The narrow corridors, the smell of oil and steel, the hum of the engines beneath his feet, it was all so familiar. It was as if no time had passed since he last stood on the deck of a warship, ready to face the enemy.

He stowed his gear in his cabin, a small space with a bunk, a desk, and a single porthole. Fred sat on the bunk, staring out at the darkening sky, and the reality of what lay ahead settled over him. The invasion would be a turning point, a moment that would decide the fate of millions.

Fred's thoughts turned to the men he had served with, those who had fallen in battle, those who had survived. He thought of the friends he had lost, the comrades who had become like brothers. He thought of Isabella, the pain of her betrayal still fresh, but now a dull ache instead of a sharp wound. He wondered if she was safe, if her children were safe. He pushed the thoughts aside. There was no room for distractions, no room for doubt.

Fred lay back on the bunk, closing his eyes. The steady vibrations of the ship lulled him into a restless sleep. In his dreams, he saw the coast of France, the cliffs rising from the sea, and the sounds of gunfire and explosions. He saw the faces of the men he would lead, their eyes filled with willingness and fear.

Morning came too quickly, the blare of the ship's horn jolting Fred awake. He rose, splashing water on his face, and dressed in his uniform. As he made his way to the briefing room, the scale of his duty settled on his shoulders. He was a soldier and a leader, always willing to do what needed to be done. The fate of the war rested on their shoulders, and he would not falter.

As he entered the briefing room, Fred felt a sense of calm wash over him. This was his world, his purpose. The HMS Belfast was ready, and so was he. The time had come. Fred Bennett was going to battle once again, and this time, he meant to see it through to the end.

Fifty Three

HMS Belfast, Normandy - June 1944

At dawn on June 6, 1944, Fred stood on the bridge of HMS Belfast, binoculars fixed on the dark line of Normandy's coast. The sea lay calm, a deceptive stillness before the storm. The Belfast, along with the rest of the Allied fleet, had taken up position overnight, their guns aimed at the heavily fortified French coast.

The operation, code-named Overlord, had been in the planning for months. Every detail had been meticulously arranged, every contingency accounted for. Fred had sat through endless briefings, listening as officers mapped out the invasion. But none of it had prepared him for the sight that stretched before him now, the vast armada of ships, the dark silhouette of the coastline, the landing craft that bobbed on the waves like toys.

Stuart exhaled slowly, his jaw tight as if he carried the burden of all the men below. "This is it, Bennett. The beginning of the end."

Fred nodded, his throat tight. "Aye, sir. Let's make it count."

As the first light of dawn spread across the water, the order was given. The Belfast's guns roared to life, a deafening barrage that shook the ship from bow to stern. Fred felt the familiar jolt of the recoil beneath his feet, watched as the shells arced through the sky, their trails cutting through the early morning mist. His eyes never left the target, the German artillery battery at La Marefontaine. This key position had to be neutralised if the landing troops were to have any chance of success.

The Belfast's guns fired in unison, a relentless barrage that pounded the enemy positions. Through his binoculars, Fred could see the impact of each shell, the explosions that tore through the German bunkers, sending plumes of smoke and debris into the air. The ground shook with each hit, the very air vibrating with the force of the assault. Fred's heart pounded in time with the guns, his blood singing with the thrill of battle.

Yet, even as the Belfast unleashed its fury on the enemy, Fred's eyes were drawn to the beach. The first wave of landing craft had reached the shore, their ramps lowering to release the soldiers within. Fred could see the tiny figures sprinting across the sand, could hear the faint echoes of gunfire and the shouts of men over the roar of the sea.

He watched as the soldiers pushed forward, ducking behind obstacles, scrambling over the rocky terrain. It was chaos, a maelstrom of noise and movement, and Fred felt a fierce urge to be among them, to be on the ground, fighting alongside his fellow soldiers. A young midshipman at Fred's side muttered, almost to himself, "God help them down there…" Fred's throat tightened. He wanted to say something, comforting, steady, but the words wouldn't come.

"Keep firing!" Captain Stuart's voice cut through his thoughts. "We need to take out that battery before it does any more damage."

Fred nodded, turning his attention back to the task at hand. The guns of La Marefontaine were still firing, their shells raining down on the beach, creating deadly craters in the sand. The Belfast's gunners adjusted their aim, focusing their fire on the heart of the enemy position. Fred watched as the shells slammed into the battery, one after another, until finally, there was a massive explosion. A cheer erupted as the battery exploded in a plume of fire and smoke. For a heartbeat, relief rippled across the deck.

"We've done it!" one of the sailors shouted, his voice hoarse.

Fred allowed himself a brief smile. The battery was destroyed, the threat neutralised. But there was no time to celebrate. The battle was far from over. The beach was still a killing ground, and the soldiers below were fighting for their lives. Fred could see the flashes of gunfire, the dark shapes that moved through the smoke. He could see men falling, could hear the cries of the wounded carried on the wind.

He gripped the railing. He had trained for this moment, yet standing on Belfast's deck, he felt helpless, a soldier trapped behind steel and distance. He was a sailor, a gunner, but more than anything, he was a soldier. And every instinct in him screamed to be on that beach, to be in the thick of the fight.

"Steady, Bennett," Stuart said, lowering his voice. "We can't be everywhere. Our guns are their shield, that's how we fight today."

Fred nodded, forcing himself to focus. Belfast's role was critical. They were the hammer that would break the German defences, the shield that would protect the men on the ground. Every shell they fired, every target they destroyed, was a step closer to victory. He knew this. But knowing didn't make it any easier.

The hours stretched on, the Belfast's guns firing until the barrels glowed red-hot, the air thick. Sweat stung Fred's eyes. His ears rang so fiercely that Stuart's shouted orders reached him as muffled echoes. The deck itself trembled beneath the endless rhythm of fire. The beach looked like hell, a scene from a nightmare, and yet, slowly, steadily, the tide was turning. The soldiers were gaining ground, pushing forward, inch by bloody inch.

As the sun climbed higher in the sky, Fred saw the first of the Allied flags raised on the cliffs. A cheer went up from the ships, a sound of triumph that echoed across the water. For a long moment, Fred said nothing, only lowering his binoculars and letting the sight burn into memory. Amid all the blood, that scrap of colour on the cliffs felt like a promise. The sight filled Fred with a fierce pride, a sense of accomplishment that washed away the doubts and fears. They had done it. They had taken the beach.

The order came to cease fire, and the guns of The Belfast fell silent. Fred lowered his binoculars, his hands shaking from the adrenaline. He looked out over the water, at the beach that was now dotted with the bodies of the fallen, at the ships that drifted, silent and sombre. The cost had been high, the sacrifice great. But they had won. They had breached the walls of Fortress Europe.

Fred's gaze drifted again to the beach, men staggering, medics carrying stretchers, the wounded crying out for water. His chest ached with the pull of it. Fred turned to Captain Stuart, his voice hoarse. "Permission to go ashore and join the forces, sir?"

Stuart looked at him, a knowing look in his eyes. "No, Lieutenant. We've still got work to do. The war's not over. I need you here."

Fred nodded, swallowing his disappointment. The captain was right.

He turned back to the sea, the waves lapping at the hull of the Belfast, and felt a sense of resolve settle over him.

Fifty Four

Portsmouth, England - July 1944

The salty Channel breeze whipped across the deck as HMS Belfast eased into Portsmouth harbour. Fred leaned against the railing, the engines thrumming faintly beneath the steel. The setting sun cast purple and gold across the water, painting the familiar coastline, a sight that filled him with bittersweet relief. They had spent thirty-three days at Normandy, thirty-three days of relentless bombardment, of watching the chaos on the beaches, of firing over five thousand shells to support the troops on the ground.

Now, as the Belfast finally returned to port, Fred felt a profound exhaustion settle over him, a weariness that went beyond the physical. The battle for Normandy had been a turning point. They had broken through the German defences and opened the way for the Allied advance into France. It was a victory, a hard-fought and costly victory, but a victory nonetheless.

As the Belfast docked, Fred saw the crowds gathered on the quayside, waving and cheering, their faces bright with hope and gratitude. He could see the relief in their eyes, the pride, and it warmed him. They had done their duty, and their country was grateful.

Some shouted names, scanning the decks for sons or brothers. Others waved flags. Fred heard a woman cry, "God bless you, lads!" and the words struck deeper than the cheers, a reminder of who they fought for.

The call came for Fred to report to the captain's office. He straightened his uniform, took a deep breath, and made his way through the bustling ship. The men were disembarking, their faces a mix of fatigue and exhilaration. Fred exchanged nods and brief words of congratulations, feeling a sense of camaraderie with his fellow sailors.

One sailor clapped him on the shoulder: "We made it back, eh, sir?" Another, younger, kept staring in disbelief. Fred returned their nods, a quiet bond of men who had survived the same firestorm. They had been through hell together, and they had come out the other side.

Captain Stuart's office was small, cluttered with charts and maps, a testament to the long days spent planning and coordinating the bombardment. Stuart himself sat behind his desk, his expression serious.

"Lieutenant Bennett, come in," he said, motioning for Fred to take a seat.

Fred sat, his back straight, his hands resting on his knees. "You wanted to see me, sir?"

Stuart nodded, his eyes assessing. "Bennett, you've done outstanding work over these past weeks. The success of the Normandy landings owes much to the efforts of you and your men."

"Thank you, sir," Fred replied. "It was a team effort. We all played our part."

"That you did," Stuart agreed. He leaned back in his chair, studying Fred. "However, I have new orders for you."

Fred felt a flicker of unease. "New orders, sir?"

Stuart nodded. "You're being redeployed, Lieutenant. You're to report to Inveraray in Scotland. Effective immediately."

Fred blinked, surprised. "Scotland, sir? I don't understand. What's in Inveraray?"

"Training," Stuart said. "The war on the front line is moving forward, and we need experienced officers to lead and train the recruits. Inveraray is one of the primary training centres for amphibious warfare. Your experience and leadership will be invaluable there."

Fred stared at the maps pinned to the wall: red arrows stabbing into France, lines of advance that others would now carry forward. He clenched his fists, the words spilling before he could stop himself. "But, sir, I want to be on the front lines…"

Stuart's gaze softened, understanding. "I know, Bennett. And I understand how you feel. But the reality is, we need to prepare for future operations. The war isn't over yet, and the skills you've gained, the knowledge you have, need to be passed on. You'll be shaping the men who will go on to fight the final battles. That's a vital role."

Fred swallowed hard, fighting the frustration that welled up inside him. He had seen so much. He had fought tooth and nail, had risked his life time and again. And now, to be sent away from the front, to be told his place was in training, it felt like a step back. But orders were orders, and Fred was a soldier.

"Aye, sir," he said finally, his voice steady. "I understand. I'll report to Inveraray as ordered."

Stuart nodded, his expression approving. "Good man. I know this isn't what you wanted, Bennett, but trust me, it's important. You'll be doing your country a great service."

Fred stood, saluting. "I'll give it my best, sir."

"I have no doubt you will," Stuart said, standing as well. He extended his hand, and Fred shook it firmly. "Good luck, Lieutenant. And thank you for everything you've done."

Fred nodded, turning to leave. As he stepped out onto the deck, he looked out at the harbour, at the ships that bobbed gently on the water, at the men who laughed and talked, glad to be home, even if just for a while. He felt a pang of longing, a desire to be back in the thick of it, to feel the adrenaline, the rush of battle. But he knew Stuart was right. The war wasn't just about the battles fought on the front lines. It was about preparation, about readiness, about ensuring that every soldier, every sailor, was equipped to do their duty.

Fred drew in the sea air, heavy with coal smoke. Portsmouth bustled around him, alive with sailors reunited with loved ones. He would not join them, not yet. His war was shifting, changing shape; from the beaches of Normandy to the quiet lochs of Scotland. He would train others, pass on what he had learned, and send them forward in his place. It wasn't the fight he craved, but it was still service. It would have to be enough.

Fifty Five

There were a few days before Fred needed to report to his new base in Inveraray. He was desperate to return to Worthing, to see his parents again, a feeling he didn't think would return. He hadn't sent word of his visit. He got off the train and walked the familiar streets. Although showing some signs of conflict, the town felt the same as when he had left. A few shopfronts were shuttered, their windows still boarded from previous raids, but the butcher's bell still jingled, and a milk cart rattled down the cobbles as if nothing had changed.

To think of the life he had experienced, and yet everything here had remained almost the same. Fred approached the front gate of his parents' house.

He walked down the path, the lavender still carefully taken care of. He opened the unlocked front door and stepped into his childhood home. His mother gasped. 'Fred!' Her hands flew to her mouth. She moved toward him, hesitant, as though afraid he might disappear. Then, in an instant, she threw her arms around him, her embrace fierce and trembling. "You're here… You're safe."

Fred held her tightly, feeling her tears against his shoulder. "Yes, Mum. I'm here."

His father, standing a few steps behind, cleared his throat, his own eyes suspiciously bright. "Good to see you, son," he said, his voice steadier than his face let on. Fred saw the pride.

"Good to see you too, Dad," Fred replied, shaking his father's hand before pulling him into a hug.

His mother stepped back, wiping her eyes with a small laugh. "Let me look at you, Fred. Oh, I'd almost forgotten what it's like to have you here. All those years... nothing but letters, wondering if you were safe, if we'd hear from you again."

Fred nodded, the memories of missed letters and long silences settling heavily between them. "I know. I hated that you didn't know where I was... especially when I was taken prisoner." He glanced down, feeling a flicker of heartache.

She reached out, touching his face gently. "We didn't know if we'd ever see you again... but here you are. Home." They lingered in the hallway for a while, all three reluctant to let go, until his mother fussed him toward the kitchen as if he were still a schoolboy come home from school.

The kettle whistled softly as Fred sat at the old kitchen table with its faded oilcloth and wobbly leg. His mother's baking lingered in the air, apple and mixed spice, the same as always. It felt like stepping into another life. One untouched by conflict. One he hadn't realised he missed quite so much.

His mother busied herself at the stove, occasionally sneaking glances at him as if afraid he might vanish again. His father sat opposite, nursing a chipped mug, eyes narrowed in quiet study.

"You've lost weight," she said. "We're all thin these days, mind: powdered egg and dried milk can only do so much. She set a plate of biscuits down. "Are they feeding you properly?"

Fred gave a tired smile. "You'd be surprised what passes for dinner these days."

His father cleared his throat. "So... what brings you back, son? We weren't expecting you."

Fred sat back in the chair, his boots still dusty from the road. "I had a few days before reassignment. Thought I'd come home. See you both."

"That's not a proper answer," his father said gently. "Where are they sending you?"

Fred hesitated, fingers drumming lightly on the edge of the table. "Scotland. Inveraray."

His mother turned from the stove, surprise blooming across her face. "Scotland?"

"I've been reassigned," Fred said, trying to keep his tone light. "They want me to help train recruits: naval operations, intelligence work, covert stuff."

For a moment, there was silence. Then his father tilted back, exhaling through his nose.

"Well, that's something," he said. "Training, not fighting. That's good."

His mother stepped forward, drying her hands on her apron. "You'll be safe, then? Not on the front?"

Fred gave a half-shrug. "Safe enough. As safe as it gets these days."

Her eyes brimmed suddenly, and she reached for his face, cupping his cheek like she had when he was a boy. "Oh, Fred. That's the best news we've had in ages."

His father stood, placing a hand on Fred's shoulder. "You've done your part. More than your part. Training's honourable work. Those lads'll need someone who's seen the real thing." Fred saw the difference in their faces, his father's quiet pride, his mother's sheer relief. Duty and love, both weighing on him in equal measure.

Fred nodded, though a heaviness settled in his chest. Inveraray wasn't going to be easy. The men they sent him would be raw, hopeful, and likely unprepared for what waited across the Channel. But for now, he let himself accept their warmth, the pride in his father's grip, the quiet relief in his mother's eyes.

Fred smiled, though his heart twisted. "I knew you'd be happy about it, Mum," he said softly, "and I'm glad I can be doing something important. But..." He hesitated, glancing toward the window. "Part of me misses it... being out there."

His father nodded, his eyes understanding. "A soldier's heart doesn't rest easy, not when there's work to be done. But Fred, you'll be saving lives differently."

His mother took his hand, squeezing it tightly. "Let us have you safe, Fred, even just for a little while. We're just so thankful you're well."

Fred looked from his mother to his father, seeing the relief in their faces, the peace his presence brought them. He forced a smile, nodding. "Yeah... I'll do my duty." He squeezed his mother's hand. "If it eases your hearts, then it's worth it."

"More than you know," his mother whispered, beaming up at him.

A quiet moment passed before Fred asked, "Have you heard from Tommy?"

His mother's expression faltered slightly. "Not for a while," she admitted. "Last visited just before Christmas. He's joined the army now."

Fred blinked. "He has? I thought he was doing clerical work, Ministry of Supply, wasn't it?"

His father gave a slow nod. "He was. Good, honest work. Organising transport and rations. Kept him out of danger, and heaven knows we were glad for it. But... well, I think it gnawed at him."

Fred raised a brow. "How so?"

"He kept saying he felt useless," his father replied. "Like he was pushing paper while others bled in the mud. Said it didn't sit right, not when his friends were in France and Italy. I think seeing so many of them go… it changed something in him."

His mother sighed. "I didn't want him to go. I told him over and over that his job was important, and it was! Supplies win wars, too. But he said if you could face what you faced and come back standing, then the least he could do was take up arms himself."

Fred looked down, swallowing hard. "He always wanted to prove himself," Fred remembered him as a boy, swaggering about with a stick for a rifle, insisting he'd join the fight one day. He'd laughed it off then. Now the memory stung.

"Yes," said his father quietly. "But I just hope he doesn't try to prove too much."

Fred nodded slowly, absorbing it all. The image of Tommy, laughing, sharp-witted, never one to take things too seriously, now shouldering a rifle somewhere on the continent, made his chest ache.

"I hope he writes soon," Fred murmured.

"So do we," said his mother, her voice soft with worry.

Fifty Six

Inveraray, Scotland - August 1944

Considering it was meant to be summer, Inveraray had greeted Fred with the chill of mist-drenched hills and the kind of sideways rain that seeped through every seam. The loch stretched out like a sheet of steel beyond the base perimeter, and beyond that, pine-draped hills rolled away into the grey distance. It was beautiful, but a rugged beauty, one that offered no comfort.

The naval training base, nestled deep in the Scottish Highlands, was a world away from the cities under siege or the shattered ruins of Europe. But it wasn't quiet. Not really. The sounds here were disciplined, boots thudding in rhythm on gravel paths, barked commands from instructors, the clatter of equipment, the occasional crack of rifle fire from a nearby range. If the front was chaos, this was controlled preparation.

Fred had arrived five days ago, and already his days ran like clockwork. Dawn. Inspections. Drills. Briefings. More drills. Each day was designed to test and shape the group of handpicked men now under his watch, young men chosen for more than just muscle or marksmanship. These were recruits bound for covert work. Espionage. Sabotage. Behind-the-lines missions that didn't make it into the papers.

Fred stood now on the lip of the training field, arms folded against the morning chill. A group of men were mid-way through an obstacle course, covered in mud, panting hard, their shoulders taut with effort. Some were green, barely out of school by the look of them, but there was fire in their eyes. That spark. He'd seen it before. In Naples. In Alexandria. In himself.

One lad, fair-haired and wiry, hit the wall with a burst of speed and pulled himself up with practised ease, but another stumbled, slid back into the mud. Fred moved closer, voice low but butting through the rain. "Don't fight the wall, use your leg. Try again." The recruit spat mud and nodded, and launched himself back up. This time, he made it. Fred didn't smile, but he filed the moment away. Resolve mattered more than grace.

"Sir!" came a clipped voice behind him. It was one of the junior instructors, Ensign Travers, efficient, bookish, but well-meaning. "Target course is set for this afternoon's stealth test. Mock village scenario, full blackout, rotating patrols as requested."

"Good," Fred replied. "Push them hard, but keep it real. I don't care how well they sneak through trees if they panic the moment someone fires a flare."

"Yes, sir. I'll brief the support staff." Travers stood in the doorway. "Was there something else?" Fred looked up from his desk.

"Sir, if I may," Travers hesitated. "Some of the men… they're struggling with the pace."

Fred studied him. "Then they're learning already. War won't wait for them to catch their breath."

Travers followed, nodded, and left.

Fred turned his gaze back to the field. Rain began again, thin and biting. One of the recruits slipped in the mud and landed hard. He got up again.

Good. Fred needed resilience more than polish.

Later that afternoon, Fred walked the edge of the loch alone. The mist over the loch reminded him of smoke rising from Naples' burning docks. Different air, same weight on his chest. He closed his eyes and almost heard Enzo's voice, that easy laugh. It faded with the wind.

The base sprawled behind him, low buildings, the clang of metal, the ever-present drone of generators, but out here, the world felt quieter. He stopped by the water's edge and watched mist coil across the surface like breath. This place… it felt like the end of the world, and yet, he knew it was where the next phase of the war would be fought. In silence. In shadows.

He thought of Enzo. Of Luciano. Of too many others.

A twig cracked somewhere up the slope behind him. Fred didn't flinch, but his instincts pricked. He turned, half-expecting a recruit trying to sneak up on him. No one.

Just the wind in the pines.

Over the next few days, the recruit's efforts began to shift. Not much, but enough. They moved faster. Slept lighter. Asked better questions. Fred had scheduled infiltration drills under moonless skies, lectures on deception and code recognition, tests in lock-picking and route-mapping. He never yelled. Never needed to. They listened. Because they knew, he'd been there.

But still, something was missing.

Not a what. A who.

He thought of O'Malley, loud, impossible O'Malley, the kind of man who'd have been barking the recruits into the mud by now. The yard felt quiet; O'Malley would see an end to that.

On the sixth day, Fred stood at the edge of the training yard, watching the morning warm-ups. The mist hung low, curling over the fields like smoke. The wind had teeth.

He sipped from a tin mug of coffee gone lukewarm.

Tomorrow would begin Phase Two: shadow exercises and mock reconnaissance. Tonight, though, he waited. For the call, the arrival, the moment that would shift everything.

Fifty Seven

The week blurred past in drills, rain, and paperwork. Fred attacked the early mornings and late nights with his usual dogged discipline, but this was different. He wasn't running through forests or slipping behind enemy lines anymore. He was laying the groundwork, building the team that would.

The men he'd been handed were raw, but not hopeless. Some had decent instincts; others were quick learners. A few had the makings of tangible assets. What they lacked was edge. And for that, Fred needed a particular kind of man.

That man arrived just after dawn, stepping off the back of a transport lorry with a duffel over his shoulder and a smirk on his face.

Fred was reviewing reports outside the barracks when he heard the lorry's engine die. A familiar voice carried over the gravel crunch of boots.

"Tell me this isn't where every bad decision I've made comes home to roost."

For a heartbeat, Fred just looked at him. It was like seeing a ghost drag itself out of memory, but a ghost that grinned, shouldered a duffel, and swore about the weather. Sergeant Colin O'Malley stood there, rain on his shoulders, wearing the same rough grin he'd carried out of a hundred bar fights.

Fred stepped forward. "Thought they told you to take leave."

"They did," O'Malley said, slinging his duffel to the ground. "But then I heard whispers you were playing schoolteacher in the Highlands and figured someone had to make sure you didn't start giving poetry lessons."

Fred shook his head, smiling despite himself. "You're late."

"Blame the driver. Got lost somewhere around Loch Awe. Or maybe he didn't want to come any closer to whatever hellhole you've signed me up for."

Fred gestured toward the barracks. "Come on then, Sergeant. Let's introduce you to the lads."

The introduction was deliberately informal. Fred gathered the recruits in the briefing hut. Their faces were tight with tension, edged with curiosity. O'Malley leaned against the wall, arms folded, surveying them like a butcher eyeing a row of lambs.

"This is Sergeant O'Malley. He'll be joining us for the rest of your training. By the end of the week, some of you will be terrified of him. That's fine. It means you're learning."

O'Malley stepped forward, voice gravelly but clear. "I don't care where you came from, what regiment you trained with, or who your uncle knows in Whitehall. If you want to survive what's coming, you'll listen, and you'll work. And if you don't... well. One of you'll make a lovely obituary."

A few of the men chuckled nervously. O'Malley's eyes scanned the group, locking in on each of them with quiet intensity. One lad sat up straighter, jaw set as if daring O'Malley to notice him. Another shrank into his collar. Good, Fred thought. Fear and pride were both sparks. All that mattered was how they burned.

"Right," he said at last. "Who here knows how to hot-wire a car?"

No one raised their hand.

O'Malley grinned. "Perfect. We'll start with the basics."

The rest of the day unfolded like controlled chaos. Fred and O'Malley ran parallel drills: one for fieldcraft and movement, the other for urban infiltration techniques. The men moved in small teams, tasked with navigating mock patrols and extracting 'intel' from scattered checkpoints. It was messy at first, stumbles, miscommunication, and more than one loud curse, but the bones of something better were beginning to form.

That afternoon, between drills, Fred and O'Malley leaned against the sandbags at the course's edge. For a while, they said nothing, just watched the recruits crawl through mud and rain. The silence wasn't awkward. It was the silence of men who had bled in the same streets.

Fred took a swig from his canteen. "How bad are they?"

O'Malley scratched at his jaw. "Not hopeless. Some of them are sharp. One or two might even have brains."

"High praise."

"I'm saving my best compliments for when no one falls over their rifle."

Fred glanced at him. "Thanks for coming."

O'Malley shrugged. "Couldn't let you have all the fun. Besides…" He trailed off, eyes narrowing on a recruit struggling through a crawl trench. "Better I'm here than sitting in some pub wondering if you were getting yourself killed again."

Fred looked away, watching the rain start to roll in across the hills. "You ever think about Alexandria?"

"Every bloody day," O'Malley said. Then he straightened. "But this is a good thing you're doing, Fred. You're giving them a chance. A real one."

Fred nodded, quiet for a moment. "Come on. Still daylight left. Let's ruin someone's afternoon."

That evening, the men stumbled into the mess hall covered in mud and soaked through. A few grumbled. Most were too exhausted to speak. But there was now a spark, a flicker of shared experience and respect. The kind that couldn't be taught, only earned.

Fred stood at the edge, watching them. O'Malley joined him with a mug of something vaguely resembling coffee.

"You know," he said, "this might almost feel like progress."

Fred nodded. "Almost."

O'Malley nudged him with an elbow. "All we're missing is a bar fight and two cabaret girls."

Fred gave a dry chuckle. "I think I'm getting too old for that."

O'Malley took a long sip. "Speak for yourself, Lieutenant."

They stood there in silence for a while, two ghosts from a different part of the war, looking out at the men who might one day carry that burden forward.

Fred wondered which of them would survive to tell the story.

Fifty Eight

They called it the Silent Hour.

It wasn't official, just something Fred and O'Malley had coined over mugs and low murmurs: a code for when the game began, when the night cloaked mistakes and made truth harder to spot.

The recruits didn't know it was coming.

Fred and O'Malley stood by the southern watchtower. Beyond them, the moor stretched into darkness, silvered in moonlight, mist curling over the bracken. The terrain had been seeded with tripwires, hidden sentries, signal flares, and dummies that could scream like dying men if disturbed.

Each recruit had one objective: slip from the forest into the compound, reach the radio shack, and extract a sealed envelope without raising an alarm.

They had one hour.

No one was told when their hour began.

Fred checked his watch: 00:12.

The first flare went off at 00:14.

From somewhere near the ridge-line, a startled curse echoed faintly. Fred didn't move. He just marked the quadrant and the name of the recruit assigned to it.

O'Malley held up his binoculars. "That's Evans. Too eager."

Fred nodded. "He breathes through his mouth. You hear him before you see him."

They watched as the recruits tried their entries. Some slithered low across the heather, ghostlike. Others snapped twigs, brushed too close to the wire, or hesitated just long enough to be seen.

Each failure lit up the darkness with flickers of consequence: red flares, shrieking alarms, and lights that swept open fields like prison-yard searchlights.

But two figures made it farther than the rest.

Fred tracked them both, Tanner, the lanky one with a background in forestry, and Sullivan, the wiry lad who barely spoke but watched everything. They approached from different angles, slipping along fence lines and drainage ditches, communicating with hand signals.

"They've been practising together," Fred said, impressed.

"They've got the patience," O'Malley agreed. "And the balls."

Sullivan belly-crawled into the shack's blind spot just as Tanner emerged from the far side. They met eyes. A silent nod. Agreement without words.

Then Sullivan vanished inside.

Watching them move, Fred felt a faint echo of his own first test. The silence back then had been heavier, almost suffocating, every twig a noose waiting to tighten. He remembered the pressure of failure, the sharp knowledge that one false step could brand you as useless before you'd even begun. These lads didn't know it yet, but the game tonight was kinder than the real thing had ever been.

Thirty seconds later, he emerged with the envelope tucked into his coat.

They retreated the way they came, fading into the grass and moonlight like shadows that had never been there at all.

Fred allowed himself the faintest smile.

By 01:45, the last recruit had stumbled back, either cursing or silent, depending on how badly they'd been caught. A few still hadn't figured out where they went wrong. Others knew exactly.

The debrief took place just before dawn, in the open under the watchtower, with O'Malley pacing in front of the shivering line of recruits like a wolf deciding who to bite.

"You all think you're clever," he began. "You had your run in the dark, dodged your fake patrols, played soldiers with rubber knives."

He stopped. Let the silence grow.

"Only two of you completed the objective undetected. Two. That's a fail for the rest of you. And if this had been Sicily, or France, or Prague, you'd be corpses by now."

A voice piped up from the line, hesitant but defiant. "But Sergeant, some of those wires, there was no way to spot them,"

O'Malley wheeled on him like a striking dog. "And you think the Germans will hang lanterns for you, do you? You think they'll give you fair warning?"

The recruit dropped his eyes. Fred stepped in before O'Malley's temper could bite deeper. "He's right about one thing: some traps can't be spotted. That's why you learn to listen for the silence that doesn't belong, or feel for the ground that gives too easily under your hand. The details save you."

O'Malley stepped in closer. "And you know what? That's fine. This is where you make mistakes. This is where you learn to get it wrong, so when it matters, you won't."

Fred's eyes looked down the line. "None of you are finished products. You're here because someone saw potential. Don't waste it."

He held up the envelope Sullivan had retrieved. The seal was still intact.

"Inside is a single photograph. An Allied scientist. In a real mission, retrieving this might mean stopping a weapon, saving lives, or exposing a traitor in your ranks."

He looked to Sullivan and Tanner.

"Well done. You'll be leading tomorrow's exercise."

The others groaned quietly. Tanner blinked. Sullivan said nothing.

Fred turned back to the group. "Dismissed."

As the recruits trudged back toward their barracks, O'Malley and Fred remained in the clearing.

"That went better than I expected," O'Malley said, hands in his pockets. "Though Evans is a bloody liability."

"I'll work with him," Fred said. "He needs focus, not shouting."

"You're going soft in your old age."

Fred smirked. "Maybe. Or maybe I've seen enough boys die to know when one's worth saving."

O'Malley didn't argue.

The mist thinned, dawn blushing across the loch. A bird called. Far beyond the hills, the war ground on. But for now, they were here. Training ghosts in the mist, for the battles no one would ever write about. As the recruits filed off, Fred's eyes caught on Sullivan and Tanner lingering at the edge of the group. They weren't celebrating, not even speaking, just standing side by side, quiet, steady, as though the test had been less a trial than a confirmation of what they already knew. Fred felt a flicker of respect. Some men were built for shadows.

Later that night, O'Malley joined Bennett in the mess, the two of them hunched over tin mugs filled with something that passed for whiskey. For a while they said little, only the crack of the fire and the rattle of wind in the rafters filling the gaps. Then O'Malley leaned back, eyes distant, and said quietly,

"You know, I nearly cashed in not long after Alexandria. Christ, I still taste the smoke when I think on it."

He told it without flourish, his voice stripped bare. "They'd dropped us along the coast, a little sabotage run, fuel depot near Tobruk. Simple in theory. In and out, blow the tanks, make the bastards walk for a change. But it went sideways quickly. Patrol cut us off. My lot scattered. I caught shrapnel when one of our own charges blew too close. Tore me open along the ribs." He lifted his shirt slightly, showing the pale scar, ridged like rope under his skin. "I lay there in the sand, blood soaking in quicker than I could hold it back, watching the sky turn black with smoke. Thought that was it. No bugles, no last words. Just sand in my teeth and the stink of burning fuel."

He poured another measure and drank it like water. "Would've been the end of me if a Bedouin lad hadn't dragged me clear. Barely older than these recruits we've been drilling. He patched me with rags and goat fat of all things. Carried me half a day to our lines. I remember staring at his face, thinking he wasn't real, just some desert spirit sent to torment me before I pegged out." His mouth twitched, a humourless grin. "But he was real enough. Left me at the wire and vanished before I could even croak out a thank you."

O'Malley looked at Bennett then, eyes hard but hollow. "That's why I drive the lads so mercilessly, why I can't stomach half-measures. Because it only takes one wrong move, one second too slow, and you're bleeding out in the sand while the world burns around you. I've been to that silence once. I won't let them go there unprepared."

For a moment, the only sound was the wind through the eaves. Bennett raised his mug slowly, touched it to O'Malley's with a soft clink, and said, "Then we'll make sure they never hear that silence."

Fifty Nine

Inveraray, Scotland - September 1944

The base settled into its night rhythm. Hammering ceased, voices dropped, and the once-bustling yards gave way to silence broken only by boots on gravel. It was in these hours, when the camp exhaled, that the hardest lessons were taught.

Fred stood in the operations tent, a map spread across the table. Pins marked entry points, guard rotations, and traction zones. A single lantern threw shadows across the canvas walls and over the faces of the men gathered.

Sergeant O'Malley leaned over Fred's shoulder, studying the layout. "Night work, then?" he asked, a grin tugging at the corner of his mouth.

Fred nodded. "They've had lots of daylight. Tonight, we'll see how they handle more darkness."

O'Malley chuckled, rubbing the stubble along his jaw."Aye, well. Darkness reveals things in a man daylight can't hide."

Fred looked up, meeting his eyes. "Exactly."

He stepped out of the tent into the cool air, calling out sharply, 'Form up!" The men, already assembled in a loose line, snapped to attention. The same young faces from earlier stared back at him, eager, restless, and a little nervous. They were learning quickly, but Fred knew that confidence was fragile in the dark.

"You've had your warm-up," Fred said, voice low but firm. "Now it's time for the real thing. Tonight, you'll operate in conditions closer to what you'll face in Europe, or Africa, or God knows where else. You'll rely on sound, instinct, and silence."

He let that hang in the air, just as rain started to fall.

"Your objective: infiltrate the old manor house on the hill. It's been converted into a communications hub for this exercise. Retrieve the coded message from the study. No lights, no help, and the 'guards'", he nodded toward a group of senior marines standing off to the side, "Won't be giving you second chances."

Fred let the words sink in. The manor was no fortress, but its echoes of old stone and long halls would amplify every sound, every misstep. In the field, the slightest slip could mean a patrol stumbling across you. Here, it would mean humiliation, but humiliation was the seed of survival.

A few of the recruits exchanged glances, their tension rising.

Fred stepped forward. "Remember what you've been taught. Move like shadows. Think before you act. Speak without sound. Fail tonight, you walk away. Fail out there…"

He didn't finish the sentence. He didn't need to.

O'Malley handed each team a small kit: a compass, a wire cutter, a blacked-out torch, and a copy of the manor's exterior layout.

One of the younger men glanced up from the map. "Sir, tripwires? Booby traps?"

Fred nodded. "Yes. Not live, but real enough. You'll know if you trip one. The enemy won't give you warnings."

As the teams split off, disappearing into the mist, Fred and O'Malley climbed a narrow ridge overlooking the manor. The sky was heavy with clouds, the moon barely visible through the grey. Fred raised his binoculars. Two men crept along the tree line.

'Too close,' O'Malley muttered.

'Too noisy,' Fred agreed. "They need to spread, keep low. If this were the real thing…"

A sudden clank echoed faintly from the field below. One of the guards had triggered a metal can alarm. A red flare burst overhead, casting an eerie light over the field. The two men froze, then scrambled back into the underbrush.

Fred imagined the lads' panic: the flare bursting above, breath catching in their throats, bodies freezing when instinct screamed to run. That moment of paralysis was more dangerous than bullets. He'd seen good men die because they hesitated when the dark lit up.

"Lesson learned," Fred said grimly.

But not all teams faltered. Another pair, moving wide along the riverbank, advanced with impressive discipline. They halted often, signalling with subtle hand movements, their footfalls silent even on the gravel path. Fred tracked their progress with growing approval.

Those two, Hastings and McBride," O'Malley said, recognising them. "Quiet lads. Always watching."

"They'll do well," Fred replied. "They're thinking like ghosts."

Minutes passed, then the flash of a signal torch blinked from the manor's rear garden, three quick pulses. Fred allowed himself a flicker of satisfaction.

"They're in."

Inside the manor, Hastings and McBride moved with methodical precision. They found the study, located the locked cabinet, and retrieved the folded message. Outside, another team laid a diversion, luring two guards away with the sound of a dropped tool.

It was not a flawless operation; one team misread the compass and ended up circling the wrong wing of the manor, but as the final man crossed the extraction boundary with the message in hand, Fred knew progress had been made.

Back at the barracks, the men gathered in silence, waiting for Fred's assessment. Their faces were flushed, uniforms damp with sweat and mist.

Fred stood before them, arms crossed. "Some of you did well. Some of you made mistakes. But all of you learned and all of you are showing improvements."

He paced slowly in front of the group.

"You felt the panic. You lost your bearings. Some of you froze. That's good. You need to feel those things here, where you can fail and stand up again."

He stopped, looking in their eyes.

"This kind of work isn't about bravado. It's about clarity under pressure. It's about knowing when to move and when to wait. When to act and when to disappear.

He opened his front pocket and pulled out the recovered message.

"This, this scrap of paper, could be the difference between success and disaster. Never forget that."

The men nodded, quiet but focused. After the debriefing, Fred lingered by the tent, watching the men as they dispersed. O'Malley joined him, arms folded.

"They're coming along," O'Malley said. "Still raw, but they're getting sharper."

Fred looked toward the hills, the wind tugging gently at his coat. "They'll need to be."

For a heartbeat, Fred saw Enzo's face, then Luciano's, their youth, their quiet courage. He thought of how quickly young men became names etched on stone. Training these boys wasn't just preparation; it was a form of penance. If they lived, maybe it would balance the ledger a little.

O'Malley was quiet for a moment. "You miss it, don't you?"

Fred paused. "I miss the clarity. Out there, it's instinct and survival. Here…I can give them a chance to live. Maybe that matters more."

O'Malley nodded. "Aye. Maybe it does."

As dawn crept over Inveraray, casting gold across the grey hills, Fred allowed himself to pause. The war would call them soon enough. But for now, in this small corner of Scotland, the next generation of silent warriors was being forged.

And Fred Bennett would make damn sure they were ready.

Sixty

Fred rubbed his eyes, pencil scratching one last note across the training report. Outside, rain tapped steadily against the tin roof of the hut. The exercise had been a success for the most part, with some navigation errors and a few protocol slips, but progress nonetheless. He pushed the file aside and exhaled, shoulders heavy.

The door creaked open behind him.

"Lieutenant," came O'Malley's voice, more cautious than usual.

Fred looked up. "Something wrong?"

O'Malley stepped in, brushing water from his shoulders. "We've got visitors," O'Malley said, his tone carrying none of the usual swagger. That alone put Fred on edge.

"Who?"

"Brass. From London. Didn't say much, but they're already on the field watching the lads. One of them's wearing the look of a man sent to measure and cut."

Fred stood, straightening his uniform. "Bloody hell. They didn't give any warning?"

"None. One's Commander Webb. The other didn't say his name, intelligence, I'd wager. Quiet sort. Cold eyes."

Fred swore under his breath and reached for his coat. Surprise inspections were never friendly. At best, they were inconvenient. At worst, they led to closures, cuts or reassignments. And if this was an intelligence officer, it wasn't just discipline they were looking at, but doctrine as well.

By the time Fred reached the training grounds, the men were halfway through a stealth navigation exercise, creeping through a fog-draped woodland path marked with tripwires and observation posts.

Two figures stood at the edge of the field, watching through field glasses. One was short and stocky, while the other was tall, angular, and as still as a statue. Fred recognised Commander Webb immediately; he'd seen his name on operational memos from Naval Command. The taller man was unfamiliar, dressed in a plain dark overcoat despite the military setting.

Fred approached briskly and saluted. "Lieutenant Fred Bennett, reporting, sirs."

Commander Webb returned the salute curtly. "Lieutenant. We decided to see this training programme for ourselves. It's been raising eyebrows at the Admiralty."

Fred kept his expression neutral. "I hope for the right reasons."

"That's what we're here to determine," Webb said, dryly.

The man in the overcoat said nothing, but his gaze flicked toward Fred with unsettling intensity.

Webb gestured to the men. "This programme, espionage, sabotage, infiltration. Useful skills, but unconventional. Some feel you're taking liberties. Especially with such young recruits."

Fred felt agitated. "With respect, sir, these lads may be dropped behind enemy lines before long. If they're not ready, we're sending them to their deaths."

"Is that your justification for lock-picking lessons and simulated break-ins?"

"No," Fred said calmly. "That's my justification for making sure they come back."

The overcoat man finally spoke, his voice quiet but sharp. "What about loyalty? Discipline? You're teaching them to disobey convention. How do you ensure that same mindset won't unravel in the field?"

Fred met his gaze. "Because I teach them the difference. When to break rules, and when not to. Espionage isn't chaos. It's discipline, measured to the inch."

There was a pause. Webb turned back to the training, watching as a team of men crawled under a low wire and into thick cover.

"We'll observe the rest of the morning session," Webb said. "No interference. Then we'll debrief."

Fred gave a nod, hiding the tension coiling in his stomach.

For the next hour, Fred and O'Malley stood off to the side as the evaluation unfolded under grey skies. Fred resisted the urge to glance sideways. He could feel the intelligence officer's stare like a weight between his shoulder blades. Every misstep the recruits made seemed to echo louder under that gaze. For a moment, Fred wasn't sure who was being tested, his men or him.

The men performed well under pressure, perhaps sensing the extra eyes. They moved with discipline, communicated clearly, and adapted when their routes were blocked or compromised. A few hiccups, one tripwire was brushed, and one team was late on extraction, but nothing disastrous.

Fred could feel the scrutiny, especially from the intelligence man, whose eyes never left the recruits. It was unnerving, like being cross-examined by a ghost.

Finally, the session ended. The men returned to the barracks for debrief, and Fred was summoned to the briefing hut.

Inside, Webb sat behind the desk, thumbing through the morning's training report. The intelligence officer stood near the window, arms crossed.

Fred remained standing, waiting.

Webb set the report down and looked up. "Your methods are unorthodox. More resistance cell than the Royal Marines."

Fred said nothing.

"But…" Webb continued, "The results speak for themselves. These men moved like veterans. They worked together, anticipating danger and improvising under pressure. I've seen fully deployed units make twice the noise and half the progress."

Fred felt the knot in his stomach ease slightly.

The intelligence officer finally stepped forward. "We'll be forwarding your protocols to Command. I suspect you'll have visitors, others looking to learn from what you've built here."

Fred raised an eyebrow. "You're expanding the programme?"

"Possibly," the man said. "But I'll say this: what you've done here isn't training. It's shaping survivors. And we'll need those before this war is done."

Webb stood and offered a hand. "Good work, Lieutenant. Keep it up, and keep them sharp."

Fred shook his hand. "Yes, sir."

Later that evening, Fred and O'Malley stood on the edge of the loch, watching the last light fade over the hills.

"So?" O'Malley asked.

Fred let out a slow breath. "We passed."

"Did they smile?"

363

"Not once."

O'Malley snorted. "Aye, that's their version of a standing ovation. If they'd frowned, we'd be packing our bags."

Fred chuckled, then grew quiet. "They might be scaling it up. Expanding the programme."

O'Malley whistled low. "We'll need more boots. And more flares."

"More everything," Fred said. "But for now, we stay the course."

He looked out across the loch, the sky now dark and full of stars. The base behind him bustled faintly in the distance, the sound of marching feet and distant drills carried on the breeze.

With eyes watching from above, he knew the stakes had just risen. But so had the belief in what they were doing.

Sixty One

Inveraray, Scotland - January 1945

Fred leafed through the day's reports, ink smudging his fingers. The office was close and dim, the coal stove giving off a steady heat that couldn't quite chase away the chill that seeped through the stone walls. Beyond the window, the loch stretched grey in the fading light, its surface shifting with a restless wind. The hills rose black against the horizon, stark silhouettes cut from the winter sky.

He rubbed his eyes and leaned back in his chair, listening to the faint, constant noises of the base: shouted orders in the yard, the metallic clatter of rifles being stacked, the measured rhythm of boots on frozen ground. The sounds of discipline, routine. He had lived long enough to know that routine was what kept men alive, whether in training halls or under fire.

It had been months since he'd last set foot on a warship, and part of him had begun to wonder if that chapter of his life was closing. Perhaps the Admiralty meant to keep him here, polishing others into soldiers while the real fighting happened elsewhere. He told himself he could live with it. Yet every now and then, in the quiet hours, he felt the sea tug at him like a memory that refused to be forgotten.

A sharp knock broke the stillness.

"Enter," he called.

The door swung open and Captain Stuart stepped inside, his uniform crisp as always, a fine dusting of snow melting across the shoulders. His presence carried a charge, a flicker of something beyond routine.

"Lieutenant Bennett," Stuart greeted with a nod. "Evening."

Fred rose slightly, then sat back down. "Evening, sir."

"I've just come from the wireless station," Stuart continued. "I hear they've taken notice of your work here. Solid results."

Fred arched a brow. "Results on paper, sir. Hardly the same as…"

"As fighting?" Stuart finished, a dry smile on his lips. "Perhaps. But your name came up nonetheless. And when London puts a name at the top of a list, I tend not to argue."

Fred sat straighter. "What sort of list?"

Stuart stepped closer to the desk, lowering his voice. "A fast posting. HMS Diadem. She sails from Scapa. Operations off the Norwegian coast."

The words landed like a hammer-blow. Fred felt his breath tighten. Diadem was no routine assignment. A light cruiser that had seen Normandy,

Murmansk, the Arctic convoys; she was forged for combat.

"Norway," Fred repeated quietly.

"Near Bergen," Stuart confirmed. "Intelligence suggests German destroyer movements. The end may be in sight, but the enemy isn't going quietly. If they're short on supplies, they may try to disrupt shipping lanes before the lights go out. Admiralty wants this dealt with swiftly and without fuss."

Fred rose, crossing to the window. The glass was frosted at the corners, and the world outside blurred. He had thought the war might let him rest here, in the quiet cold of the Highlands. He should have known better.

"And the base?" he asked, turning back.

"O'Malley will take command," Stuart said. "Promotion to lieutenant came through this morning. Admiralty was impressed with him: his steadiness, his instinct. He'll keep Inveraray running."

Fred allowed himself a faint smile. He remembered O'Malley's rough edges when he'd first arrived, the temper that flared quicker than it should. Yet the man had tempered with time, forged by hardship. If anyone could keep the place steady, it was he.

"Good man, mind if I tell him?" Fred asked.

Stuart studied him carefully. "You take the lead on this one, Bennett."

Fred gave a short laugh, bitter at the edges. "The things I could tell you about O'Malley."

"I bet, and the things I am sure he could tell me about you," Stuart laughed, his voice relaxed. "You've seen too much, Fred and survived too much. Admiralty trusts you to finish clean. That's why your name is on their lips."

For a moment, the two men stood in silence, the coal stove ticking softly in the corner. Fred felt the chill pass through him again, one that had nothing to do with the snow outside.

He drew a breath. "When do we leave?"

"First light," Stuart answered. "Scapa Flow in 3 days. Final briefing aboard Diadem."

Fred nodded once, slowly, as though sealing a pact with himself. He stepped forward to take the orders from Stuart's outstretched hand, but the older man didn't release them right away. His expression changed, just slightly, as if bracing himself for what came next.

"Oh," he added casually, "one more thing."

Fred looked up.

"You're promoted," Stuart said. "Effective immediately. Captain Bennett."

Fred blinked. The word echoed in his chest like a drumbeat. Captain. He should have felt pride, but instead, there was only a curious heaviness. The title carried no glamour here; only responsibility, sharpened by the knowledge that not all his men would come back.

"I…" He faltered, then recovered. "Thank you, sir. I won't let the rank down. Or the men."

Stuart smiled, a brief but genuine expression. "I know you won't. You've earned this, Fred. Every inch of it. Now gather your kit. You'll brief your detachment en route. We'll have transport ready by 0500. And bring your winter gear, it's bitter up there."

Fred finally allowed himself a faint smile. "Aye, sir. I'll be ready."

Stuart stepped back toward the door, then paused. "They say the last battle changes you," he said over his shoulder. "Make sure it changes you for the better."

Then he was gone, leaving Fred alone with the flickering hearth, the smell of leather and damp wool, and the sharp awareness that everything had just shifted.

He turned back to the window. Snow was falling harder now. Below, his men were laughing, unaware of the changes coming to their training.

He squared his shoulders, the new weight of command settling onto them like the snow outside.

The mist had started to roll low across Loch Fyne, the water as grey and flat as sheet metal. Fred walked the narrow track just beyond the barracks, boots crunching over snow-covered gravel, the aroma of pine and peat smoke drifting in on the wind.

In his coat pocket was a folded envelope, edges softened by the journey from the south. He had received it earlier in the day but hadn't had a chance to open it. Tommy's handwriting was as sloppy as ever, uneven, rushed, but somehow comforting.

Dear Fred,

I imagine by now you've fully assimilated into Highland life, grumbling about the weather, teaching fresh recruits how to tie knots while knee-deep in freezing loch water, and surviving on black pudding and spite.

Rumour has it you're running a covert ops course. Very fancy. Do the lads know their instructor once passed out in a pub toilet in Dover?

Your mum wrote, sweet lady. Sent me biscuits, I ate them in your honour. She mentioned that she told you about me joining the front line? Sorry, I hadn't mentioned it. Just got on and did it.

I am currently with the forces under Field Marshall Montgomery, we're holding the northern flank of the Ardennes. The Germans are continuing their counteroffensive, but we are holding strong; we might be here for a while, mind.

I've no idea what you'll be assigned to next, but if history's any guide, it'll be cold, risky, and classified. So please, for God's sake, don't get shot again. You've filled your quota.

And remember: if you die, I'll come up there and kill you properly.

Stay sharp. You're better than you think you are, even if I'll never tell you that twice.

Yours in sarcasm,
Tommy

Fred smiled, a slight, reluctant curve of the lips that faded too quickly. The warmth of it flickered, then gave way to the weight he'd been carrying.

He missed the laughter and loved how his friendship had been unshaken by war. He could almost hear Tommy's voice again, ribbing him for the way he added whisky to his tea as if it were the most natural thing in the world. Memory and reality overlapped for an instant, and it was almost enough to make him laugh. Almost.

The loch outside the window was still, but Fred's thoughts were not. He folded the letter from

Tommy and tucked it into his coat. The call to report had come with little warning.

Sixty Two

The coal stove had burned low in the night, and the office felt more like an icebox than a command post when Fred opened the door at first light. Frost traced the inside of the windowpanes, curling in delicate feathers that no warmth could chase. He set his small pack down on the desk, the total of what he would take north. A spare uniform, razor, and writing kit. He had learned long ago not to carry more than he could walk away with.

The loch outside was still, a sheet of pewter beneath the pale dawn. A mist clung low over the water, drifting between the black shapes of the hills. The camp was stirring now: the muffled thud of boots, the clang of the cookhouse bell, a shouted order cutting across the yard. The day was beginning as it always did, though for Fred the rhythm would end in only a few hours.

A knock at the open doorway drew his eye.

"Morning, sir."

O'Malley stood there in his greatcoat, breath steaming in the cold. The sergeant's cap was pulled low, shadowing eyes still heavy from the early hour. But there was a sharpness in his stance that Fred had come to rely on.

"Come in, O'Malley," Fred said. He gestured to the chair opposite his desk. "Close the door. We'll have a word."

O'Malley obeyed, dragging the chair back with a scrape of wood on stone. He sat, leaning forward, forearms on his knees. "You've got that look about you, Fred. Like a man with news."

Fred allowed a smile. "You've a good eye. I do have news. The Admiralty have pulled me out."

O'Malley blinked, then let out a short, sharp laugh. "You're joking."

"I rarely joke before breakfast." Fred reached into his desk, drew out the sealed envelope Stuart had delivered the night before, and slid it across. "Orders came in yesterday. HMS Diadem. Sailing from Scapa Flow within the week."

O'Malley's hand hovered over the envelope before he touched it, as though he half expected it to vanish. "The Diadem? Christ, that's no milk run. She's been in the thick of it since Normandy."

Fred nodded. "Which is why they want men who won't lose their heads when it turns ugly." He paused. "That leaves Inveraray in need of someone to keep it standing. And that, O'Malley, is where you come in."

The sergeant's brow furrowed. "Me?"

"Not as sergeant." Fred reached again into the drawer, producing another folded document, stamped and signed. "Congratulations, Lieutenant

O'Malley. The promotion came through this morning."

For a moment, O'Malley just stared, mouth slightly open. Then he gave a low whistle and rubbed a hand through his dark hair. "Well, I'll be damned."

"You've earned it," Fred said. "I've watched you since Alexandria. You've steadied, sharpened. The men trust you. They'll follow you."

O'Malley gave a crooked grin. "They follow because you drive them like a bloody cattleman. I've not your bite."

"You don't need my bite," Fred replied. "You've got something better: their respect. You'll do fine."

For the first time, a trace of nerves flickered across O'Malley's face. He looked down at the commission in his hands. "I'll admit, sir... I always thought I'd finish this war taking orders, not giving them."

Fred leaned back. "None of us finishes where we think. The trick is to finish at all."

Outside, voices carried across the yard, young and eager, a reminder of the men whose futures rested now with O'Malley.

"Have you told them yet?" O'Malley asked.

"Not yet," Fred said. "That's this morning's task. I'd like you there when I do."

O'Malley nodded slowly. "Aye. They'll want to hear it from you."

The parade ground was glazed with frost, the packed earth white beneath the morning sun. Breath steamed from every mouth as the trainees formed up, stamping their boots to keep circulation in their toes. Rifles slung, collars up, they stood in ranks that only weeks ago had looked more like a rabble than soldiers.

Fred walked out with O'Malley beside him, the weight of silence pressing on the gathered men. He stopped before them, hands clasped behind his back.

"Men," he began, voice carrying clear across the yard. "You know I'm not much for speeches, so I'll give it to you straight. Orders came last night. I've been reassigned."

A ripple of murmurs ran through the ranks. Fred raised a hand, and they quieted.

"I'll be shipping north to join HMS Diadem. That means I won't be here to see you through the rest of your training." His gaze swept across their young faces, some surprised, some uncertain, all intent. "I want you to know something before I go. In the short time I've had with you, I've seen grit. I've seen discipline take root where there was none. You've proved yourselves ready to stand, not as green lads but as fighting men. And that counts for more than you yet realise."

The cold air bit his lungs, but he kept his voice steady. "From this day, you'll answer to Lieutenant O'Malley. He's earned that rank, and he's earned the

376

right to lead you. He'll take you further than I could here. Listen to him, trust him, and trust yourselves."

He let the words hang a moment, then gave a firm nod. "That's all. Dismissed."

For a heartbeat, the yard was silent. Then came the sound of boots stamping the ground in unison, not in regulation, but with respect. The sound echoed off the stone walls, a rough salute in place of words. Fred felt it strike deep, an unspoken farewell.

The ranks broke, and men dispersed toward the barracks and mess. O'Malley lingered at his side, arms folded, expression unreadable.

"You've left me a fine mess, sir," he muttered at last.

Fred gave him a sidelong glance. "You'll manage."

O'Malley snorted. "Manage? You mean carry the weight you're running off to drop on Jerry's doorstep. Aye, I'll manage." He paused, then added with a crooked grin, "But don't think this lets you off the hook. You'd better bring me back a souvenir from Bergen. A German cap will do nicely. I'll hang it in the mess, proof you didn't just sneak off for a cushy cruise."

Fred barked a short laugh, shaking his head. "You've a strange idea of a cushy cruise."

"Strange ideas are all that keep me sane." O'Malley's grin softened. "Truth is, sir... I'll miss having you here. Place won't be the same without your scowl."

Before Fred could answer, the distant growl of an engine cut across the yard, and a navy staff car rolled through the gates, tyres crunching over the frozen earth. The driver pulled up smartly, stepped out, and saluted.

"Lieutenant Bennett?"

Fred straightened. "That's me."

The driver reached for his pack, but Fred waved him off and lifted it himself. He turned once more to O'Malley.

"Well, that's it then."

O'Malley clasped his hand firmly, grip strong. "Go on, sir. Leave the paperwork to me, and I'll leave the heroics to you."

Fred smiled at that, a warmth spreading through him despite the chill. "Take care of them, O'Malley."

"I will," the Irishman said.

Fred climbed into the back of the car. The door shut with a heavy thud. As the vehicle pulled away, he looked back through the rear window. O'Malley stood in the yard, a lone figure in a greatcoat, already turning to bark an order at a straggling trainee. The base shrank behind him, the loch opening vast, the hills watching in silence.

Sixty Three

Off the coast of Bergen - January 1945

The winds off the Norwegian coast screamed over HMS Diadem, rattling halyards and cutting through every layer of wool and oilskin. The sea rose in great, glassy swells beneath a sky the colour of gunmetal. It was a bleak, savage beauty, harsh and indifferent to the ships that dared to cross it.

Fred stood on the bridge, gloved hands behind his back, the collar of his greatcoat turned up against the cold. Through the binoculars, he could see only waves and mist, broken occasionally by the pale gleam of distant snow on the fjords. Somewhere out there, hidden in the veil of the North Sea, were three German destroyers. And Fred had been sent to find them. The ache in his shoulder throbbed harder in the cold, a reminder of chains and stone floors, of a cell where his war had nearly ended. He thought of Naples burning, of sandstorms in the desert, of blood washing into the surf on the beaches of Normandy. Each battle had taken men from him. And now, here, at the ragged edge of the war, he wondered if this sea would take him too.

The Diadem was not alone. HMS Mauritius, another light cruiser, steamed alongside her port side at a careful distance, their formation steady. Both ships bore the scars of long service, worn paint, and battle-patched hulls, but their crews were sharp, experienced, and ready.

"Captain, we're approaching the Norwegian coast," reported Lieutenant Greene, stepping up beside him with a clipboard tucked under one arm.

Fred turned slightly, nodding. "Thank you, Lieutenant Greene. Anything from radar?"

"Still tracking three contacts, roughly sixteen miles bearing south-west by west. Speed: variable. Could be feints."

"They're testing us," Fred said quietly. "Trying to draw us closer or force us into rougher waters."

He lowered his binoculars and turned to the chart table. The coast near Bergen was riddled with hazards, reefs, narrow straits, and ice. Not the place for a careless pursuit. He tapped a gloved finger on the chart.

"We'll hold the current heading. Inform Mauritius to maintain port position and keep radio discipline tight. I don't want to give them any advantage."

"Aye, sir."

As Greene moved off, Fred took a deep breath, the cold air sharp in his lungs. Below him, the crew of the Diadem moved with quiet focus. Deck crews were busy checking gun mountings. Signalmen worked the lamps and flags with frozen fingers. Below decks, tea brewed in the galley, a small comfort for those not yet at their posts. A warship preparing for battle was not loud, but there was a hum to it, a vibration of purpose that ran through every bulkhead.

Torrens stepped up beside him, breath misting in the cold. His voice carried the flat calm of a man who'd watched too many ships vanish into the Arctic night. "They'll be waiting. Kriegsmarine's desperate now. And a desperate wolf bites hardest."

"I know," Fred replied. "Which means they'll fight until they break."

Torrens gave a small grunt of agreement, then added, "Crew's ready. Guns primed. If it comes to it, we'll give them hell."

Fred didn't answer immediately. His eyes lingered on the sea. The ache in his shoulder from Italy flared in the cold, a ghost of his time in a cell.

He had survived the Mediterranean Sea, the desert, the ruins of Naples and the invasion at Normandy. And now here he was, back at sea, at the edge of the war, one last time.

"Good," he said finally. "Let's make this clean."

A sharp voice broke over the intercom: "Bridge, radar contact now twelve miles and closing. Enemy likely approaching visual range."

"Helm, maintain speed and heading," Fred said. "Gunnery crews to action stations. Load high-explosive. Keep the secondary guns hot."

Lieutenant Greene returned, cheeks flushed, a glint of adrenaline in his eyes. "Signal sent to Mauritius. They're holding formation. No sign of enemy aircraft yet."

Fred nodded. "Then they're coming by sea alone. It'll be gun against gun."

The minutes passed slowly, stretching like taut wire. Every sailor aboard Diadem knew what might come next. Quiet conversations stilled. Eyes turned toward the horizon. Fingers gripped steel.

Then,

"Contact!" shouted the lookout from the foremast. "Enemy ships sighted, three destroyers, bearing 240 degrees!"

Fred spun his binoculars toward the horizon. There, emerging from the fog like ghosts, came the silhouettes of the Kriegsmarine. Sleek, dark hulls slicing through the waves. Gun turrets like staring eyes.

He could almost feel the change ripple through the ship.

"Helm, bring us about. Course two-four-oh," Fred ordered, his voice sharp now. "Gunnery, lock targets. Prepare to fire on my command."

He turned to Greene. "Signal Mauritius: we are engaging."

"Aye, Captain."

As Diadem pivoted, her great guns began to shift, turrets whining as they aligned. Fred felt the vibrations under his boots, the deep, predatory hum of a warship ready to strike.

"Fire."

The deck lurched as the forward turret opened fire, a blast that seemed to tear the air apart. Smoke clawed across the bridge windows, acrid and heavy. Fred felt the shockwave in his chest before he heard the scream of the shells, a sound like the sky itself ripping open. To port, Mauritius answered with her own thunder, her broadside flashing like a second sunrise against the grey horizon.

A moment later, the German destroyers replied in kind.

Flashes lit the horizon. Shells burst in plumes of seawater.

The sea erupted.

Flashes of light blazed across the waves as both British and German ships unleashed hell. Fred stood firm on the bridge of HMS Diadem, his gloved hands gripping the rail, and the thunder of the guns rolled through his chest. The ship shuddered with every salvo, her hull vibrating as if she were a living thing roused to anger.

Shells screamed overhead, some landing wide, throwing up geysers of salt and steel, others too close.

"Hit confirmed on lead destroyer!" shouted Lieutenant Greene, ducking back from his observation post. "Portside guns request reload!" Greene shouted. "Recoil's thrown the sights off!"

"We don't wait," Fred barked. "Keep pressure on them."

He could see the German formation clearer now, three destroyers moving fast, zigzagging through the mist to break targeting locks. One had already taken damage: black smoke trailed from its stern, but it kept moving, guns blazing in retaliation.

"Sir!" came a voice from the comms station. "Mauritius has taken a hit to her aft turret. She's still operational, requesting covering fire while she adjusts course!" Every decision here was a coin flip with men's lives on the other side.

Fred didn't hesitate. "Helm, starboard fifteen. Bring our port-side batteries to bear. Gunnery, concentrate fire on the second destroyer. Keep those bastards off Mauritius."

The Diadem turned, her bow slicing through the waves, exposing her broadside to the enemy. Her guns roared again, high-explosive shells arcing through the cold air like meteors. One struck near the second German ship's forward deck, resulting in a burst of flames. Fred caught a glimpse of men scrambling, then disappearing into the smoke.

"Enemy retaliating!" Greene called. "Brace!"

The deck jolted violently as a shell exploded just off the starboard bow, sending a curtain of seawater crashing over the bridge. Fred was thrown sideways but caught himself on the railing, coughing through the mist.

"Damage report!" he shouted.

A petty officer appeared, soaked to the skin, blood trickling from a cut on his temple. "Minor damage to the forward plating, sir. No breach. Engine room reports full function."

"Good. Keep it that way."

Another shout came from below deck, "Medical team to mid-deck! We've got injured!"

Fred clenched his jaw. There was no time to dwell. Men would live or die without him. His job was to win this fight.

A new sound cut through the roar, rapid, sharp. The German destroyers had switched to smaller-calibre fire, 20mm and 37mm anti-aircraft guns now trained horizontally, sweeping across the decks in search of soft targets. A barrage of tracers flew across the waves, bright green and orange slashes in the mist.

"Deck crew, keep your heads down!" barked Commander Torrens. "This isn't a parade!"

Then came another explosion, this one from their own side.

"Direct hit!" Greene called. "One of ours scored a clean strike amidships. She's slowing!"

Fred raised his binoculars. One of the German destroyers was dead in the water, smoke pouring from her midsection. She was listing to port, men leaping overboard.

"Concentrate fire on the remaining two. If they're falling back, we finish what we started!"

But the Germans had other plans. As if on cue, the two remaining destroyers suddenly veered west, engines straining, smoke canisters deployed behind them to mask their retreat.

"They're running," Torrens muttered. "Cowards."

"No," Fred said quietly. "They're survivors. Same as us."

Lieutenant Greene stepped forward. "Captain, shall we pursue? Mauritius is requesting your orders."

Fred didn't answer right away. He looked again at the sea. The Diadem had taken hits, nothing critical, but her hull bore fresh scars. Her crew was alive, but blood had been spilt. Mauritius had damage to her turrets. The enemy was limping, but leading them further into Norwegian coastal waters was dangerous. Mines, torpedo traps, shore batteries, it was a gamble.

One hard push, and he could end it. Destroy them here, now. But at what cost? He thought of the bodies already being carried to sickbay, the young ones who hadn't yet learned how thin the line was between duty and waste. He weighed the scales. Was vengeance worth it? Would finishing the kill bring victory any closer?

"No," he said firmly. "Signal Mauritius: negative on pursuit. We regroup. Let them crawl back to Bergen."

Greene hesitated, then gave a sharp nod. "Aye, sir."

As the orders were relayed, Fred exhaled slowly; the magnitude of the command was heavier now that the firing had stopped. He could still hear it, though, the echoes of gunfire, the screams of metal, the frantic shouts of men in combat. Battle left a residue in the mind.

One of the young signalmen approached, eyes wide. "Sir, what do we tell the men?"

Fred looked at him, really looked, barely nineteen, cheeks still round, but a streak of soot across his forehead that made him look older.

"Tell them we did our duty," Fred said quietly. "And we lived."

The Diadem began to turn, slowly, deliberately, back towards the open sea. The sky above was still grey, but somewhere beyond the horizon, dawn waited.

Fred walked out onto the deck, the cold wind tearing at his coat. He looked back once, toward the mist-shrouded coast, where the enemy had vanished into smoke. He thought of all the battles past, North

Africa, Naples, Normandy. The fallen. The saved. The hollow victories.

Torrens joined him a moment later. "You made the right call," he said gruffly. "They'll fight another day, but so will we."

Fred nodded. "The war's nearly over."

"Not for everyone. They'll remember today, though. Not the glory. The fact that we came back."

"No," Fred agreed. "But it will be. Soon."

From below, the sounds of repair crews echoed up through the deck: hammers, orders, and the hum of welding torches. Life returning, even as the memory of death lingered.

"Set course for Invergordon," Fred ordered at last. "We'll return for resupply and report."

Greene relayed the order, and the engines of Diadem surged to life once more. She turned her bow toward home, leaving the smoke and fire behind.

Fred stood at the prow as the wind tore through his hair. The war had taken so much: his friends, his innocence, his peace. But it had given him something too: purpose, honour, and a legacy written not in glory, but in survival.

As the sun rose, faint and pale over the North Sea, Fred allowed himself one final thought:

Is this really my last time?

Sixty Four

Fred stood on the deck of the ship, his eyes fixed on the receding Norwegian coastline. The sun was setting, casting a golden glow over the water, but he barely noticed. His thoughts were far away, lost in the memories of war and betrayal. The sea breeze tugged at his hair, but it did little to soothe the turmoil within him. After years of conflict, he was finally returning home.

The war in Europe was almost over. For him, it already was.

The words felt unreal, almost meaningless. For so long, his life had been defined by the relentless struggle, by the fight for survival, and by the need to complete his mission. Now, as the ship cut through the waves towards England, Fred felt an emptiness gnawing at his soul, a void that victory could not fill.

He looked down at his hands, his fingers tracing the rough, calloused skin. Scars crisscrossed his knuckles, each one a testament to the battles he fought. His body was a map of pain, but it was the scars on his heart that hurt the most. Fred clenched his fists, his jaw tightening. He had tried to forget, tried to bury the memories of Isabella and what she had done, but the betrayal lingered like a poison, seeping into every corner of his mind.

As the ship approached the Scottish coast, the rolling hills of Invergordon seen in the distance, Fred felt a pang of unease. This was the moment he had dreamed of, the end of the war for him, but it felt hollow. The cheers of his fellow soldiers filled the air, their faces alight with joy and relief, but Fred could not share in their happiness. The war had taken so much from him: his innocence, his trust, his belief in the goodness of people. Isabella had taken the rest.

When the ship finally docked, Fred disembarked with the other soldiers, his steps heavy on the gangplank. The docks were crowded with families, their faces bright with smiles, their arms outstretched in welcome. Fred's eyes scanned the crowd, knowing that he wouldn't know anyone. He only had his parents, and they lived a long way from Scotland.

Fred slung his pack over his shoulder, his expression blank as he moved through the throng of people. He could hear the cries of joy, the laughter, the tears of reunion, but they felt distant, like echoes from another world. He made his way through the bustling streets, his footsteps carrying him towards the train station. The roads of Invergordon were crowded with soldiers and civilians, a sea of faces that blurred together, but Fred barely noticed. His mind was elsewhere, lost in the memories of the war, of the men he had fought alongside, of the ones who had not made it back.

The train ride to Worthing was a long blur, the countryside flashing past the window in a haze of green and gold. Fred stared out at the fields, his eyes unseeing. He could hear the conversations around him, the excited chatter of the other passengers, but he felt disconnected, as if he were watching from a distance. The world had changed, yet he felt as if he were still in the past, trapped in the shadows of war.

When the train pulled into Worthing station, Fred stepped onto the platform, his heart heavy. The town was much the same as he remembered, but to Fred, it felt different, as if he were seeing it through a veil. He walked through the familiar streets, his footsteps echoing in the quiet.

Fred stood at the gate, looking up at his childhood home, a modest brick house, with ivy trailing warmly over its walls. The garden, though a bit overgrown, was still bright with flowers his mother had planted long ago, and he could see the familiar lace curtains in the windows, slightly faded but lovingly kept. A soft smile tugged at his lips as he took it all in. This place, with its creaking gate and worn path, held memories that felt like a warm embrace.

Pushing the gate open, Fred walked up the path, feeling an unexpected surge of excitement. This time, he knew he would be home for longer, that he would get a chance to spend real time with them. The time away made him realise how much his parents meant to him.

He fumbled with the key, his fingers trembling just slightly, and finally opened the door. The familiar smells of home greeted him as he stepped into the hallway, where the old clock ticked steadily, its rhythm grounding him. Faded photographs lined the walls, each one a small piece of his history, and the carpet beneath his feet was worn but comforting.

"Fred!" His mother's voice called from the sitting room, filled with disbelief and joy. She appeared in the doorway, her eyes welling with tears as she took him in. "It's you…"

Fred smiled, pulling her into a tight embrace. "I'm home, Mother. For good this time." He buried his face in her shoulder, breathing in familiar air, the scent of home. For the first time in years, he allowed himself to lean into someone else's warmth.

His father joined them, his expression both proud and relieved. "Look at you, Fred," he said, clapping a hand on his shoulder. "Back where you belong, and we didn't have to wait as long to see you again this time!"

They settled in the cosy sitting room, tea steaming on the table, as they caught up on everything they had missed. It wasn't long before their conversation turned to family, to memories of loved ones they had lost over the years. Fred listened as his parents shared stories, some he'd never heard, about aunts, uncles, and cousins now gone. There was a quiet comfort in realising that, in this moment, it was just the three of them, a family bound by memories and an unbreakable connection.

"We're all we have now," his father said gently, looking at Fred. "That's why we're glad you're here. Funny thing, I could've sworn I saw Rose walk past the window this morning."

"Maybe you did see her. I see people from my life, Dad, every day. Life feels different now, doesn't it?"

His mother nodded, her eyes soft with hope. "It's time to think about the future, Fred. Maybe even settling down."

Fred looked between them, a warmth filling his chest at the thought. He'd never imagined this path for himself, but here, surrounded by love and memories, he felt a glimmer of possibility.

"Yeah, maybe it is time," he said, smiling as he took his mother's hand. "We'll make sure there's a future for this family yet."

He made his way to the small bedroom at the back of the house, the room he had grown up in. The bed was neatly made, the curtains drawn. Fred sat on the edge of the bed, his head in his hands. He carried the memory of the past, pressing down on him, the memories of the war, of Isabella's betrayal, a constant presence in his mind. He had thought coming home would bring him peace, but he felt no relief. Only a deep, aching emptiness. The silence pressed in on him. No gunfire, no engines, no voices, just the ticking of the old clock downstairs. It should have been comforting, but it only reminded him of how empty the room felt without the ghosts of the men he'd lost.

Days turned into weeks, and Fred struggled to adjust to civilian life. He spent his days wandering the streets of Worthing, his nights haunted by nightmares of the war. The sound of gunfire, the smell of smoke, the faces of the men he had fought alongside, everything came rushing back in the dark, the memories vivid and unrelenting. Fred would wake in the middle of the night, drenched in sweat, his heart racing. He could still feel the cold steel of the cell, the echo of their voices in his ears.

He tried to distract himself, taking up odd jobs around town, but nothing held his interest. His mind was elsewhere, always drifting back to the past, to the war, to Isabella. He thought of her often, her dark eyes, her warm smile, the way she had made him feel alive. The pain of her betrayal was still felt in his chest, a pain that had softened but still present. He couldn't understand how she could have done it, how she could have sold him out to the Gestapo. He had trusted her, loved her, and she had broken his heart.

Fred avoided company, withdrawing into himself. He had no desire to talk, to explain, to relive the memories that haunted him. His friends and neighbours gave him a wide berth, sensing the darkness that surrounded him. They whispered about him behind closed doors, their voices filled with pity, but Fred paid them no mind. He didn't need their sympathy. He didn't need anything. His parents were understanding. His mother would worry about him, but his father had told her to give him space and time.

One afternoon, as Fred walked along the beach, the waves crashing against the shore, he felt a sudden urge to escape. The vast expanse of the sea called to him, a promise of freedom, of a fresh start. He had spent too long in the shadows of the past, in the grip of pain and betrayal. He needed to find a way to move on, to let go of the memories that bound him. He needed to find a way to forgive not only Isabella but also himself.

Fred stood at the water's edge, the cold waves lapping at his feet. He stared out at the horizon, his heart heavy. He had survived the horrors of combat, the pain of betrayal, but now he had to face the most brutal fight of all, the battle for his peace, for his future.

As the sun dipped below the horizon, Fred made a silent vow. He would find a way to heal, to forgive, to move forward. He would not let the past define him, would not allow the darkness to consume him. He had faced the fires of war and come out the other side.

Sixty Five

The evenings came early in January, wrapping the little seaside town in long hours of dusk. Fred had grown used to the quiet rhythms of home again: the smell of coal smoke drifting from the neighbours' chimneys, the clatter of pans in the kitchen, the tide whispering against the shingle. He had been back a while now, but the days still passed in a kind of limbo, neither quite peace nor quite belonging.

That night, the three of them sat down together in the small parlour where the dining table stood near the fire. His mother had set a pot of stew on the trivet, steam curling into the lamplight; the smell of carrots, beef, and pepper settled warmly in the air. Fred's father, his pipe resting in its usual spot by the mantel, ladled generous portions for each of them before lowering himself carefully into his chair.

They mainly ate in companionable silence. The fire crackled. Outside, the wind tapped lightly at the windowpane. Fred's mother glanced at him from time to time, her eyes soft, her hands busy breaking bread and passing it across. She didn't ask questions the way she had when he first came home, when every quiet moment had threatened to collapse into the unspoken. Instead, she let the meal unfold like an old habit, filling the spaces with little mentions of

397

neighbours, ration books, the vicar's sermon last Sunday.

Fred listened, chewing slowly. The warmth of the food sat heavily in his stomach, comforting yet strangely distant. He was here, safe, alive, surrounded by the things he had once longed for, but part of him remained adrift, as though his body had made it home while his mind was still at sea.

His father cleared his throat. "I know I say this a lot," he murmured, his voice thickened by age and pipe smoke, "but I am truly so glad you are home."

Fred looked up. His father's gaze held his steadily, a weight of sincerity that needed no embellishment. For a moment, Fred wanted to speak, to thank him, to say something about how much it mattered, but the words stalled, stuck in the same place where everything seemed to catch these days. He only nodded, quietly, and forced a small smile.

His father accepted it with a faint nod of his own, turning back to his plate.

The warmth of the fire pressed against Fred's skin, and for a moment, he thought the evening would slip into its usual gentle lull, his mother knitting, his father with the paper, Fred staring into the flames. But then came a knock at the door, sharp and unexpected, rattling the air.

His mother frowned. "Who on earth?"

She rose, wiping her hands on her apron, and crossed to the door. The latch clicked. The door swung wide.

And there he was.

"Surprise!"

Tommy barrelled into the room, grinning from ear to ear, his uniform jacket hanging open and an arm in a sling. Snowflakes clung to his hair and shoulders, melting into damp spots as he stomped the cold from his boots.

"Tommy," Fred said, rising in disbelief.

"In the flesh," Tommy replied, laughter bubbling in his throat. He thumped Fred's good shoulder with his free hand before pulling him into a lopsided embrace. "Blimey, look at you! Still brooding like a philosopher, I see. Some things never change."

His mother gasped and ushered him inside, clucking over the sling at once. "What have you done to yourself?"

"Nothing much, Mrs. Bennett," Tommy said, his grin never dimming. "Just a scratch. Ardennes gave me a little souvenir, that's all. Nothing to worry about."

"Nothing to worry about, he says!" she exclaimed, bustling to fetch another bowl from the cupboard. "Sit yourself down this instant. You'll eat with us."

Tommy didn't need telling twice. He dropped into the spare chair, shaking out his hair like a dog. "Smells like heaven in here. Army rations don't hold a candle to your stew, Mrs. B."

Fred sat back down slowly, still blinking at him. "You're supposed to be in France."

"Not any more," Tommy said, tearing off a hunk of bread with his good hand. "They gave me some time off to recover. Thought I'd surprise the old gang. You were top of the list."

Fred felt something stir in his chest, relief, warmth, something close to joy but quieter. Tommy's energy filled the room like a fire flaring suddenly higher, chasing away shadows. He had always been that way: at school, at the docks, in every scrape and every laugh they'd shared. To see him alive, sitting at their table, was like sunlight breaking through a long, grey sky.

They ate together, Tommy talking with his mouth half-full, his mother fussing at him to slow down. He told stories of the Ardennes: the bitter cold, the snow so deep it swallowed boots whole, the way the sky lit up red when the shells came in. But he spun even the darker parts into something lighter, finding humour in the mud, in the absurdity of trucks breaking down, in the way one of his mates insisted on brewing tea in the middle of a firefight.

"Nearly got us all blown to kingdom come," Tommy laughed, slapping the table with his good hand. "But he wouldn't let go of that tin mug. Said if he were going to die, he'd die with proper tea in his belly."

Fred managed a smile. His mother laughed too, though she shook her head in disbelief.

"Honestly," she muttered, "men and their foolishness."

But as Tommy launched into another tale, Fred caught the flicker behind his grin, the way his eyes hardened for a moment before he pushed the darkness back down. He knew that look. He had worn it himself.

They talked late into the evening, the stew pot scraped nearly clean, bread crumbs scattered across the table. For the first time in weeks, the little parlour felt alive, filled with voices and laughter instead of silence.

When at last the fire burned low and the clock chimed the hour, his mother rose, gathering plates. "That's enough excitement for one night. Bedtime for me"

Tommy yawned, stretching his legs under the table. "Feels like I could sleep for a week. Haven't seen a proper bed in months. Thanks for dinner, Mrs. B. You're an angel. I'll head off now."

She tutted, but her eyes shone.

Fred climbed the stairs slowly, the laughter fading into the hush of the house. He slipped into his room, closing the door behind him. The bed waited,

401

sheets crisp, pillow plumped by his mother's careful hands.

Sleep came quicker than he expected.

And then he was back on the ship.

The Channel stretched grey beneath the hull, the wind snapping at his collar as he leaned against the railing. Around him, men talked of home; pubs, warm fires, the taste of bread not made from rations. They laughed, voices rolling across the deck, and Fred smiled politely, nodding when they caught his eye. But the sound reached him like echoes through water, distant, belonging to another life.

Relief stirred in him, thin and fragile, but hope refused to settle. He watched the sea churn white beneath the prow, the sun glinting on each crest like a promise he couldn't quite believe.

Faces swam before him: Enzo, eyes bright with conviction; Luciano bleeding in the shadows; Isabella, her voice soft as she called his name. They drifted past, never lingering, never close enough to hold.

When the coastline appeared, silvered with mist, he braced for a rush of joy. But nothing came. The land stretched before him, familiar and foreign all at once. He stepped ashore carrying the war in his bones, every laugh behind him fading like smoke.

Fred stirred, caught between dream and waking. The sound of waves lingered in his ears, the salt sting of sea air sharp in his lungs. Then it faded.

Morning light crept through the curtains, casting a pale gold hue on the walls. A robin perched on the sill, chest puffed red, singing a bright, cheerful trill into the cold air. Fred blinked at it, surprised by the softness of the sound after the harsh echoes of his dream.

On the bedside table stood a cup of tea, still steaming gently. His mother's doing, no doubt.

He lay back against the pillow, listening to the robin's song, the warmth of the tea drifting upward. For the first time in a long while, the morning felt lighter.

Sixty Six

The seafront in Worthing was peaceful. The sun hung low in the sky, casting an angelic light over the water, and a gentle breeze swept in from the English Channel, rustling the leaves of the trees lining the promenade. Fred strolled, hands in his pockets, eyes on the horizon. The familiar sights of home brought calm, though memories still pressed heavily.

It had been years since the end of the war, but Fred still found solace in these walks. The sea was a constant, its waves washing away the edges of his thoughts, giving him space to breathe. He had tried to rebuild his life in Worthing, to carve out some semblance of regularity, but the scars of his past lingered. He had taken up work as a fisherman, finding comfort in the simplicity of the work, the rhythm of the tides. Each day was a reminder that life went on, even after so much had been lost. He had been offered further military training positions, including back at Inveraray, but it hadn't interested him.

He turned onto the main promenade, where families strolled and children played, their laughter ringing out in the salty air. Fred nodded to a few familiar faces, offering polite smiles, but he kept to himself, preferring the quiet of his own thoughts. As he walked, his mind wandered, memories flickering like shadows at the edge of his consciousness. He thought of the men he had served with, of the friends he had lost, of the battles he had fought.

And then, inevitably, he thought of her.

Isabella.

Even after all these years, her face was etched in his mind. The way her eyes sparkled when she laughed, the softness of her voice, the warmth of her touch. He had tried to forget, to bury the pain of her betrayal, but her memory was a ghost that haunted him still. He had never forgiven her, never found peace with what she had done. She had been the love of his life, and she had destroyed him.

The sound of the sea masked the footfalls behind him. But it didn't mask the shift in the air, the old intuition. He turned, not quite expecting what he saw.

Fred sighed, pushing the thoughts away, focusing instead on the gentle crash of the waves. He was nearing the pier now, the air filled with the smell of fish. He glanced up, his eyes scanning the crowd out of habit, when he saw her.

For a moment, he thought he was imagining it, a trick of the light, a mirage conjured by his restless mind. The sea wind whipped at his coat. Salt stung his lips as he stared at the silhouette, impossibly familiar, framed against the pier's edge.

405

As he looked closer, he felt his heart stop. There, just a few paces ahead, stood Isabella. She was older now, her hair touched with silver, lines of worry etched on her face, but it was her. The years had changed her, but nothing, not time, not betrayal, could strip away the familiarity that hit him like a blow to the chest.

Beside her stood two young adults, a man and a woman. Fred's breath caught in his throat as he recognised them. Marco and Sofia. The children she had once spoken of with such love and fear. They had grown, no longer the small, vulnerable children he had imagined. They looked healthy, strong, their eyes bright with the light of youth. They were no longer the frightened shadows he remembered from whispered conversations in Naples, but flesh and blood, a living proof of the choice that had broken him. A pang of emotion shot through Fred's chest, relief that they were alive, a reminder of the price that had been paid.

For a long moment, Fred stood frozen, his mind reeling. He felt a surge of emotions: shock, anger, pain, and something else, something he couldn't quite name. He had never expected to see her again, had convinced himself that chapter of his life was closed. Yet here she was, flesh and blood, a living reminder of everything he had suffered.

As if sensing his gaze, Isabella turned, her eyes meeting his. For a moment, time seemed to stop.

Her face paled, her eyes widening in recognition. The colour drained from her cheeks, and she took a step back, her hand instinctively reaching for her children. Fred saw the fear in her eyes, the shock mirrored in his own.

"Fred?" The word was barely a breath, almost lost to the wind.

Fred felt his heart hammering in his chest, the blood roaring in his ears. He took a step forward, his gaze locked on hers. The years seemed to melt away, and he was back in Naples, feeling the warmth of her touch, hearing the soft murmur of her voice. He had loved her with all his heart, had trusted her, and she had betrayed him.

"Isabella." His voice was low, bitter. He looked at Marco and Sofia, then back at her. "I thought I'd never see you again."

Isabella swallowed, her eyes darting between Fred and her children. She straightened, her chin lifting slightly, as if bracing herself for what was to come. "Neither did I," she admitted, her voice trembling. "I didn't expect… Fred, I thought you were…"

"Dead?" Fred finished, his tone cold. "I might well have been, thanks to you."

Her face crumpled, the gravity of his words striking her like a blow. She closed her eyes, pain etched in every line of her face. When she spoke, her voice was thick with emotion. "Fred, I did what I had to do. For them."

Fred's jaw clenched, anger flaring in his chest. He had spent years trying to make sense of her betrayal, trying to understand how she could have turned him over to the Gestapo. Hearing her say it so plainly, with such finality, was like a knife twisting in his heart.

"For them," he repeated, his voice laced with bitterness. He looked at Marco and Sofia, standing protectively by their mother's side. "You sold me out to save your children?"

Isabella flinched at his words, but she did not look away. Her eyes were filled with tears, her hands trembling. "Yes," she said, her voice barely audible. "I had no choice. They were going to kill them, Fred. I couldn't let that happen. Not to my children."

Fred stared at her; his chest felt hollow, and each word froze the air between them. He understood the desperation that had driven her, the fear that had clouded her judgment. But it didn't lessen the betrayal, didn't erase the scars that had been left behind. He had loved her, trusted her, and she had made her choice.

He turned away, unable to bear the sight of her, the memories flooding back with brutal clarity. The cell, the beatings, the endless questions. The knowledge that the woman he loved had betrayed him. He had thought he could never feel anything for her again, but standing here, seeing her, he felt a tidal wave of emotions threatening to drown him.

"Fred," Isabella's voice was pleading, desperate. "I never wanted to hurt you. I loved you. I still do."

He closed his eyes, his hands clenching into fists. He wanted to scream, to rage at her, to make her understand the depth of his pain. But he couldn't. The words stuck in his throat, a knot of anger and sorrow.

When he spoke, his voice was quiet, filled with a deep, aching sadness. "It doesn't matter. What's done is done. I survived, that will have to be enough."

He turned to leave, his heart heavy, the impact of the past pressing down on him. As he walked away, he heard Isabella's voice, soft and broken, calling after him. "Fred, please, "

But he didn't turn back. He couldn't. The wounds were still too fresh, the pain too deep. He had survived the war, but some battles could never be won.

As he walked along the seafront, the wind whipping at his face, a tear slipped down his cheek. He wiped it away, burying the ache that threatened to break through. He had loved Isabella once, but that love lay buried in the ashes of betrayal.

The sea stretched out before him, vast and unending, a reminder of the world beyond, of the life that awaited him. Fred took a deep breath, his eyes fixed on the horizon. Behind him, the sound of Isabella's voice dissolved into the wind, swallowed by the crash of the waves. Ahead, the horizon glimmered, a promise he wasn't sure he believed in, but one he would walk toward all the same.

Sixty Seven

The sea whispered beside him, endless and unbothered. Fred walked along the edge of the promenade, wind tugging at his coat. Beneath his boots, the stones were warm from the afternoon sun, but the heaviness in his chest gave the day a hollow feel.

He had left Isabella standing behind him, and yet, not. Her presence still clung to him like a song unfinished, each echo of her voice stitching itself through his thoughts.

He hadn't planned to go back. But some part of him, the part that had resisted so many deaths and betrayals, couldn't walk away from her words, not without knowing what had truly happened, not without understanding what had broken them.

He turned.

She stood near the old stone steps that led down to the beach, her figure stiff against the shimmer of the water. Marco and Sofia were beside her, older now, yes, but their posture still childlike.

Isabella was speaking to them, her hands moving gently, as if trying to keep the conversation from breaking apart. Fred moved slowly toward

411

them, each step louder than the last. When Marco noticed him first, he touched his mother's arm.

She turned.

"Fred," she said, voice soft, uncertain.

They stood in silence for a moment, the afternoon wind curling between them like a thread pulled too tight.

"I need the truth," Fred said. "No guessing, no holding back. I've carried the ghosts long enough. I need to know what happened, all of it."

Isabella nodded slowly. "Alright," she whispered. "Come with me."

They walked away from the children, only a little, just enough to speak. A bench overlooked the surf, and they sat side by side, though not touching.

Her voice trembled at first, then settled into rhythm, not rehearsed, but remembered. She spoke of the night the Gestapo came, how they had taken Marco and Sofia from their beds. She hadn't known who to trust. Luciano had gone underground. Neighbours stopped answering their doors.

"They told me I had twenty-four hours to deliver something useful," she said. "Or they'd disappear forever. Not arrest them. Not prison. Disappear."

Fred's hands clenched on his knees.

"I thought you'd find a way out," she continued. "I told myself if I gave them what they wanted, it would buy time. That I was protecting everyone, you and the children. That maybe it wouldn't lead to anything."

Her voice cracked, but she pressed on. "When I heard later you'd survived the prison break, the escape, I was relieved. But also terrified. I knew I couldn't undo what I'd done. I didn't hear anymore. I knew you were in a bad way and…"

Fred's throat tightened. He opened his mouth to speak, then closed it again. His hands shook slightly, betraying the calm he tried to wear.

"You could have told me," he said eventually. "We could've planned together. Trusted each other."

"I couldn't think," Isabella said. "I am a mother, and that was all I was in that moment, a mother with no choices. Every decision felt like a knife-edge. I… I had to choose the lesser harm, not what was right for me, for us, for you."

Fred turned his head toward her. Tears were spilling silently down her face. He felt himself soften for a moment, wishing he could embrace her, but something in him recoiled, a spark of old pain that refused to be extinguished.

"I know what they did to you," she added. "I can't forgive myself for it. Not ever. But I swear to you, Fred, I didn't betray you because I stopped loving you. I betrayed you because I couldn't bear to lose my children."

He looked down at his hands. Pale scars lined his knuckles now, the kind that didn't fade. He thought of the cell, of the beatings, of the days blurring together. And then, unexpectedly, he thought of her laughter. Of the café. Of the children drawing chalk horses on the balcony walls.

"I've hated you for years," he said quietly. "And I've missed you just as long. I don't know what to do with either of those things."

Isabella closed her eyes. "Then just sit with me," she said. "We don't have to fix it. I just needed you to know."

A shadow passed over them. "Is this a bad time?"

Fred turned, slowly.

A familiar face stood at the edge of the path, his coat loose around broad shoulders. A scar trailed just below his left eye. He looked tired, cautious, but the warmth in his eyes was unmistakable.

Fred stared at him in disbelief. "Luciano…?"

"I didn't mean to interrupt," Luciano said. "I just… I needed to see this for myself."

"You're alive." Fred stood. "I thought they said you were dead."

Fred's fingers lingered for a moment on his friend's shoulder. For all the wounds they carried, seen and unseen, this was one reunion that hadn't come too late.

"Nearly was," Luciano admitted. "Somehow, when the walls collapsed, the walls fell around me. I got away with it." He offered a half-smile. "I've always had a habit of surviving when I shouldn't."

Fred blinked, trying to absorb it all. The timing. The sudden clarity. The way Isabella stood now was not startled, not apologetic, but quietly at ease.

"You're together," Fred said, his voice low.

Isabella stepped beside Luciano. Her hand found his, instinctively.

"Yes," she said. "It happened slowly after you left. After everything."

Luciano stepped forward. "I didn't come over to make this harder," he said. "But I needed to thank you, Fred. You gave more than any man should've had to. You saved lives. Mine included."

Fred looked between them, a part of him aching, but another part finally still. The weight of relief, jealousy, guilt, he carried it all at once, but he forced himself to breathe and make a choice. Forgiveness didn't come easy, but it began here, in the act of letting go.

He nodded. "You make a good team," he said. "I mean it."

Luciano reached out. Fred took the hand. Firm grip. No resentment. No triumph. Just men who had survived something unspeakable.

"Take care of each other," Fred said. "And take care of the children."

"We will," Isabella said softly. "I promise."

Fred walked down to the sand.

The beach was nearly empty now. The horizon glowed pale gold. He stood at the water's edge for a long while, the tide washing against his boots, the sea breeze pulling at his coat like an old friend urging him forward. He thought of the past, pain, love, and betrayal, and let himself feel, acknowledge, and release it.

The past hadn't disappeared. But it had been faced and spoken aloud. And perhaps that was the weight he'd carried all along, silence.

Fred took a breath so deep it hurt. And then he smiled. Not because he had won anything. But because he had chosen survival. Chosen life.

The sea roared on, endless, uncaring. Fred drew a long breath, steady and unbroken, letting his feet lead him. He didn't look back.

About the Author:

This is Luke Osborne's debut novel. Having written many children's and educational books before, this lights up a new path.

Having studied at Brighton University and being a lover of history, this spy thriller represents 20 years of imagining what his first novel would read like.

Printed in Dunstable, United Kingdom